A Fairy Tale

Ginger Robinson

NEWMAN SPRINGS PUBLISHING
320 Broad Street
Red Bank, NJ 07701

First originally published by Newman Springs Publishing 2022

ISBN 978-1-68498-191-5 (Paperback)
ISBN 978-1-68498-192-2 (Digital)

Printed in the United States of America

THIS BOOK IS DEDICATED TO my Lord and Savior Jesus Christ; to my husband, my one-in-a-million love and editor, Benjamin Robinson Jr. (you fussed at me many a day to take chances and be crystal clear in my writing); to my beautiful children—Benjamin III, Kelsey I, and Chelsea★—and our foster daughter, Angel; and last but not least, to my ultimate push, the one that kept me "accountable," Vermantha Lizana.

Chapter 1

"So what happened?" Miss Justine sits at her desk, looking sternly at Rookie.

"You know what happened. You were there," Rookie states.

"I was there, yes, but you need to explain this to me for the house's records. I need to know that you understand what took place with you and Tracy."

Rookie gives a long sigh. "Well, Tracy always comes into group therapy, thinkin'"—Rookie turns her head dramatically—"she runs the thang." She looks at Miss Justine for response and gets none. "She said that I didn't have any business thinkin' that I could go home."

She runs the scene back in her mind. *In your mind, you are so suavay*—Tracy accentuated the word *suave*—*that you think you can go home anytime.*

Rookie looks at Miss Justine again. "She called me Queen Chaos. Queen Chaos, and you didn't do anything about it."

"Rookie."

"I just jumped. I jumped and tried to claw her eyeballs out!" Rookie leans forward in her plastic chair. "She screamed and tried to get me off, and then when she got me off her eyeballs, I went for her body and banged on it!"

"Rookie." Miss Justine looks at Rookie, eyes stern and voice all business. "You won't be allowed to go to group therapy. This is your second fight."

"That first one wasn't even really a fight," Rookie says quietly.

"This is your second documented fight, so no more group therapy. It will be just you and I. You are counted as a tier 2 group risk due to your antisocial issues." Miss Justine closes the folder, indicating the conversation is over.

"Antisocial, huh? Whateva."

Nights later, Rookie's sweaty fingers grip the cold steel of her bed rails. In, in, and in, her breathing comes shallow in what feels like life-threatening intervals. In and out, she tries to remind herself to breathe, but it just isn't working, hasn't been working for quite a while.

You disgust me. I used to adore you, and now I just wanna spit on you! Rookie Simpson uses the flat institutionalized pillow from her bed to wipe the tears from her dripping face and lie in the darkness of her room, thinking over the last words her husband had spoken to her.

Her heart mercilessly constricts when she reflects over her questionable life.

"Maybe Tracy is right. I am Queen Chaos."

Finally, with much concentration, her breathing becomes controllable. She smirks cynically, for it has been six years since she has seen him or the six children they have. The dreams are a constant reminder of the critical offenses she's committed. The punishment, it seems, is that she has never forgotten her family; however, until recently, she's only experienced fleeting memories, easily pushed back into the recesses of her mind with reminders to herself that she'd return soon.

"I have cried many a night for all the things I've done wrong," Rookie told her court-appointed counselor, Miss Justine.

Rookie was nineteen, and Jeoff was seventeen when they met. The initial goal of speaking to him was to see if she could make the pastor's son her love slave. He seemed so wholesome. With his mellow disposition and impressive good looks, he made the perfect trophy for the time, or so she thought.

Rookie looks at the ceiling, moist tears forming in her eyes.

Jeoff is so sweet and rebellious. He is the youngest of Pastor Simpson's three children, but he always seemed older. Still, Rookie was able to use her alluring figure, large olive-shaped eyes, and husky, soft voice to woo him into giving up a scholarship out of state and moving into a tattered small Section 8 apartment with her and her infant son, Duran.

Now openly weeping, Rookie whispers into her pillow, "I'm so sorry."

"You are a sorry loser! I'm sick of this house, this jail, and these kids! I wanna have fun and be free!" A twenty-year-old Rookie yelled these words to her husband.

Rookie didn't know how to be a wife and mother. The first time she got pregnant with Jeoff's child, an eighteen-year-old Jeoff surprised her by proposing marriage.

"Girl, he comes from a good family!" her friends told her. "He's gonna be rich one day," they continued. "Plus he's a good babysitter!" They all laughed together.

Jeoff had another girlfriend when he and Rookie met. But he would plot and plan to get to Rookie, and she knew it was only a matter of time before he was all hers. Rookie, the product of a Black mother and a Mexican father, has long, wavy black hair; large eyes; wide hips; and a small waist. Her full lips are always sensuous, and her eyelashes are still unbelievably long and curled at the end, giving them an artificial appearance. Her lightly bronzed skin once had soft freckles sprinkled on her left shoulder. Just slender now, then she had the Coke-bottle figure a lot of women swore they wanted and had known what to do with it since she was thirteen.

When they got married, both worked, but Rookie never kept a job.

She would constantly call in sick or tell Jeoff, "They hate me there, and I quit. I only need a job until income tax time anyway, and then, baby, we're gonna be paid!"

"I wish you'd stop thinking so basic. Income tax is only a lump sum. What about the rest of our lives?"

She rolled her eyes as he continued.

"And I know you wanna have fun, but I'm struggling here. I'm trying to keep my classes straight and work, and you won't even work half the time, Rook!" Jeoff yelled at her.

Still a toddler, Duran stared blankly at the television while an eleven-month-old Ni Ni and newborn Devon screamed.

"Okay, Daddy, whatever you say!" Rookie yelled to Jeoff.

After Jeoff went to sleep, Rookie walked out that night and many different nights, returning after the parties were over and all the clubs had closed. She flinched when she thought about the hours or days she would stay gone, depending on who wanted to have a better time than Jeoff.

Every day, when Jeoff would leave to go to class or work, Rookie would wait and leave about thirty minutes later. She remembers being excited because she'd met a cutie named Devon Keyes.

"Everybody says you've been seeing some guy," she remembers Jeoff saying to her sadly.

"Are you accusing me of somethin', Jeoffy?" Rookie said condescendingly to him. She fluttered her eyelashes and put her hand on her hip.

"I'm just tellin' you what I hear," Jeoff said. He turned to walk away and then turned back determinedly. "Are you messin' around, Rook?" His eyes simultaneously pleaded with her to tell him the truth and not to tell him the truth.

Rookie rolled her eyes and pursed her lips. "Where'd you hear this mess from, Jeoff? Ya momma? Well, I'm married, and I like havin' fun, but not that much fun." She turned and walked away from Jeoff.

Two weeks later, Jeoff surprised her and Devon at a gas station and, after the encounter, went to his parents'.

Rookie surprises herself as she feels shame for that night.

She slashed his tires and threatened that he couldn't see the kids if he wouldn't come home. She didn't like the idea of being left. When she threatened him, there was silence. She guessed he didn't like being threatened.

As Rookie's memories refuse to let her mind go, she remembers Jeff sincerely telling her, "Look, I miss the kids, and I don't wanna be without them…or you."

Rookie's stomach burns with acid, recalling how she was always running off somewhere whether it was a man or just to be away, yet Jeoff would constantly come and find her.

No matter how she tries to shut it off, these nights have been a glimpse in the mirror of her own soul, and she isn't liking what she is seeing and definitely that she had to see it at all.

4

Rookie opens her eyes and closes them.

"Why don't you just go on home, li'l boy?" Devon had yelled out to Jeoff in his drunkenness. He stood up, snatched three-month-old Ni Ni and Duran, and handed them to Jeoff. "Here, you can take your kids. You're the only one who wants 'em. I ain't got no use for 'em."

Rookie thought Jeff was going to throw up as he looked at her.

"Are you comin' home?"

She paused, looked at Devon looking sexy and older, and then looked at good old solid Jeoff. Jeoff was her "home man" who cooked dinner and took care of the kids; Mr. Mom, she loved to call him. She turned from the door, got the children's bags, and gave them to Jeoff. His tired eyes gleamed with hope, then dimmed with sadness as she turned and closed the door between them.

A couple more weeks passed before Rookie decided she wanted to return home. She had been with Devon off and on for several years, but he just wasn't as solid as Jeoff was. She walked to their apartment, and when her key worked, she merely sauntered in.

"Jeoff, I wanna come home," she stated.

"You're here," he said flatly.

She touched his chest. "Jeoffy, I am sorry for…everything, all of the drinking and the partying. I realize that I just want to be with you. I love you, Jeoff. I've loved you since the first time I met you." She looked up at him.

Jeoff was a handsome young man. He had milky-smooth skin the color of a Hershey bar and deep-brown eyes that had such depth they appeared black. His eyelashes, although shorter than hers, were curled at the ends, making his eyes appear as though someone had skillfully put a fine eyeliner to them. He was 6'2" and leanly muscular and could throw on any outfit, and everyone followed suit. His naturally wavy hair was cut into a bob that he brushed regularly. He loved to have fun and was considerate and, at times, breathlessly romantic and affectionate; yet Rookie stood flat footed and lied to him regularly.

"I'm really gonna try this time. I mean it. Whatever it takes to keep us together."

Jeoff's parents helped him emotionally and financially during their marriage, and Rookie could feel the tension every time she saw them. She began to feel the hold she had on him loosening and figured they were finally getting Jeoff to consider leaving her.

"Jeoff, I want to stay at home and be a better mom for the kids and wife to you."

These words were spoken in desperation. Job offers would begin to come as Jeoff only had a year left, and that summer, he committed to an internship and had moved them to a slightly larger apartment. So Rookie thought it best that she try to hold on to this good thing. Despite the stress in his life, he was proving to be a promising student. If all went as planned, in a year, Jeoff would have his architectural design degree; and then he'd really have a good job.

Ni Ni was only six months old when Rookie discovered she was pregnant again.

"I want a blood test when the baby's born," Jeoff told her, stone-faced and serious like a drill sergeant.

"If you do, Jeoff, we're through!" Rookie shrieked in a panic.

"Don't play with me like I'm stupid, Rookie. You've been on a tear since I married you, and you know full well, if it ain't mine, then we're through anyway."

Her eyes got wider, and Jeoff's features got even harder. He sighed and gritted his teeth.

"I've made our marriage that horrible for you?" She looked at him with moistened eyes. "Baby, I'm so sorry. Please?"

She touched his hand and tried to look in his eyes. He had them deeply veiled with his own thoughts.

"Please let this baby be our new beginning? I know in my heart he's yours."

She touched his hand, and he pulled away.

"Please?"

Jeoff didn't answer but never got the test.

Looking around the room, Rookie is never so glad to wake up. Sighing, she gets up and heads to the showers. The day runs past so quickly. Rookie finds herself returning to the same room slowly putting on her nightgown. Without a television, the hum of the fluorescent lights in the hallway lulls her straight to sleep.

"The doctor found drugs in your system." Jeoff choked on the words as he spoke to her as Rookie stared at him blankly.

"They made me take a drug test to see if I would be fit to take the kids home with me!"

He breathed heavily as he tried to get his emotions in check. "There won't be any criminal charges, but you'll have to stay in the hospital for the rest of the pregnancy."

"What? You can't let them do this to me!" Rookie screamed. "You've got to fix this, Jeoff," she pleaded.

Rookie shakes her head, trying to wake.

"I told the doctor that I didn't have full tabs on you, but somebody probably slipped it in your drink because you don't do stuff like this." Jeoff glared at the wall as he contemplated the lies he was telling himself and Rookie.

"You know I'd never endanger our baby."

He looked at her.

She shrank back and said quietly, "I was just experimentin'."

Jeoff just stood, glued to his same spot on the floor looking at her.

"I'm not a hype, M&M."

"Stop calling me that."

M&M was her short version of Mr. Mom, the nickname she sometimes called him.

"You liked it when we first got married," Rookie said sweetly.

"I liked a lot of things when we first got married, and we're not newlyweds anymore, are we?" Jeoff breathed heavily out of his mouth and bit his lip.

"Do I really have to stay here?"

He nodded.

"Jeoff, you do believe me, don't you? I wouldn't hurt our baby."

Jeoff nodded blankly and left.

Day after day, Rookie remembered begging Jeoff to come and see her.

"Hey, whatcha doin'?"

"I'm studyin' right now, Rook. You know I don't have much longer, and my classes are gettin' harder and harder," Jeoff answered.

"Well, where's the kids?" she asked, trying to make small talk.

"Duran's outside on the swings. I had to have the neighbor watch him so I could bring Ni Ni in with me to answer the phone in case it was the hospital," he said.

"Well, why don't y'all come over here? Y'all can spend the day with me. It's boring here, and—"

"I can't. You know that. I've got the kids, and I still need to study." His voice stayed dry the whole time.

"You don't have to be so mean, Jeoff!" she fussed.

"I'm not being mean. I'm being truthful." He said matter-of-factly. "We'll come in a couple days after my test, okay?"

Before he had finished his words, she had already slammed the phone down.

Breathing heavily and taking in a deep breath, Rookie wakes herself. "I just can't take it anymore!" She swings her legs over the side of the bed and sits with her elbows on her knees.

Rookie recalls calling back in ten minutes.

"Yes?" he answered the phone.

"What do you mean yes? You don't know how to answer a phone anymore?" she snapped.

"I knew it was you, Rook. What do you need?" he asked.

"A couple days'll be fine," she said softly. "I'm just tired, Jeoffy. I'm…sorry. Okay?"

"All right. Now can I go back to studying and taking care of the kids?" he asked, his tone sounding a little softer.

"Yes." She paused and then said, "I love you, Jeoffy."

"I love you too, baby."

Rookie's almost-conscious mind tries to shake her out of sleep, but while in sleep, her mind tortures her with memories.

The next week, Rookie called the house at eight o'clock, and nobody answered. She called every ten minutes until ten thirty when Jeoff finally answered the phone talking softly.

"Hello?"

"Where have y'all been!" she screeched. "I've been callin' since eight!"

"Calm down before you throw yourself into labor," he said, still talking softly.

"Why're you talking so low, and where've you been?" she repeated.

"I went to a reception for the students. I thought it'd be a good networking opportunity." He sighed. "Look, I'm tired and have class in the mornin', so—"

"You're not gettin' off that easy! Why're you rushin' me off the phone, and why're you talkin' so soft?" she demanded.

"I told you I'm tired, and if you must know, I have Ni Ni in my lap asleep, and Duran is on the couch too. I didn't have a chance to put them in the bed because the phone was ringin'." He sounded slightly amused.

"I don't see anythin' funny! That's a real good story, but—"

Jeoff cut her off furious. "No, no buts. If I wanted to cheat, I could've done it all the times you been gone. Now get off the phone before anybody says anything they're gonna regret, and I'll talk to you tomorrow after my class."

She got quiet. "Good night."

The next morning, she called again.

"Hello!" Jeoff snapped.

"What's wrong with you?" She heard Ni Ni fussing in the background.

"You hear the baby. What do you want?" he asked, still upset.

"Jeoffy, can you bring me some books to read and some of those puzzle books to work on? I'm bored."

Jeoff sighed loudly. "When I get outta class, Rookie. Now let me go."

"You can't bring them before class? It's kinda on your way," she said sweetly.

"No, I can't bring them before class."

By this time, Ni Ni was screaming.

"I told you I'll see you after class! You know I have a test, and you still *keep* calling! Hold on."

He set the phone down and, after a few moments, returned. She could hear Ni Ni cooing on the other end.

"Well, excuse me for bein' a bother to your day! I told you I was bored!" she screamed, almost breathless. "Don't even bother comin' after class. I can't stand you!"

She slammed the phone down. She called right back, but Jeoff was gone. She cried for a while and then picked up the phone and made a call.

"Bring me somethin' to take the edge off of this."

The delivery was a primo marijuana mixed with crack cocaine pieces rolled into a small joint, which Rookie smoked in the bathroom.

Tears streaming down her face, Rookie rouses from sleep. "My, my, my." She can either lay in the bed and cry or go back to sleep.

The result of the drugs was nausea, vomiting, and premature labor of their baby at five months.

She spitefully named him Devon and told Jeoff, "The doctor said it was stress. If you would have come and seen me more often, this wouldn't've happened."

Rookie seemed so hurt and angry that Jeoff didn't get the blood test. The fact that Devon was born premature, there wasn't even a full year between him and his older sister, Ni Ni; and Jeoff was so embarrassed because, when people saw the children, they always assumed he and Rookie were rabbits.

The next day, Rookie tells Miss Justine, "I'm livin' in a nightmare."

Later that night, the dreams return right on schedule.

"I want you to stop dropping off the kids at Mom and Dad's and not returnin' to pick them up. This is the second time I've come home from school and work to find them at their house." Jeoff gave Rookie a look of scorn. "They think we're some child abusers over here." He paused as though contemplating something and then seemed to mentally shrug. "What are you doing all day anyway?"

"Look"—Rookie brushed her hair back from her face—"I'm sorry about leavin' the kids at your parents. I had some errands to run." While Jeoff eyed her suspiciously, she began to ramble, "I went to the community college to see what kind of classes I could take and—"

"You went to the college," Jeoff repeated.

Even though Rookie hadn't left in a long time and Devon was doing well, ever since the two weeks with Devon, Jeoff didn't trust anything she did and, for the most part, didn't have a problem saying as much.

"So what did you see at the college?" he asked.

"I just wanted to see if there were any classes that I'd be interested in takin' so that I can help out more here."

Jeoff just eyed her tiredly.

"I know I don't seem like I have goals, but I do, Jeoffy," she rambled on. "Plus I wanted to plan some quality time with you." She pulled a black nightie from a bag. She advanced on Jeoff and kissed him gently on the neck. "I've been thinkin' 'bout you all day."

As Rookie pulled back from her kiss to witness Jeoff characteristically melt, he merely went to check on the kids.

When he returned, he lay on the couch and said, "You can have the bedroom."

Rookie went into the bedroom, and her mind immediately began to swirl into a panic. If he wouldn't share a bed with her, he must have wanted to split up.

Turning over her sweaty flat pillow, Rookie falls back into her fitful sleep.

In a month, Jeoff would graduate and already had a job offer.

His parents must've convinced him to leave when he graduates and take the kids!

Devon was seven months old and a happy chubby child. She had been breastfeeding, but they switched him to formula because the doctor said he was doing very good.

What am I supposed to do if he wants to split up? she thought to herself.

She tries to not remember as she lay on the bed for a while longer, watching the light from the television outside the door. Finally, she walked into the room and stood in front of the television.

"Jeoff, I feel like we're drifting apart."

He raised an eyebrow and leaned on his elbow.

"Why won't you sleep with me?" She leaned her head to the side. "Don't you love me, Jeoff?"

When he didn't answer, she looked angry and grabbed his drinking glass from the coffee table and threw it at him. When it hit the wall, she screamed as though it hit her.

"Why don't you just tell me you don't love me anymore!" She threw the picture frames that held their wedding pictures and the ones that held their children's pictures. "Why don't you love me anymore? Why don't you want me?"

Jeoff stood, his breathing intentionally slow to calm his frustration.

She ran to the kitchen and began to smash dishes, crying uncontrollably. "If you're leaving me, you're not taking anything with you!"

Jeoff grabbed her at first angrily and spun her around to look at him.

"Have you lost your mind?" he asked.

"You don't show me any emotion anymore! And you definitely don't show me any passion! I said I was sorry I was gone all day, but you act like I was out cheatin'. I just figured that, since you'd be out of school soon, that I could do somethin' with myself. You're just on your mean tangent!"

When he still refused to answer her, she pulled her arm back to slap him. He caught her arm, and they stood suspended in time. He leaned down and kissed her tear-stained cheeks, moving to her full lips, and when their passion ignited, Rookie's future was secured. Not long after their marriage was reconsummated, Rookie became pregnant with the twins.

"In order for this marriage to work, you have to stop all of the drinkin' and anything else you've been doin'." Jeoff looked completely serious when he stated what he wanted.

"I'm not usin' drugs, M&M."

He gave her a warning look.

"Jeoff," she stated.

Jeoff wasn't pleased about the next pregnancy, but he said he loved her. Now he had a good job, so they'd be all right.

Rookie squeezes her eyes shut as tight as possible and grits her teeth.

"I need to know I can trust you, and you know these kids need their mommy."

It killed her, but she remained somewhat a good girl through the whole pregnancy. She remembered being in the hospital with Devon and didn't want any more episodes like that. At the conclusion of nine full months, she delivered fraternal twins, naming the boy child Jeoffrey Adam Simpson Jr. to make up for Devon and his fraternal twin Marianna Topaz to kiss up to his mommy.

Chapter 2

THE YEARS ARE SHOWING ON Rev. Simpson. He is going to be six-ty-five soon. Dealing with the congregation God had entrusted to him, his marriage, and his children, it is a wonder he doesn't look eighty. To anyone on the outside looking in, he is a pretty normal Black man, slender with an older man's pooch. His chocolate complexion has worn well over the years. He always has a vibrant smile sparkling with his three gold teeth—one with a diamond in the center, one with his initials, and an open faced, all next to one another. He has the good looks of an older man, weathered throughout the years with naturally wavy hair always cut short close to his scalp.

He is a charismatic man, one people are naturally drawn to. He guards his heart as the Bible charges, spending the bulk of his time with his family. He learned over the years to not trust too many people and take his cares to God.

Rev. Bruni Simpson stands firmly on the fact that he is thankful for all that he has, and he is especially thankful that Jeoff's divorce will be final that coming Friday. The turmoil in Jeoff's life has been hard on all of them. He will never be able to forget the day Jeoff showed up at their door, unshaven and fifteen pounds lighter, confessing that his wife had been gone for six months and he wasn't sure if he could handle six children alone. At the time, he was twenty-six years old. Most men his age are still tossing women to the side and struggling with commitment, yet here he was with six children, a career trying to take off, and no one to depend on. He had always prayed that the Lord would separate those two, yet watching his son fighting through tears of frustration and the humiliation of having to come home, he wondered why God chose this method.

Rubbing his hand across his forehead, a habit he has when he is thinking, Rev. Simpson remarks to his wife, "The kids should be home today, huh? It'll be good to see the three of 'em together in the same place. It's been a while."

Marianna Simpson walks around the breakfast bar and kisses her husband on the cheek. "Yes, it's been a long time since all of our kids were in the same house, but it's supposed to be a surprise." She winks one of her beautiful dark-brown eyes at him as she heads for the kitchen.

"Nobody needs to know that Cha Cha told us."

Cha Cha is their nickname for Sienna, Joeff's youngest. When she was a toddler, Jeoff's grandma, their great-grandma, said she reminded her of the dancer Charro. She'd shake when she danced and talked so fast like the famous dancer that it sounded as though she were mixing languages. Ma Mee called her Charro. Little Mari called her Cha Cha because she couldn't pronounce it, and the name stuck. Cha Cha can't keep secrets, and Christmas time nearly kills her because she wants to tell all of the business. It is so cute to watch her struggle to not tell all of the gifts she knows.

Rev. Simpson walks to the kitchen table and sits staring at his wife.

"What?" she asks, looking concerned.

"Now I know it's none of my business, Mama, but what's goin' on with Jeoff and that Pete girl?" He shifts in his seat sideways, his long legs crossed as he tries to look into the future. "They've been close friends for a long time now. They go everywhere together. She helps him with the kids, and he helps with her baby."

He looks frustrated, and Mari giggles.

"Now I just think she's a beautiful Christian woman far better than…what he used to have." He pauses at the thought of Rookie as though saying her name was too much in their house. "They've been inseparable for three years as far as I know, and I want the boy to be happy." He looks at his wife appreciatively. "I want him to have what I have."

Mari, he is sure, God has sent to him. He can talk to her about anything, and they share everything. At sixty, she has aged well with her tall, shapely frame and shoulder-length salt-and-pepper gray hair that is pulled back into a bun. She has a walk that commands attention like the soldier she was when he first met her. Her smile lights up a room with an open-faced gold that matches her husband's. She exudes a confidence that many women envy and isn't afraid to show the deep love she feels for her husband, knowing that he has just as deep a love for her. After almost forty years of marriage, they still enjoy each other's jokes, are each other's confidant, and know each other's needs.

"I think Jeoff is just being cautious, baby. He's been through a lot." She sets a plate of fresh fruit and eggs in front of her husband. "He must be committed to Melasan. He won't date anyone, and they take trips together." As she walks away, she turns and looks at her husband searchingly. "You know that's her maiden name you keep callin' her by, right?"

"She's single now," he says like an insolent child as he absently picks at his food.

"Well, either way, you know yourself we have to let him work this out for himself." She reaches the stove and says almost softly, "He could take off his wedding ring though and finalize his divorce."

She looks at Rev. Simpson again, and they enjoy a chuckle together, knowing they want so much for their son so much less than the pain he still endures from time to time. Court has drudged on for several years as they said he had to prove he had diligently searched for Rookie since there were children involved.

Mari fixes her plate and sits with her fork in the air, thinking about the whole situation. She has always felt a little sorry for Rookie as she doesn't have the advantages Jeoff has. It was always her and her mom and several men in and out of their house. The lady's group at church had tried several times to reach Rookie's mom when Rookie was only a child, but she seemed to only be interested in her men and her drink. She wouldn't even allow Mrs. Simpson to take Rookie to church without her. The first time Rookie came to their house, she seemed to be in awe, like a servant at a castle. There were times Mari wanted to take her in her arms and hug her, and there were times when she just wanted to shake her.

The moment she found out she was pregnant the first time, she went to God and asked for His intervention and protection for Jeoff. This obviously is Jeoff's journey with the Lord as it took many years and many prayers. She knows Jeoff will be responsible as he is his father's child. That's why he and Bruni have such a hard time getting along; they are too much alike.

"Hey, Ma, I'm going over to the church and check on the new addition. I'll be back in time to be surprised for the kids, okay?" Bruni smiles and kisses his wife on the lips, heading for the front door.

"All right, Bruni," Mari says distractedly.

Bruni always take things with Jeoff harder, especially regarding this whole issue with Rookie. They have two other children, Bruni Jr. and Cee Cee, but Jeoff is their youngest. Bruni is protective of his children and blamed himself for Jeoff seeming to "slip" through the cracks and giving up his scholarship to Florida to marry Rookie. She flinches slightly as she remembers the night Jeoff told them that Rookie was pregnant.

"Boy, you're only eighteen. Don't expect me to raise this child for you," Rev. Simpson angrily stated to him.

"I don't. I'm gonna marry her and go to Tuskegee forty-five minutes from here," Jeoff said all of this with a straight face, but Mari knew he was shaking in his shoes.

"What? Are you crazy? What about your architectural scholarship?" Bruni Simpson looked as though he was going to have a heart attack. "Is it yours, boy?"

Jeoff looked green, and Rev. Simpson was practically hyperventilating. So Mari took over for him. She continued throughout the years to smooth their rocky relationship. Although Bruni has always been a man of God and has been pastoring almost all of their marriage, she knew he would absolutely blow up and say something he had no business saying to Jeoff. She kept him from killing Jeoff every time Rookie ended up pregnant, all four times Rookie ended up pregnant. She couldn't explain to her son that they knew better than he did, that Rookie was securely locking herself in with Jeoff by having these children. They learned to sit politely and painfully through visits with him and her. They believed in their hearts the marriage wouldn't last, but as the years still dragged on, they wondered if maybe they wanted it to end but it possibly wasn't God's will for it to end.

They learned the hard way to keep their noses out of it. When the two first got married, Mari found out that Rookie was cheating. She saw her with a young man, and they were too cozy for a mere friendship. She told Jeoff, and he blew up. It took them a couple months before they saw the kids again. She and Bruni Sr. vowed to stay out of it unless he asked, which he never did.

"Why do you stay with her?" she heard Bruni Sr. yell at him.

"Because marriage is forever," Jeoff said.

Rookie brought the children over more than Jeoff at times. Mari retired long ago and loves having them around, so she took advantage of that. They both knew Rookie didn't have a job, but Mari wouldn't dream of confronting her about why she was bringing them. One day, she left them far longer than usual; when Jeoff got finished with his classes and work, he had to pick them up. They didn't see the kids for months after that as well. She assumed he was ashamed of what was going on and didn't want to admit it to them.

Mari pushes her chair back and carries her half-eaten plate to the sink. "I thank God for the day when my grandbabies stop paying for her disappearance."

Chapter 3

"WHAT MAKES YOU THINK THAT, after six years, your kids want to see you?" Miss Justine, the counselor, sharply questions.

"I have a right, you know! They're mine. They'll always be mine!" Rookie's eyes shoot fiery darts at Miss Justine. "I thought you were on my side."

Miss Justine sighs. "Rookie, you've been in this halfway house for three years, which means you had three years prior that you could have been a mother to your children." She looks at Rookie sadly. "You have to take their feelings into consideration. What type of memories do you think they have of you? Your youngest child may not even remember you." Miss Justine leans forward and touches Rookie's hand. "You have scarred them."

Rookie stares at Miss Justine angrily and suddenly breaks into uncontrollable sobs.

The crying evolves into a panic attack, with Rookie clutching her chest and breathing spastically, her eyes darting at Miss Justine for assistance, who hands her a paper bag.

"Breathe, baby. Breathe. Slowly, slowly." She rises and rubs Rookie's back. "That's it. Calm down, slowly."

She places her chair next to Rookie's as the breathing becomes less labored. The crying also subsides, and Rookie breathes in heavily, looking away as though ashamed of her display of emotion.

"I...know I've been gone a long time. But I always wanted my daddy when he left. I always—" She stops as Miss Justine looks at her.

"It's normal for a child to want the parent who is gone, to want that completion, but what reason are you giving them to want to forgive you?" Miss Justine leans forward in her chair.

"To forgive me?" Rookie's eyes get wide. "I'm their mother. Of course they want their mother." She looks at Miss Justine, uncertain. "I mean…" She looks back at Miss Justine and sighs, pulling her feet into the chair. "I know I may have hurt them and all, but I had to get myself together. I had to get away. I just wonder how they turned out, ya know?" She looks out the window. "I know Jeoff did a good job with 'em. I wonder if any of 'em looks like me." She smacks her lips pondering. "I wonder…" She pauses as though scared to say the words. "Do they think about me?"

"I'm sure they do." Miss Justine says.

Rookie looks at her angrily. "I know what you mean by that!" She puts her feet on the floor. "I don't know why they make us come here!" She bites her lip in frustration.

"Have you heard from your mother?" Miss Justine rolls her pen in her fingers, looking at Rookie.

"You know I ain't heard from that woman! She's the reason my marriage didn't work." She turns back and forth in her chair. "And don't talk to me 'bout ownin' up to my own mistakes either." She turns the chair toward Miss Justine. "She's gotta own up to her mistakes too, right?" She smacks her lips in determination and then licks them, frowning.

Miss Justine sets the pen down and scratches her neck. "There is such a thing as accountability, but this isn't about her. She doesn't have six kids in another state." She stops scratching as Rookie turns her head angrily toward her. "What do you plan on saying to these children if you get the chance to see them? That you just wanted to know what they looked like?"

"No," Rookie mumbles.

"What are you going to say when they ask where you've been and why you left?"

"I'll cross that bridge when I come to it," Rookie continues to mumble.

"You need to cross it now," Miss Justine says. "What about your eldest?"

"My who?" Rookie asks.

Miss Justine sighs. "Your oldest child."

"What about him?" Rookie asks.

"He has to remember you best. What does he remember about you?"

"Look," Rookie snaps, "I wasn't the greatest momma, but I loved him. He *should* remember that I loved him." She looks away and then looks back. "He does remember I loved him."

"That's very touching, but what will he really remember?" Miss Justine probes, looking deeply into Rookie's eyes.

"What are *you* sayin' will happen?" Rookie's skin blotches with emotion, and she holds her head.

"Happen?" Miss Justine looks slightly confused. "I'm not a psychic, Rookie. I know you have questions. However, they"—Miss Justine adjusts in her seat—"your family, has more cutting questions than I do. You've been gone six years." Miss Justine accentuates all of her sentence while looking at Rookie. "You can't possibly tell me that you've been contemplating some big return and they're supposed to be just like you left them. How do you know they even live where you left them?"

Rookie sighs heavily. Miss Justine always has some hard-hitting questions, but ever since the day Rookie disappeared from the apartment, she had kept track of their lives as best she could. She always planned to return in a couple of weeks like she usually did, but somehow she ended up gone longer.

She looks out the window, hearing, "Momma, where you goin?"

"I'll be right back. I'm gonna get the mail," she remembers answering.

She looks back at Miss Justine with a stab of shame. "I know they still live in Montgomery. Jeoff has kept the same phone number all these years." She looks at Miss Justine with a child's hope. "He kept the same phone number for me. He's been waitin' for me. What more proof do you need? We're still married."

Chapter 4

"I CAN'T BELIEVE YOU'RE ALL here!" Mari stares at her three children standing in the living room looking like small children all over again. "Bruni, can you believe our babies are home?" She looks at her husband.

When he smiles, she begins to laugh, knowing their secret.

"What's so funny?" Bruni Jr. asks.

"Nothin', son. Just excited to see y'all." Rev. Simpson looks slightly guilty and steps forward to hug his oldest. "So how long are y'all staying?" He steps back, pretending to calculate months and months' worth of a visit.

"Daddy," Cee Cee smiles at her dad, "we know Sunday is your anniversary at the church and then next week is your fortieth wedding anniversary, so me, John, and the kids'll be here for two weeks, and Bruni…" She looks over at her brother.

Bruni smiles at his parents, rubbing his chin. "We'll be here for two weeks."

The room gets caught up in the excitement as they hug and talk at the same time, trying to catch up on lost time.

"Hey, Pop, we barbecued in the back, so let's go back there. Everybody's there."

Bruni grabs Jeoff by the neck, and they all head out with their mom and dad on permanent smiles and absolutely ecstatic.

"Man, I can't believe Duran is sixteen! The boy is super lanky!" Bruni says to Jeoff while sitting down with his stacked plate of barbecue.

Jeoff looks at Bruni's plate with one eyebrow raised and smiles. "Yeah, the boy is all feet and legs." He sticks a fork into his equally stacked plate. "I can't get him to commit to whether he wants to go to college or what."

"Lighten up, Baby J. He' s only sixteen. Besides, I don't think that one's gonna leave you. He's always been your keeper." He holds his fork in the air. "Well, all of them are your keeper, but he definitely is one that I don't think is goin' too far. Anyway, don't rush him. Have fun with his teenage years."

Jeoff rolls his eyes, making a face.

"What's that for? Girls?"

"Man, the girls ain't stopped callin' since he turned fourteen!"

Bruni laughs, digging into his plate some more.

"They call like it's a matter of life or death, but I told him he couldn't date until he turned sixteen, and here he is," Jeoff says, shaking his head.

"Any dates?" Bruni asks in the midst of chewing.

"Yeah. Me and Mel've been stuck droppin' him and a different girl every weekend off at the mall to go to the movies. Sometimes we just stay and watch a different movie from them so we don't have to come back from the house."

"I'm glad mine are still young. You know you got Ni Ni comin' up behind him though." He laughs boisterously, almost turning over his plate.

"Yeah, and you got one that won't be too long either. Time flies, big brotha. Believe you me."

"Yeah, but mine ain't never gonna date. She loves her daddy too much for all that nonsense." He winks an eye and nods his head at Jeoff while Jeoff shakes his head otherwise. Bruni looks at him knowingly, and then turns his attention to Melasan. "I see your friend is here this evening for our family function. Is there somethin' I need to know? I mean, I know so much already, but is there somethin' I officially need to know?" He nudges Jeoff, who doesn't get a chance to answer as Melasan heads to their table.

"It's good to see you again, Bruni." She smiles at Bruni as he nudges his brother again. "It's so many people here it's hard to believe they're all the same family."

"Yeah, Mom and Pops have quite a few grandkids, especially with you and Jeoff's." He smiles sneakily at Jeoff.

Jeoff looks away from him.

"Hey, Mel!"

Melasan, saved by Cee Cee's call, excuses herself and heads her direction.

"I know what you're doing, Bru, but me and Mel are just friends," Jeoff says to Bruni.

"It's been a long time for a friendship, and you won't even date anybody, so she must be the one." He smiles at Jeoff mischievously.

"I'm still married, so of course I'm not datin'."

"Tell me the truth. Do you have feelings for her? Y'all came to see me, Celeste, and the kids in Louisiana together."

Jeoff starts to protest.

Bruni continues, "And we all went to Disney World together!" He looks at Jeoff and raises an eyebrow at him. "So what's up with that?"

Jeoff looks around the busy crowd as though someone is listening in and leans close to Bruni. "Yeah, she's pretty special to me, but I wanna take my time. I mean, we have taken all of these trips together, but we never stay in the same room."

"Yeah, that's how playas do it." Bruni starts laughing boisterously.

Jeoff looks around as though everybody hears them.

He ignores Jeoff frowning at him and continues, "It's been three years that you've been spending time with her. You're worse than me and Less." Bruni calls his wife by his nickname for her and leans in to Jeoff. "Don't move so slow that somebody can move in, Baby J," Bruni teases, calling Jeoff by the childhood nickname he and Cee Cee call him at times.

"Court is Friday. I'm not divorced yet," Jeoff states flatly.

"Do you think that woman is gonna show up or somethin'?" He looks at Jeoff almost harshly. "Don't be a fool. You couldn't possibly still want her."

Jeoff shakes his head.

Bruni continues, "Well then, what are you waitin' for? I admire your gentlemanly ways and all, but three years is a long time for a woman to wait for a man." He smiles, showing all thirty-two of his teeth. "And it's been six years for you, my brotha."

Jeoff looks at his brother and smiles sheepishly. "I know how long it's been, and I have enjoyed Mel's company."

Bruni laughs again. "I hope you're more romantic with her than you are with me 'cause you're killin' me!" He pokes his brother, and they continue eating. "Seriously, though, Jeoffrey, y'all have a pretty serious relationship goin' on. The kids call her Mimi, and her lil' one is a part of this family too and calls you Papa J, so y'all have got some serious soul-searching to do." He cuts his meat and waves it in the air for emphasis. "Those kids are in this relationship too, ya know?"

"I know they are, man, and believe me, I didn't plan on everythin' gettin' tied up this long, but once this divorce is final, I'll get everythin' ironed out." Jeoff sighs heavily and cracks his knuckles.

"Have you expressed all of this to your wife in waitin'?" Bruni laughs at his own joke and goes back to eating as Jeoff frowns at him.

"My actions speak louder than my words. Don't you worry 'bout me, Bubba." Jeoff calls Bruni his childhood nickname.

Bruni raises his eyebrows.

Across the yard, Cee Cee and Melasan hug one another.

"It's been a while since I've seen you, girlfriend."

They both pull back and look at each other.

"So how's life been treatin' you?" Cee Cee asks Melasan.

"Can't complain." Melasan's face lights up with her vibrant smile.

She and Cee Cee sit down in some lawn chairs.

"How 'bout yourself? I see you, John, and the kids are still lookin' good."

Cee Cee nods. "Yep. God is still good to us." She smiles thoughtfully at Melasan. "So are you goin' to court with Jeoff Friday?"

"No, but I'll be at his house for the surprise party. You too, right?" She asks Cee Cee.

Cee Cee rubs one of her eyebrows, an old childhood habit she has never dropped. "So what kinda plans do y'all have for after the divorce is final?" She turns in her chair toward Melasan, waiting for an answer.

"I'd imagine the same plans we always have, travel and maintain our friendship," Melasan answers. "Why? Did you hear somethin'?" She wants to ask but remains quiet.

"Well, I just thought y'all had perhaps discussed the future, ya know? Y'all have kids and all." She looks slightly embarrassed. "I mean, not together, but y'all are a family, and I just thought…" She trails off, looking uncomfortable as Melasan looks uncomfortable. "I'm sorry. I should leave all of that business to you and Jeoff. I just think y'all look so good together, ya know?"

Melasan nods, smiling slightly and thinks to herself, *Yeah, I know.*

Chapter 5

"ROOKIE ETHEL SIENNA SIMPSON? ROOKIE Ethel Sienna Simpson?" The judge lawfully calls Rookie's name.

Jeoff reflexively looks around a courtroom that is completely void of Rookie. One wouldn't believe it literally took years as the judge easily and quickly puts his pen to the divorce papers and hands them to Jeoff's attorney. It was final. Final. What now?

"Surprise!"

Jeoff looks genuinely surprised as his brother stands beside him and the children bombard him at the door of their townhouse. He looks at them through softened misty eyes. Duran, now sixteen, is the child/man who, through the years, has always taken care of his dad and the other kids. He has been Jeoff's live-in babysitter who saved him many times from having to drop out of college without even knowing it. Duran is tall and lanky, already six foot tall, with wavy dark hair and gray eyes with long, curled lashes over them. His bronze complexion and lackadaisical attitude give him a "cool" aura. He's sensitive and caring, and the phone never stops ringing with calls for him. He's the commanding force as the oldest, and even if the kids don't want to listen to him, they do.

After Ni Ni was born, he called himself Big D, explaining, "Cause I'm big, and she's little." It was so funny to both Jeoff and Rookie that they sometimes called him that. Domininisierra, Ni Ni for short, is fourteen and a half. One must always remember the half. She'll no doubt give a reminder. She looks exactly like Rookie, with the exception of having Jeoff's chocolaty complexion, with long, wavy hair; olive-shaped eyes; and full lips. Jeoff constantly admits to himself that to have such beautiful daughters makes him nervous. Unlike Duran, she hints at dating right now, and he either sidesteps the idea or has finally evolved to outright striking it down. With the exception of strong boy craziness, she tends to be more mature than her years and has grown very close to her older brother and her dad. She always keeps perfect grades and is quiet until she becomes comfortable, then the conversation doesn't stop. She often writes poetry; and sometimes, even though nobody but Duran knows, she writes letters to Rookie.

Devon is thirteen and three-fourths and next in line to Ni Ni. There's only a few months between Devon and Ni Ni, so at a certain time of year, they're the same age. They share the same complexion, but Devon is the wild child and great at every sport he tries. He's always making plans for his future; and Jeoff's sure, the minute he graduates from high school, he'll leave to travel the world. He has mischievous dark eyes and wavy dark hair. His hair is always thicker than the other children, with Jeoff having to cut it often. A few times, at his constant begging, Jeoff has let him grow his hair into a curly 'fro, with Ni Ni braiding it. He's already five feet four, with huge feet and a vibrant personality. Mari, his grandma, always tells people, "He don't meet no strangers." He always talks loudly and claps like he's trying to get the crowd amped.

The twins—Jeoff and Marianna, Mari for short—are twelve. People often think they're Jeoff's youngest because even Cha Cha is taller than them. Mari has long, wavy reddish hair and innocent wide brown eyes with flecks of gold in them. She has the same light complexion as her twin, freckles, very petite features, and tiny fingers. Her babyish cheeks always get slightly red when she gets excited. She loves to play the piano, and Jeoff can never seem to imagine how those tiny fingers move across the piano with such ease. They both have knobby knees and love to roughhouse even though they're smaller than other kids.

Jeoff Jr. is a wiry, small-framed child. His reddish-brown hair has blond highlights year-round, and his dark eyes are always thinking up the next prank. His face is speckled with numerous freckles, and his small muscles have been forged from years of playing soccer and basketball as he loves just as many sports as Devon. He has a little darker complexion than Mari; and everybody comments that, although he's a "redbone," he looks like Rev. Simpson. Maybe it's from spending so much time with him because he loves to spend time with his grandpa. He tries to go everywhere with him, even to the church constantly, talking his head off. When he was just a toddler, everybody would laugh because, as soon as Rev. Simpson would move, even if it was just to the kitchen, Jeoff would throw up his arms, saying, "Go? Go?"

Last of Jeoff's crew is Sienna, known as Cha Cha. She's eight years old. She's taller than the twins, slender with a potbelly from eating every snack she can get her hands on. She has long, wavy black hair that's braided in two braids down her back. Her gray eyes sometimes turn brown when she's upset. She has the attention of everybody at church because she began playing the drums for the youth choir when she was five. All of Jeoff's children have some function in the church, and they love being there. That was where they found their peace after Rookie left.

When he and Mel started spending time together, Adrienne, Melasan's only child, became one of his. They have tried not so hard to let her get attached to Jeoff as a father figure. However, she naturally fit into the family even though she's younger than Cha Cha. Adrienne and Cha Cha have an understanding that nobody else seems to be involved with and love each other. Being the baby, she gets toted around by the Simpson clan. They enjoy annoying the older children, especially Duran when he's on the phone. They seem to both carry the title of Jeoff's youngest daughters with no argument from either. When Boo, one of Adrienne's many nicknames, was a newborn, the children spent lots of time with her even though Melasan's family lives in Montgomery. Jeoff was in the delivery room when she was born, and when people ask him if she's his, he says yes and moves on. Adrienne has a caramel complexion and shoulder-length hair that Mel always put barrettes in for her to shake and lose.

"Daddy, I kept it a secret!" Cha Cha scoots up to him and loudly whispers in his ear.

"You didn't keep it a secret! Nobody told you 'til today!" Lynnie, John and Cee Cee's daughter, tell on Cha Cha.

They run away laughing with Adrienne at their heels.

Jeoff is still smiling when Ni Ni walks up to him. "Daddy, Mimi and Boo are here to celebrate with us. I hope you don't mind."

He kisses his daughter and smiles. "Of course not. We're all family. I wouldn't have it any other way."

Ni Ni looks deeply into her daddy's eyes, and he lowers them in attempt to hide his feelings.

"It's over now, huh, Daddy? I guess she's never coming back." Her eyes draw Jeoff into them, and she says softly to him, "I'll always be a little sad that she never came back, but I'm glad we have Mimi and Boo. Mimi's the best mom in the world."

"So you think of Mimi as your momma?" Jeoff asks, already knowing the answer.

Ni Ni nods. "I don't have any other momma. Never will."

Jeoff looks at Ni Ni walk away and can't help but think, *She's just too grown.*

His grandma always said she'd been here before. There were times when Ni Ni could look right into your soul.

Jeoff walks out the glass door of his kitchen and smiles at how they pulled together this party at his own house. He spies Melasan across the backyard and can't help but notice that she looks absolutely beautiful with her caramel-colored skin and jet-black bobbed hair streaked by the summer sun. She's a vibrant and very pretty woman with full lips that seem to always hold a smile and a soft feminine shape that's accentuated by the lime-green summer dress she has on. Her brown eyes seem to always be serene, and sometimes Jeoff finds himself drawn into them, fighting back the desire to kiss her on several different occasions. His appeal to her isn't anything like the appeal he had to Rookie. He thinks about how he thought being married to somebody everybody wanted would make him a superstar and winces.

As he winces, he reminisces about how he always kept the same phone number even when he and the kids moved in with his parents for two years. He moved the phone line to his bedroom just in case Rookie called and wanted to come home. Every time the phone rang, it was never her. It took him three years after her disappearance to file the divorce papers, and then it took another year to actually go through everything because she called her mother a couple of times.

When she contacted her drunkard mother, Miss Phyllis contacted Jeoff and said Rookie was coming home. He couldn't count how many nights he was consumed with loneliness and how many nights he dreamed that she would come home a completely changed woman, ready to be a wife and mother. It never happened, and his heart remained broken for many years.

Finally, three years after the disappearance of Rookie, Melasan reappeared in his life. She's always been there. She is a member of the church they attend, and his dad pastors. His family always assume they met three years ago because that's when they began to spend so much time together. However, Jeoff met her when he was nineteen and she was fifteen. She was just a kid to him but more than a help with the kids as Devon was a newborn then. She seemed to know things about kids that Rookie didn't even think about. Sometimes he couldn't pay her, and to this day, he is sure he still owes her babysitting money.

Melasan looks over at Jeoff while she talks to his mom and smiles. He smiles back and continues to reminisce.

One night, when he got off work, Bruni was waiting for him.

"What are you doin' here?" he remembers asking.

"I figured I'd pick you up since I've been in town two days and you never come home," Bruni answered.

"I work and go to school," Jeoff said, getting quiet.

They drove around for a while just talking about life, and then Bruni stopped at a gas station. When he pulled up, Jeoff immediately saw Rookie in a skimpy minidress inside the gas station hanging all onto some dude.

He ran in and grabbed her arm. "What's goin' on here?"

She looked shocked and didn't answer.

"Where are the kids?"

"Don't you question me!" She yanked her arm back and almost fell as she was drunk.

He remembered asking her before if she was cheating on him because he heard things, but she denied it. Jeoff walked closer to her;

and the guy, who turned out to be Devon Keyes, stepped into his way.

Jeoff pushed Devon. "Man, this is my wife!"

Devon stepped back arrogantly and said, "Well, she's with me."

Devon went to say something else, and Jeoff hit him so hard they both crashed through the glass door at the gas station. Blood sprayed everywhere as Jeoff tried to take out his frustrations by beating Devon silly.

"Stop it! Stop it!" he could hear Rookie screaming.

Finally Bruni, Jeoff's brother, pulled them apart; and Rookie clumsily helped Devon up.

"I don't care if you never see those kids again! We're through!" she slurred.

Jeoff began to walk away.

"Do you hear me?" She staggered behind him. "You're an animal! There's nothin' goin' on! We're just friends!"

Devon laughed in the background, and Rookie continued to walk behind Jeoff. Jeoff turned around and looked at her. The look on his face made her stop talking.

"We're through, right?"

She didn't say anything, just kind of swayed.

"Then get on somewhere!" He snorted and walked away.

He had Bruni take him back to his car, and he went to the apartment thinking she might've cooled down and returned. When he found out she hadn't, he went back to his parents' and stayed a few days to cool himself down. When he returned after his hiatus, she still hadn't returned, so finally he asked around to find out where Devon stayed and went to get her and the kids. She didn't come, but he got the kids. Ni Ni was only a few months old when that happened, so he couldn't rationalize with himself that marriage was getting to her.

The two weeks that she was gone seemed to actually move smoother. He and the kids found their rhythm. He found a sitter in Tuskegee because, in those days, Melasan wasn't his sitter. He was able to pick up the kids after he got out of class. One of the neighbors was his sitter for when he had to work, and everything was progressing like a well-oiled machine.

When Rookie returned, he wouldn't touch her. He wouldn't sleep in the same bed with her and had made up his mind that he and she could just be roommates. She was intoxicating to him, and staying away from her just didn't seem to work for him then. He sometimes felt like he had to rescue her from herself and that, if he gave her enough love, she'd be able to do better. When she returned, she looked at him sadly and made her plea, said something about wanting to be a better mother for the kids. It was the same thing every time, maybe not word for word, but the same nonetheless.

"Why do you drink so much!" he yelled at her.

He knew Rookie was a drinker when he met her, but he thought she was just a social drinker like most people. She was normally drunk on most weekdays when he got home from school or work.

When he would tell her about it, she would say, "What's wrong with a few drinks? That's your problem, Jeoff. You're a square! Big ole L7!" Then she'd laugh and turn over on the couch.

She made fun of him constantly for being the solid person in their relationship and sometimes made him feel ashamed of that fact. Jeoff remembered not actually wanting to try with Rookie, but after Devon, she got pregnant with the twins. He wanted out but felt he owed the kids a two-parent family. That's what he had growing up. The smothering feelings weren't stronger than the guilt he felt for wanting out of the marriage. He'd work through his conflicting emotions and admit that he still loved her and needed to work out their differences.

He remembered, during the pregnancy with the twins, she seemed to be really trying. He still didn't trust her and would start arguments so she would leave, but she hung in there. She found her typically sporadic job and cooked and cleaned. For Jeoff's birthday, she took him out, and they even had a good time like they used to. Even though Jeoff was getting close to finishing his degree, he was getting tired. He was missing classes to get more hours at his job, and at one point, he contemplated quitting school and getting a full-time job. Even though Rookie was working, she was still undependable with her end of the bills. She would have her check direct deposited and then would constantly take money out of the bank with no excuse as to where it went to. When Jeoff asked her what she was taking money out of the bank for, she would deny taking any out.

"I don't think you should quit Tuskegee." Years ago, Mel sat in his living room, talking to him.

The kids were all asleep, and they were just sitting and talking.

"I don't have any choice. I have five kids, and you can see right now that girl ain't never here!" He looked at Mel desperately. "All she does is party and say she's goin' to work. I know she's not workin'! And even when she is, she don't pay no bills!" He put his head in his hands.

"You have choices, Jeoff. Don't say that." Mel sat beside him, looking so innocent and pleading with him.

"*You* have choices. You're still young and know what you want to do with your life. Florida A&M all the way, huh? Where I should've been. You have prospects." Jeoff looked at Melasan like a trapped rat. "I gave up my scholarship to Florida A&M for all of this." He waved his hands around sarcastically and looked around the dinky apartment. "I got five kids! I just have to stop going to school for a while." He looked as though he was going to throw up.

"You don't have much longer, Jeoff. Why don't you ask your parents to help you?" she asked.

"My dad was so mad when I gave up my scholarship, and he has a heart attack every time she has a kid. They think I'm stupid. I am stupid. Thank God she got her tubes tied after the twins, but as potent as she is, she's probably pregnant right now for all I know. She's always pregnant." He looked quickly at Mel.

"You just said for all you know, so you have a chance. You have a good babysitter." She smiled. "And you don't have much longer, really. You have companies gunnin' for you right now, so you got a chance, don't you think?" Mel questioned him. "Jeoff, you need to let your family help you."

He shook his head. "I could kick myself for getting into this!"

Mel looked at Jeoff with admiration and love he couldn't see. "Don't say that. You have your children, and if it wasn't for you, Duran wouldn't have a father. Since you won't let your family help you, I'll keep watching the kids, and you know Momma and Daddy'll help." She turned to face Jeoff. "If you quit now, you may never finish. You're almost finished. You have your three years invested, and if you can just hold on, you can graduate this spring."

Jeoff looked deeply into Melasan's eyes. It was just a three-year architectural program, and talking to Mel, he felt like he could hold on. Her presence in watching Devon and then hanging in there for the birth of the twins gave him the strength to hold on.

The room seemed to heat up as they looked at each other.

"You know, talking late at night is something married people normally do." He paused and swallowed, noticing himself getting cotton mouth. "Mel, you are the best thing that has ever happened to this family." He paused and looked at her.

Her eyes were partially closed, and she seemed to just be waiting for him. He leaned toward her on the couch and kissed her. She had the sweetest lips he had ever tasted, and they seemed to melt into his. He rubbed her back and felt her body pressing into him.

He thought to himself, *This is too good to be true.*

As he thought, he was jolted back into reality; this was too good to be true. He pulled back from her, and they both looked at each other, shocked.

"Mel, this can't happen. Even if Rookie doesn't respect this marriage, I have to, and I most definitely have to respect you."

As she left that evening, he wanted to cry.

The job offers started coming, and Jeoff had the joy of graduation being ever so close, only a month away. Then he found out that Rookie was pregnant.

"All you are is a baby-making factory!" he blew up at her.

She wasn't even gonna tell him. He caught her throwing up and saw that familiar gray-faced look he dreaded so well.

"You ain't no help! You don't spend any time with your own kids! You don't do nothin' but drink and party!" he screamed at her. "How could you do this to me? Ain't the twins enough?" His brain started processing things, and he said to her, "What were you doin' while you were supposed to be gettin' your tubes tied? While I was gone to that training class? You were messin' around with somebody else while we all thought you were being responsible and gettin' your tubes tied!"

She started to cry and told him, "I wasn't messin' around, I swear! I went to get them tied and changed my mind. I wanted—"

"What? You wanted what?" Jeoff said maliciously. "You wanted to pull me in deeper. There's no deeper than this baby! You planned this just like you planned all these other kids!"

"Planned?" she screamed. "Like you some prize!" She walked toward him angrily. "You're slow, a square, don't like havin' fun anymore! Every kid I've ever had with you has held me back! This baby is holding me back!" She pointed at herself.

"Well then, have an abortion," he said.

Rookie stopped cold as though Jeoff had slapped her.

"We can't afford another mouth in this house!" he screamed at her.

When she didn't answer him, he packed his clothes and moved to his parents' house.

"It's over," he told them.

Chapter 6

REV. SIMPSON LOOKS AROUND THE yard at his children and grand-children and feels his eyes moisten with joy.

"Oh, it does me good, Mama!" he says to Mari.

He looks at John and Cee Cee and watches their children run around the yard with the rest of them. They have Lynnie, who's eight and a fireball. She and Cha Cha argue constantly because Lynnie, being the oldest of her brood, feels she has to run everything. Then there's John John, who's the same age as Adrienne, and she chases him around the yard for him to slow down every so often to punch her. He laughs every time he sees it happen. Ayanna is their youngest. She sits on the ground by herself. Everybody calls her a diva because she acts as though she believes she's too good to stoop to the level of playing with the other kids. She's perfectly content. She reminds him of Cee Cee. Every time she talks, he can hear his baby girl.

"Gumba." Her big eyes look at him as she tries to shake her thousand barrettes every time she talks. "Gumba, those kids keep running into my toys."

He smiles at the name they've given him. When Duran started talking, he called them Gumba and Grinny. The other kids liked it, and over the years, it stuck.

He smiles at his other grandkids as he makes them leave Lynnie's toys alone. Bruni and Celeste had taken a while longer to have kids. It even took Bruni longer than any of their other kids to get married. He started dating Celeste when he was twenty-four, and they got married when he was thirty. It took them three years of marriage to have Bruiser, Bruni III. Just six months ago, they had a little girl named Teena. Rev. Simpson laughs outwardly as he sees Celeste try-ing to clean mud out of Bruiser's mouth. He's all boy and true to his nickname. He walks like a weight lifter and looks like one. When he was just starting to walk, they called him Hercules, and he'd dance for them, his chubby legs bouncing up and down to the beat of their voices. Yes, Rev. Simpson reflects, he is blessed with his family.

At times, he feels closer to Jeoff's kids because they lived with them for a while, but he's always careful not to show any favoritism. The boys are always around if Gumba needs anything done around the house, and he appreciates that. He looks over at Jeoff and wonders what he's so deep in thought about.

Hopefully he's thinking about marrying that girl, he thinks to himself.

Jeoff, still deep in reflection, looks at Cha Cha running around and laughing and thanks God she's still alive. He can still feel a chill run down his spine when he remembers that he asked Rookie to abort her. He stayed at his parents for two months. When he would try to see the kids, Rookie would tell him that, if he didn't want this last one, he didn't want these either and she wouldn't let him see them.

How would Mel feel about one more child? he asks himself.

He keeps thinking about that kiss and what kind of future would he have with her if he weren't in this mess.

Jeoff remembers ignoring her for a few weeks and asking his parents to help him see his kids.

"I don't want her anymore," he told his mom.

"Well, Jeoff, I understand your anger, but if you're gonna fight to see the kids, do you want to see the last baby?"

That question jabbed him like a well-sharpened knife, and he thought about it constantly. He wanted to be free though. What was more important, the kids or his freedom?

One day, Rookie called and said he could have the kids for a weekend. He knew it was because she wanted to go out, but he was fine with it. She dropped a bomb on him though.

"You can have everybody but Duran."

"Why not Duran?" he asked.

"He's not your son, and I don't want him hurt like this last baby," she said vindictively.

When the kids got to the house, Jeff felt hollow with one child missing. While he was with the kids, they saw Melasan at the grocery store and later went to the park. At the park, they saw one of Rookie's little running buddies, and Jeoff knew there was gonna be trouble.

At the end of the weekend, Rookie came and calmly picked up the kids; but later that night, she came back. Jeoff frowns slightly as he remembers being groggy and hearing something like heavy rain against his window and then hearing it smash. He ran down the stairs in time to see Rookie throwing mud packs at the house and screaming, "You think you're slick, don't cha? Taking my kids around that girl! Well, you're not replacing me that easy!"

She pelted more mud packs and then proceeded to smash out his front window. Just as Jeoff was starting to head out of the house, Rev. Simpson stopped him.

His dad stopped him from doing anything stupid that night, and they called the police. Jeoff, of course, wouldn't press charges against her. He put clear plastic on his back window and rode looking through the large cracked circle in his front window. Later that day, Rookie came to his job.

"I'm gonna move to Florida," she said.

"Why?" he asked.

"Because I can't deal with seeing you with other people while I'm pregnant with your child." She cried as she finished her statement.

"I'm sorry for leaving and for asking you to get an abortion."

She nodded.

"Why'd you smash my windows?"

She looked at him, wiping her eyes. "I was messed up, and you know how crazy I get when I drink."

"Why are you drinking with *my* child in your stomach?" Jeoff yelled at her.

She flinched. He sighed, not wanting to get into it. The next day, he moved back to the apartment; and for once, his dad even seemed like he understood.

Rookie was once again the devoted wife during the pregnancy; and Melasan, of course, was no longer allowed to be their babysitter. Jeoff let his and Melasan's friendship drift apart and devoted his time to his marriage and his kids. Before the pregnancy was over, he made sure to officially adopt Duran. They always called him Simpson, even at school; but he knew, if he didn't wanna go through the same type of drama with Rookie again, he had to make it happen.

"Hey." A smiling Melasan walks up as Jeoff is thinking. "What you thinkin' so hard about?"

Jeoff smiles at her. "Nothin' really."

The two sit down on a picnic bench, looking toward the children.

"So…" Mel begins.

"Yeah?" Jeoff asks.

She looks away slightly and then looks back toward the kids. "So your divorce is final today, huh?"

Jeoff nods his head, and Mel looks at him.

"How're you feeling?" She looks a little embarrassed. "I mean, are you excited, sad…?"

Jeoff looks at her quickly and can't believe he's nervous. *I've spent all of this time with this woman, and here I am, nervous!* he tells himself.

Out loud, he shyly says, "I'm happy to be free."

He sits smelling the scent of Obsession on her skin and sees the flecks of gold glittering lotion and loses his train of thought.

"Well, I mean…" She drifts off and then picks at the wood on the picnic bench. "Are you gonna start dating?" she asks.

Jeoff smiles at her and says, "Yeah, I think I may start dating. Do you think I should?" He clears his throat and grabs her hand. "Mel?"

She looks at him and is breathing so shallow he can barely hear her.

He feels like he is leaning toward her, and then he says, "You've been the best friend I could've had through all of this. I want to know if you want me to date because I value your opinion."

Value your opinion? he thinks to himself. *I sound like I'm doing a survey.*

Mel looks a little upset and says softly, "Yeah, Jeoff, you should date since you're free and all." She gets up and walks away.

Jeoff looks confused.

He stands up to follow her, and Devon walks up.

"Hey, Dad!"

"Hey, son," Jeoff answers dejectedly.

"Dad," Devon asks, smacking on a chicken leg. "are you gonna ask Mimi to marry you?"

Jeoff looks at him with a slightly annoyed look on his face.

"We kids just wanna know so we can plan our next step." He smacks.

"Number one, son," Jeoff says to him, "you need to stop smackin', and number two, what is y'all's next step?"

"Well, Dad"—Devon swallows—"we need a house if we're gettin' a woman."

Jeoff Jr. calls to him.

"Hold on!" he yells. "And…" He looks a little nervous. "Can we switch from Mimi to Momma?"

Jeoff raises his eyebrows and smiles slightly. "Well, son, we just have to wait and see what happens. But I'll be sure to put in some good plannin' if we're gettin' a woman." He smiles and grabs Devon in a bear hug.

Devon struggles to get out and says, "I gotta go, but I'll talk to ya later, okay?"

Jeoff watches him walk away and smiles again.

"Hey, baby brotha'." Cee Cee sits down on the bench beside Jeoff. "I saw you lookin' like somebody stole your dog. What's up?" she asks.

"I don't have a dog," Jeoff says sarcastically.

"Okay then, since you wanna be funny, I just saw Melasan leave from over here, and you looked upset. What's going on?"

Jeoff sighs. "Now that I'm divorced, I don't know how to talk to her."

He looks at his sister like a small child, and she laughs.

"What do you mean you don't know how to talk to her?" she asks, still smiling.

"I mean, it's not like we're friends anymore. I'm divorced." He throws his hands up and looks at Cee Cee.

"Oh, Baby J." She pokes her lip out in a fake pouty face. "Why don't you just say, 'Will you be my girlfriend?'" she jokes and then gets semiserious as Jeoff looks even more upset. "You really don't know how to talk to her?" She turns in her seat and looks directly at Jeoff. "You know that's silly, right? I mean, you've been with her all this time. Just tell her how you feel."

"Cee, what if she doesn't feel the same?" he asks.

"Jeoff, now you're just being ridiculous. That woman has been here for three years and hasn't dated one person. Of course, she feels the same. You just need to go over to her right now and ask her on a legitimate date."

"It's a bit more serious than that." Jeoff reaches into his pocket and pulls out a ring.

"Oh, Jeoff, that ring is gorgeous. If she says no, can I have the ring?" Cee Cee asks.

Chapter 7

"HELLO, JEOFF." ROOKIE LOOKS SHEEPISHLY at a shocked Jeoff.

"What are you doing here?" Jeoff looks dumbfounded as though she is an apparition. He rubs his hand across his face, looking troubled. "I thought you—"

Rookie places two fingers gently on Jeoff's lips. "I know what you thought." Her eyes search Jeoff's for some recognition of the love they shared and finds it when their eyes lock. "I am so sorry for all I've put you and the kids through. I don't know where to begin..." Rookie's words trail off as she gets lost in emotion.

Jeoff steps close enough for her to feel his breath and smell his masculine scent. "I don't want an explanation right now. I just want to know if you're real."

Rookie melts and cries soft tears of joy as he touches her hair and softly kisses her tears. "Six long years, I've waited for this day—"

Rookie wakes up smiling as though still feeling Jeoff's hands. "There's still a chance. I've gotta go home to my family."

She jumps out of the bed feeling greater purpose than she has felt in years. It has been far too long; they could put all of the bad memories behind them. She muses; Jeoff has always been such a patient and caring man.

"I know in my heart there's still a chance for us."

Rookie floats into Miss Justine's office and announces, "I'm ready to go home." She looks proud of herself. "I got a sign from God," she says, flouncing into a chair.

"I didn't know you were a Christian woman," Miss Justine says calmly.

"I'm not, but I know a sign when I see one," Rookie says, still smiling. "You can say what you want, but it was a sign."

Miss Justine raises her eyebrows slightly. "What was the sign, if I may ask?"

Rookie gives a lovestruck sigh. "Well, I went to Montgomery and saw Jeoff, and"—she sighs again—"he still loves me."

Miss Justine moves her chair, and Rookie jumps at the sound.

"Is this a sign, or is it just a fantasy?" she asks.

Rookie looks angry. "I knew you'd have some wet blanket to throw on this, but it *is* a sign."

Miss Justine leans forward, her keen eyes focused on Rookie. "If you dreamed that one of the children were sick, would you still be ready to return?"

"Well...yeah. I mean..." Rookie gives a look of confusion, which quickly turns to one of determination. "Of course I would!" She smiles and sits back smugly.

Miss Justine sits back in her chair. "It's going to be a momentous step going back," she says.

"For me as well as for them. It's been too long, far too long. I can't hide my feelings any longer." Rookie looks distant, remembering the crystalline hope of her dream.

"If your mind is made up—" Miss Justine begins.

"Oh, it is!" Rookie says anxiously.

"You need to devise a plan." Miss Justine's sensible words snap Rookie from her reverie. "Do you have a plan?" she asks.

"No," Rookie says.

"Well, you will need funds as your family is in Alabama and we are in Arizona, worlds apart. You'll also need to contact your family."

Rookie looks dejected. "I didn't think about all that." Her excitement fizzles like a deflated balloon.

"Don't lose heart. Your time is almost up here, and I think I may have a way to help you find the money you need."

Rookie smiles as the clouds open with a ray of sunshine for her. She can't remember ever feeling so elated.

"You need to get in touch with them and let them know your plans," Miss Justine says to her.

"What do you mean?" Rookie says, mortified at the thought. "I don't know where Jeoff lives for sure. I...I just know his phone number," she replies.

"Well, you said his parents are responsible people. Send them a letter," Miss Justine answers.

"Why do I have to send anything? I can just show up," Rookie retorts.

"Well, if you plan to just show up, then I can't help you," she quickly states and sighs. "Rookie, you haven't helped this man at all over the past six years, and you just want to show up on his doorstep because of a dream you had." She shakes her head.

"I'll write the letter," Rookie says angrily, standing up.

"Good," Miss Justine answers.

Rookie shakes her head and walks out the door.

A few days later, Rookie is back in Miss Justine's office.

"You called for me?" she asks.

"Yes, I've gotten you a job at the law library on campus," she answers as Rookie smiles. "I called in a favor, and I explained to them that this is only a temporary job for you, okay?" She looks at Rookie.

"Okay!" Rookie beams.

"Although I don't agree with your theory that this is going to be a love nest reunion, I do believe you should go see your children," Miss Justine says to her.

"Thanks!" Rookie bounces off, her mind swirling with her own thoughts. "I need some new clothes, to get my hair did. Oh, and I wish I still had my ring!"

Chapter 8

"So, girl, are you gonna go out with my cousin or not? Every time he sees you, he asks about you nonstop. And he's a good catch, girl," Arika, Melasan's friend and hairdresser, says. "You said, if Jeoff didn't say anything yesterday, then you'd let all of this chase go."

"It's not a chase," Mel says softly, curling her hair.

"Well, all I'm sayin' is that I don't know anybody who would wait on a brotha this long." Arika looks at Mel, pulling a stocking cap over her short cut hair. "Which wig do you think Derek will like?"

"I haven't been waiting for anything. It's been a friendship," Mel says, sounding frustrated. "Plus, has Derek even seen your real hair?" She smiles slightly at her eccentric friend.

Arika is the type of person who changes her hairstyles with the wind, whether it requires her real hair or not.

"If I've told ya once, I've told you a thousand times. It's the right of a Black woman to have variety in her life. And yes, he's seen my real hair and everythin'." She swishes her hips. "I have to offer. I think he's my soul mate," she says, grinning. "Maybe that's what your problem is with Jeoff." She looks at Melasan.

"Don't start," Melasan says, shaking her head.

"I know you're a nice girl and go to church and all, but I'm sure even God thinks y'all have waited way too long. Why didn't you ask him out yourself?" She shakes her head as Melasan ignores her. "Anyway"—she smacks her lips and thinks for a minute—"so are you gonna go or not? If you and Jeoff are just friends, then what difference does it make if you go on the first real date you've been on in at least three years?"

"Okay, I'll go if you go to church with me," Mel says, smiling knowingly at Arika.

Arika's definition of going to church is to "meditate" on the week to come in the privacy of her own home and preferably while in sleep mode. Melasan is sure she will say no, and that will be the end of it.

"Okay." She smiles as Melasan looks completely shocked. Arika smacks. "Humph, yeah, I know you didn't think I'd do it, but this'll give me a chance to see lover boy and get you out on this date." She puts on a curly, long golden-blond wig reaching to the middle of her back and says, "If you're as sprung"—she accentuates the word *sprung* and twists her head—"as I think you are, then a sista needs to see what her cousin is up against." She sits at her vanity and begins to put on her makeup. "So should I tell him to pick you up Saturday?"

Melasan looks sick and nods. "What time should I pick you up Sunday?" Mel asks.

"Oh, I'll be ready, honey. Never you fear." She puckers her lips and looks in the mirror. "Besides, I may look so good you may have to worry about all the single men in y'all's church!" She laughs.

Melasan returns to her own apartment after talking with Arika. It is only a little while before she will have to pick up Adrienne from summer camp. These few little precious hours from running are a breather to her. She throws her keys on the kitchen table and lies on the couch.

I don't really wanna go out with her cousin, she thinks to herself. *He's probably a greasy scrub for all I know.*

Melasan reflects on how, years ago, she had left for college without so much as a goodbye from Jeoff.

I shouldn't even be worrying about him.

She couldn't believe he had so many babies with that…woman. When she got to Florida A&M, she vowed she would completely forget about that boy/man she had fallen in love with as a teenager.

Upon getting to college, she met Henry St. Cyr, the star defensive tackle for Florida A&M. He was so good at what he did that his nickname at school was Head.

When she asked him about the name, he said, "It's because I'm good at bustin' heads!"

They had a whirlwind romance and got married a year later, and within a year, he was the third-round draft pick for the Miami Dolphins. Their lives were on the move. Mel was right on track to graduate and transferred to Miami to finish up with her culinary of arts degree and be with Henry. She was absolutely ecstatic.

Mel sits up on the couch and walks to the kitchen to get some water. She can almost hear the knock on her door just like that day and even instinctively looks at it. She was in their small apartment combing her hair for dinner that evening when someone knocked on the door. It was Henry's aunt Florese. The coach had contacted Henry's parents, who then sent his aunt who lived in Miami to tell Melasan that Henry had died on the field during practice with an aneurism. Mel still barely remembers the funeral or her parents coming to take her back to Montgomery and then finding out that she was pregnant with her dead husband's child.

The phone rings, shaking Melasan out of her memories.

"Hello? Oh, yeah, I can pick her up. We'll meet you at your office. All right, no problem." She hangs up the phone with Jeoff, and her mind turns to him.

When she returned, she found out that Jeoff had been left with six children. She decided she wouldn't trouble him, but they ran into each other at a revival. His parents insisted they all go to dinner, and they wound up playing catch-up that night. He revealed to her that he had shunned church and God for some months and then finally let God take care of him. As they talked, she realized that he had matured so beautifully and had a powerful testimony. It was amazing how their lives had split and then come back together in such tragic yet fluid movement. She remembers going furniture shopping with him as his career took off and helping them move into the duplex they are now in. She smiles as she thought of how she and Adrienne became fixtures at Jeoff's place, cooking and cleaning.

Jeoff was there when Adrienne was born.

The doctor calmly handed Adrienne to him and said, "Here you go, Dad."

Jeoff didn't even correct him. He also helped her a lot. When they first got back in touch with one another, she was grieving over

Henry, and Jeoff helped her not turn her back on friends or God. She was also doing a lot of cooking for a catering company and traveling back and forth to Birmingham to Culinard to finish up her degree. When her schedule would get too hectic, Jeoff would pick up Adrienne as though she was his. A few times, it had to be explained to Adrienne that Jeoff wasn't her dad because she saw him so frequently; and sometimes, only sometimes, Melasan felt guilty for wanting to tell her it was all right to call him Daddy. She stopped talking to Jeoff at all in anger, so they consented to allow her to call him Papa J. Amusingly Adrienne, being very strong willed, still sometimes calls him just Papa or Daddy, correcting it only when her momma is looking at her.

Since Melasan was pregnant when she saw Jeoff again, she was amazed that he carried on the friendship and wasn't bitter at the obvious addition to his family. He was the only daddy Adrienne knew, and he was so sweet and never asked for anything. The kids and rest of the family automatically adopted her and Adrienne, babysitting and giving her the nickname Boo. Jeoff's kids began calling her Mimi after Adrienne was born, and the name just stuck. She knew they longed for a mother, so she filled the role, not even thinking how she and Jeoff could both be playing dangerous games with their children. Their families became one complete unit from day one, and she can't help but hope marriage will seal the deal; plus she can't forget the kiss they shared years ago. Sometimes, when she and Jeoff got caught in tight spots in his small kitchen, it would seem as though they shared moments. When they would sit up late at night watching television, she would catch herself waiting for him to kiss her again.

She is trying to be considerate of his feelings because she knows she has mourned her husband and she can't fathom how much time it will take for him to mourn someone when there is no closure. They aren't even sure if she is alive or not. Jeoff is so complex to Melasan. She can't understand why a seventeen-year-old boy would marry a nineteen-year-old girl with a baby and one on the way. She also can't understand why he is so responsible and why it isn't him who left rather than Rookie.

She remembers seeing Rookie and how other guys think she is so alluring. She is this Hispanic chick that has a body like a Greek goddess. She has the outward appearance of a young Sophia Loren with a Beyoncé body and never seems to gain any weight with the zillion kids she had with Jeoff. She understands what the sexual appeal is to her, but she doesn't understand why Jeoff stayed after the obvious cheating and drugged-up drunken sprees. He never discusses it with her, just said he was a fool and now had to sleep in the bed he had made.

Jeoff has shown some feelings for her a few times over the years, but she isn't sure if that is just because he hasn't had companionship in so long. Melasan sighs, remembering when they went to Louisiana to see his brother. They were on the deck drinking lemonade and talking.

"Sometimes I feel like my degree is a waste," he'd said to her.

"What do you mean?" she asked, sipping her lemonade and gazing at the sunset.

"Well, being on the board of architects, you have to take classes continually, and that makes my four years at Tuskegee seem somewhat a waste." He gazed at her. "I wanna be able to do something important with it, something that helps the people, you know what I mean?"

She nodded. "I know exactly what you mean. I don't want to be in the corporate world forever. I want to start my own catering company, partner with public schools, and give Montgomery teens who don't have their diplomas a chance to work with me and get their GEDs in the process. They can gain the training to be able to make some good money and get them off the streets."

Jeoff smiled at her and leaned forward in his chair.

"There's a lot you can do for people with your degree. It'd be nice to put some affordable housing up," she said, pondering.

"I'd like to buy at least a hundred acres somewhere and give families a chance to purchase a home regardless of their credit." His brow crinkled in thought. "'Cause it's not about that score on paper. It's really about your true character, which can't be calculated in numbers."

She nodded in agreement, and then it seemed to get comfortably quiet outside. It was late, and she didn't really want to go to bed because that meant she wouldn't see Jeoff until the morning. In the midst of her thoughts, Jeoff leaned in and kissed her softly on the lips. She could hear her heart longing to tell him how she felt about him.

She pulled back though, remembering their first kiss, and he looked bewildered.

"I need to check on the kids." She flinched, almost wishing she'd let that kiss continue, but she had to think clearly for the both of them.

He was still married, and what if they were ruining a friendship just to fulfill a momentary physical desire?

"I guess I was right." Melasan gets up distractedly and then flops back down. "If he wanted me for real, then he would've said somethin' yesterday, somethin' other than he's glad I want him to date."

Melasan knows her old feelings have been rekindled, and although she has loved her husband, she is very aware that she is in love with Jeoff. She wants to give him time, but now with the divorce final, she can feel her patience wearing thin with roller-coaster speed. She wants him to be the man she needs him to be—her husband, lover, and best friend. Many nights, after leaving his house, she wondered if he wanted to be her lifelong companion as well. He seems to be so much stronger than she is, and sometimes that hurts. She wants him to take her in his arms and impetuously say that he can't make it without her. That isn't his personality though. Jeoff is a virtuously self-controlled man in her eyes. She wonders if he's always been that way or if hurt played a part.

Jeoff and she have discussed their faith in God, and she knows they have grown both singularly and together.

She sits back and thinks about how Arika asked if she had asked him out. "Should I have?"

Melasan looks at the clock, grabs her keys, and leaves to pick up Adrienne and Cha Cha. The other kids are with their Uncle Bruni and Aunt Celeste. Today is the last day for summer camp, and Adrienne and Cha Cha want to pick up their "art," painted pieces of plaster of Paris, thousands of baked painted pieces that would be all over her and Jeoff's homes. She cringes and thinks of the different relatives she can mail them to and the ways she can throw them away without either of them finding out.

Well, she thinks to herself, *even if Jeoff doesn't want me, I know the kids appreciate me.*

Chapter 9

Rev. Simpson, Mari, and Cee Cee come into the house slamming the front door, almost breathless.

"Daddy, did you see that house?" Cee Cee asks her dad.

"You know I saw it." Rev. Simpson smiles, showing all his gold. "I'm just glad that Jeoff is finally gonna do this. I had no idea he was building a house and proposing to Melasan all in the same! This is the best anniversary me and your mom could ever have, I think."

As they are all smiling overseeing the new house, John comes in the door. "Mail call!" He hands the mail to Mari and walks over to Cee Cee, putting his arm around her waist. "That house is somethin' else, ain't it?"

Rev. Simpson sits in a kitchen chair and stares at the blue stationary in his hand, looking bewildered.

"Baby, what's wrong?" Mari steps closer to her husband and tries to look over his shoulder.

"What kind of silliness..." Rev. Simpson hands the stationary to Mari.

"Daddy, what is it?" Cee Cee's voice rises as she sees the shocked look on Mari's face.

"Dear Rev. and Mrs. Simpson," Bruni Sr. and Mari read together. "My name is Justine Moira. I am the counselor for your estranged daughter-in-law. She has been in the Arizona correctional system for the past three years. I have the understanding that Rookie has been gone for a total of six years, and at present, she has no idea where her family is." Rev. Simpson snorts, and they continue to read, "I have urged her to contact you for herself. However, this correspondence from myself seemed to be the easier process and will pave the way for any further correspondence she intends to send herself. In our counseling sessions, I have noted that she has gained a stronger sense of responsibility, which has been conveyed in her fervent desire to return to her family."

All four say at the same time, "Family?"

"She's got some nerve," Cee Cee grumbles as John nods his head in agreement.

Mari's breathing heavily as she and Bruni Sr. finish the letter. "I believe she has made considerable progress in her rehabilitation as she no longer has a drug abuse and drinking problem. At the completion of next month, Mrs. Simpson will have fulfilled her obligation to this state and, at that time, will make her journey to Montgomery, Alabama. I have consulted with my superior, and we both believed that contact was imperative as there needs to be time to emotionally prepare your son and the children if possible. If you have any questions, please feel free to contact me. If any of the family desires to contact Rookie, she can be reached at the above number and address. I thank you for your time and apologize for any confusion or strain this may have placed on your lives. Best regards, Dr. Justine Moira, PhD."

"Who does Rookie think she is?" Cee Cee asks angrily. "I get the impression she wasn't gonna let us know she was coming by the way this doctor talks." Cee Cee looks around the room angrily. "She has the nerve to still call herself Simpson! She needs to go back to whatever her name used to be."

"Marevangepo," Mari says sadly.

"Huh?" Cee Cee asks, confused.

"That's her maiden name, Marevangepo. That's the name she needs to use." Mari looks at Bruni Sr. "Will you get me some water, baby?"

He nods and gets her water.

She sits at the table, drinking. "I can't believe, after such a beautiful day and such beautiful news, this"—she points at the letter—"happens."

"What are we gonna do, Dad?" John looks at Rev. Simpson with wide eyes.

"They're divorced," Cee Cee says to her parents, wide-eyed. "Is there any point in telling him? They're divorced." She continues to repeat it as though it may not be true.

"Bru, who does this girl think she is? Hasn't she done enough?" Mari can feel her head pounding as her blood pressure is rising by the minute. She looks at her husband for answers. "You know"—she laughs sarcastically—"I remember when she asked me to watch the kids so that she could go get her tubes tied."

Everybody nods.

"I kept those babies four days." She looks around the room. "Remember Jeoff was gone to Baton Rouge for training?" She rubs her temples. "Well, I kept them while he was gone, and then when he gets back, she turns up pregnant with Cha Cha!" Mari shakes her head and rolls her eyes, remembering. "She left my babies and Jeoff six years ago!" She is almost screaming, and frantic tears have begun to stream down her face. "What'll this do to Jeoff?"

Bruni Sr. walks over to his wife and holds her face in his hands. "Calm down, Mama. It's gonna work itself out. You know Jeoff is much stronger than all of this." Without removing his hands, he speaks to John and Cee Cee, "You know none of us like what has happened, but we're gonna do what we know to do, pray, pray, pray, and pray some more."

They all nod.

"God has a great plan in all of this, and healing is on the way. Stay prayerful."

The four sit in the kitchen as the excitement from the day has drained out of them. Bruni Jr. and Celeste walk into the kitchen from the deck, wet, and smile at everybody.

"When'd y'all get here? We were talkin' with the kids about goin' to the water park later since they've been terrorizin' us outside with water balloons and anythin' else they can find. Where'd y'all go?" He stops smiling as he notices their facial expressions.

"What's wrong?" Celeste asks.

Mari holds out the letter, and Celeste and Bruni Jr. read it together silently.

"You know, this is all so strange," Celeste says, looking amazed.

"What do you mean?" Cee Cee asks.

"Well, when we were outside, Mari said to us that she had a dream her mom came back." She looks at her husband. "I thought it was strange 'cause they try so hard to not discuss her anymore and they were all such babies, but we talked about it for a while because it bothered her, and now this."

"Do you really think she'll come here?" Bruni Jr. asks.

Bruni Sr. nods his head.

Bruni Jr. sighs. "Well then, when are we gonna tell him?"

"I'll talk to him tonight. Jeoff can take this. These past few years, he's learned to trust in God far more than he used to. The hard part is gonna be tellin' the kids."

The conversation in the room continues as Rev. Simpson reflects on when Jeoff had to move in with them six years ago.

"Baby, Jeoff is in the living room," Mari told him. "He says he needs to talk to you. He doesn't look too good," she informed him.

She took the kids to the bedroom with her to watch television while Rev. Simpson went into the living room.

"What's goin' on, son?" Bruni tried to sound lighthearted, but the years had been stressful with him and Jeoff.

As he looked at Jeoff, he noticed his skin color was gray and sickly and his body looked broken in pieces.

It has to be that girl, Rev. Simpson thought to himself.

He looked Jeoff over and noticed he was much slimmer—in fact, skinny—and had dark rings around his hollow eyes.

"Dad." Jeoff got choked up.

As the tears fell from his eyes, Rev. Simpson looked at his hands, and Jeoff looked down. When he finally got his composure, he looked up.

"Rookie's been gone for six months."

The revelation took some wind out of Rev. Simpson, and he sat silently for a minute. "I don't know if I can say I'm sorry she's gone."

Jeoff looked away, gritting his teeth, and Rev. Simpson sighed, thinking how he wished Mari were in the room to run interference.

"What happened, son?"

"I came home from work and school at eleven at night, and the kids were there by themselves. Duran fed and took care of 'em. They told me that she left after lunch sayin' that she was goin' to get the mail and never came back." He looked at Rev. Simpson with tears threatening to fall again. "If Duran hadn't taken control, I could've lost the kids. Anything could've happened!" He looked at his hands and picked at his nails and resumed talking, "I know you think I did this to myself by lettin' her have so many kids." Jeoff looked up at his dad.

Rev. Simpson didn't remark.

"I don't know what to do. I haven't been able to go to work for the past few days or go to my continuing ed class because I can't afford a sitter." He looked down again. "I've even left them at home alone a few times, but I can't concentrate like that." He paused. "She left her keys. I don't think she's coming back, and nobody knows where she is. I've asked."

"Well, Jeoff, what do you wanna do?" Rev. Simpson rubbed his head.

Jeoff looked agitated and said, "I'm comin' to you 'cause you're the man of the house."

His eyes challenged Rev. Simpson, and his dad couldn't help but feel angry at him for a minute. Then he backed down as he looked at him. He had never seen his son look so fragile. It was time to set aside all the differences of the past and just be there for him.

"Son, I just asked what you wanna do to see if you have a plan. I'm not just the man of this house. I'm your daddy, and I love you."

Watching Jeoff struggle, he felt anger in his heart toward this irresponsible girl who loved to make babies but didn't love taking care of them.

"I don't know," Jeoff said.

"Well, son, you need to always have a plan of action. Have you prayed about it?" he asked him.

"Pray? I just knew you'd go there," Jeoff said angrily.

Rev. Simpson looked at him, confused.

"I guess this is just like the day you came by the apartment to tell me I needed to get back to church?" Jeoff glared at him.

"No, I don't think it's the same, boy." Rev. Simpson could feel himself getting agitated.

He began to pray. *I can't handle this*, he told God. *You have to talk for me 'cause I'm gonna choke this boy. I don't have any patience with him or his situation. Please, Lord.*

He felt himself calming and looked at Jeoff. "What's wrong with prayer, Jeoff? Son, me and your momma can help as much as we are able, but only God can fix this and carry you through," he stated, looking concerned as Jeoff was still agitated, moving about the room in jerky motions.

Jeoff turned and looked at him, no longer glaring and unable to control his tears. "Where was God when I met her? Huh, Dad? Why'd He let me get into this mess! Where was He when she just kept having babies or when she kept cheatin'! Where was He when she just kept leavin' and wouldn't help with any bills? Where was He then?" Jeoff was screaming hysterically.

Rev. Simpson just watched, letting him vent.

"I've asked for help, and things have just gotten worse!" He sat on the couch and quickly got up, pacing again like a caged animal. "What am I gonna do with six kids? It's been just me all this time, and God can't help me! He can't help me!"

Rev. Simpson got up and walked over to Jeoff.

The moment he touched him, Jeoff collapsed into his arms, sobbing. "Daddy, why won't He help me?"

It had been years upon years since Jeoff had called him Daddy, and now just hearing it, he knew it was in desperation. That night, Rev. Simpson put his son to bed like a five-year-old. When he told Mari what happened, they both went to Jeoff's old bedroom, where he slept. She cried when she saw the kids crammed into the room with him. Some were in the same bed, and the ones that couldn't fit slept on the floor around the bed.

They both got on their knees on the floor in Jeoff's room and prayed for him and the children. When they stood up, they went to his apartment and began packing for him. By the next day, they had his belongings moved into their basement. It took months for the kids to stop sleeping in the same room with Jeoff. When Cha

Cha would nap after kindergarten, no matter where Mari put her, she would wind up lying in front of the front door, waiting. After a while, despite the extra bedrooms in the house, not to mention two in the basement, Jeoff and the kids slept on the basement floor, and it broke his heart every time he saw it. By the grace of God, Jeoff was able to keep his job and keep up with his continuing education classes.

Rev. Simpson smiled. As a result of Rookie leaving, he got to have a stronger relationship with his son than he ever had. He never understood his decision to marry her, but now he admired him for being responsible enough to finish college and take care of not only one child but six. She could come back, but he knew in his heart Jeoff could take it.

Chapter 10

"Hey." Jeoff looks at Mel, and his eyes crinkle into a smile. "It's good to see you."

She feels her body tingle as he speaks to her and smooths her linen Capri pants.

He leans in to hug her, and Mel feels herself lingering for a whiff of his cologne.

She whispers into his collar, "I love you." When she pulls back, she can almost swear Jeoff kissed her neck.

I am so out of it, she thinks to herself.

"Daddy, can me and Boo go to the lunch room and get some victuals?" Cha Cha asks.

"Stop sayin' that," Jeoff admonishes her.

"That's what Gumba says," she answers.

Jeoff looks at Melasan again and then back at Cha Cha. "Well, your name ain't Gumba, is it?" He shakes his head. "Let me give you little bugs some change."

He hands her two-dollar bills, and the girls bounce off.

He turns and looks at Melasan. "I designed a house for a young couple, and the building process is completed, but a few finishing touches have to be put in it. It needs a woman's touch." He looks at her and smiles, his eyes lingering for a moment with Mel's.

I can't stop looking at him, Melasan thinks to herself. *He looks different somehow*. She sighs and thinks, *Gorgeous*.

"You look beautiful today." Jeoff looks at her and then turns as they head into his office. He sits at his computer with Melasan sitting in a chair in front of his desk. "Hey, goofy, you can't help me way over there. Come over here so that you can see my screen."

Melasan moves closer to Jeoff and his computer and smiles slightly as the scent of his Curve cologne washes over her body. She looks at him, and his lips are just inches away. So she moves back a smidgen, deciding she'll be embarrassed if he catches her fantasizing about nibbling one of them.

"So what do you need from me?"

"Well, she's into the culinary arts like you, so I need to design the kitchen so it'll be the most feasible to her and her children, and I need help designing the bedroom. It's already set up as a loft bedroom, but I need some feminine colors to put into it." He leans in closer to her. "I thought, if their bedroom were somewhat in its own little world away from the kids, they would like that, know what I'm saying?"

Melasan feels Jeoff's breath moving her hair like soft wind.

"You know, Mel, I like your cologne. You smell so nice, real sweet." He brushes her hair softly with his fingers.

Is he flirting with me? Melasan thinks to herself.

Out loud, she gives him as much input as possible. "Well, if she's anything like me, she will like lots of yellows, blues, and brilliant white." She gets carried into the home in her imagination. "Some of the blues you would want to make a little darker so he doesn't feel like he's sleeping in a girlie room. And in the kitchen, I hope you put lots of room for the pots and pans and lots of storage and stuff." She leans into the screen. "Oh, I see you did. Oh, my goodness! It has the eight-burner stove! And the storage, so much storage!"

"I took some ideas from the Embassy Suites where you work."

She raises her eyebrows, impressed.

"The house has lots of extras and is cozy in spite of having to be large."

"Jeoff, this house is so beautiful. It looks like my absolute dream home. I know they'll love it." She smiles at him. "Where is it built?"

"Well, they bought a piece of land in Prattville."

She sighs happily as though picturing it.

Jeoff smiles. "It's near the river, and from the master bedroom, you can see it in the distance."

"It just sounds absolutely peaceful. If I were her, I'd put a small garden in the back for her herbs and fresh vegetables." She looks distant, thinking about it. "I love how you put the window seat in there and the office upstairs with the master bedroom. How many square feet does it have?"

"Two thousand nine hundred thirty-seven," Jeoff replies.

Melasan takes in her breath. "Oh, Jeoff! Can I see it?" she asks.

"As a matter of fact, you just reminded me. We're havin' Momma and Daddy's anniversary party there, so you'll see it then," he replies.

"Why there?" she asks, confused.

"Well…" Jeoff fumbles, feeling his face get warm, "because Prattville has asked us to help with their future building and growth, so I figured…" He pauses, searching for words.

"Oh, I get it. If everybody sees the house, then the people who come to the party will think about either building in Prattville or just plain ole' movin' there," she finishes for him.

He inwardly sighs.

"They have one of the best school systems in the country, you know?" she says.

Jeoff nods, looking at his briefcase.

"She should feel like a queen in that loft. Did you ask them what they want?" she asks.

"Well, the husband wants the small touches to be a surprise to the wife, so I can't really ask her for much."

As Mel nods her head, Jeoff leans close to her, putting his hands on the arms of her chair. "Would you wanna be surprised like that?" He leans forward so that their lips again are millimeters apart.

Melasan can swear she feels them lightly touching, like little butterfly kisses.

"With your own custom-designed house?"

Melasan nods as though in a trance, and they stay like that for what seems like hours. She just can't seem to find the strength to move.

I want to touch his face, she thinks.

As her hand instinctively moves, she holds it down with her will. Jeoff's eyes are searching deeply into hers, and the smell of his cologne is intoxicating. She can't figure out if he's messing with her or if he wants to make contact the same as she does.

Jeoff's breathing gets shallow, and he says, "I was thinking—"

Just then, the children burst into the room with their snacks.

"Daddy—Papa J," Adrienne corrects herself and smacks. "They didn't even have the hunka chunkas like they used to."

Jeoff leans back into his own chair, smiling softly at the girls, and Mel feels her heart sink in disappointment. She looks at Adrienne.

"Mommy, I had to get a kitty cat."

"She means a KitKat," Cha Cha says knowingly. "We made a list of who's gonna get our statues…"

Cha Cha's voice drifts off endlessly as Melasan looks at Jeoff. She can't quite put her finger on it, but Jeoff seems to look agitated.

"Hey, Cha?"

She looks at her daddy.

"You and Boo go to the waiting area, and we'll be right out, okay?"

Cha Cha doesn't answer, but she and Adrienne take off again.

Jeoff grabs his briefcase and looks at Melasan. "There's a time and a place for everything right?"

Mel nods, confused.

"I mean, you know that you mean a lot to me and the kids, right?"

"Oh, of course, yes. Y'all mean the world to us too," Melasan answers.

"I mean, uh, do you wanna do somethin' tonight?" Jeoff asks, logging out of his computer.

"Well, yeah. Me and Pooty can be by your place at about seven," she says.

Jeoff stands up, getting a better grip on his briefcase, and stands in front of her. "The kids are gonna stay with Momma'n'em, if that's all right with you?"

Mel nods.

"I know we haven't gone much of anywhere without them, but don't you think we should?"

Mel nods again, catching a whiff of that cologne again.

"So, six thirty'll be better, and then we can drop the kids off with the old peoples."

He smiles as he picks at his parents, and the two of them head out the door.

Jeoff stops right outside of the office door. "Oh, man, I forgot!"

"What's wrong?" Mel asks.

"I haven't finished tellin' you about the party. It's gonna be Saturday for their church anniversary and wedding anniversary party. We got them that cruise I was tellin' you about. We figured this Saturday because, that way, we can just chill out the last week, plus the kids wanna go to Talladega for the car race. That'd be somewhere nice we can all go as a family, right?"

He looks at Melasan, and she understands she's supposed to go. *Are we going out on a date?* she thinks to herself.

"Mel, did you hear me?" Jeoff asks.

She looks at him, and then it registers what he said. "Oh, yeah, this Saturday is fine." She smiles at Jeoff distractedly. "This'll be great exposure for that gorgeous house, huh?" she asks.

"Well, I'm tryin' to give you some exposure," Jeoff says and blushes. "I mean, can you coordinate and cater the food for me? I'll give you a key to the house so you can see how you want things set up and all that. There's still a few rough edges to the house, but they'll be done in time for the party."

"I'd be honored," Melasan answers.

"Great. This'll help with that catering business you were thinking about, right? I mean, that's what I meant by exposure."

Melasan smiles. *He's so cute*, she thinks.

Jeoff shocks her by leaning over and kissing her cheek. She jumps and looks at him. He looks happy, and she looks confused again.

"So are you still gonna help me out with this house?"

She nods. "Why do you need my help anyway?" she asks.

"Because I value your opinion. You have some good ideas that'll put this house together. Plus I don't really know much about putting colors together. You have a flair for that. He wants softer colors in the kitchen area because that is a place of sanctuary for her. He also wants

64

the bedroom to be a gorgeous suite that touches her heart. This'll be their first house, ya know?" Jeoff looks uncomfortable, sensing he has said too much.

They head out the door.

"I mean, the first house they're having built. He wants it to have a lot of her personality. I guess she's his sweetie pie, huh?" He smiles at Melasan.

Chapter 11

"ALL RIGHT, Y'ALL." JEOFF LOOKS around the Surburban at the kids. "Duran and Jeoff are already at your grandparents'. I expect y'all to act like you got good sense." He smiles at Melasan in the passenger seat and winks. "Like they know what that is."

"Daddy, me and Boo wanna stay the night. Can we stay the night?" Cha Cha asks.

"Can we, Papa J?" Adrienne asks.

"You have to ask them," Jeoff answers her. "Everybody is there anyway, so I don't think it's gonna make any difference."

He pulls into the driveway, and they get out and head for the door.

"Hey, kinfolk!" Jeoff yells out.

A gang of kids come running his direction. "Uncle Jeoff!"

He sees Bruiser duck his head around the corner and wave, and Jeoff heads the direction of the men. As he gets to Bruni Jr., Rev. Simpson comes up and punches him on the shoulder.

"So is this the night, boy?"

Jeoff smiles big.

"Now you know ya gotta be tender and—"

"Pop, how you gonna be tryin' to give Jeoff pointers? When's the last time you pitched woo?" Bruni Jr. grins as he asks him.

"Oh, I pitch woo all the time. How ya think I keep that good-lookin' woman in there? I might be a preacha, but the ole man's still got his game tight." Bruni Sr. nods toward the kitchen, where Mari, Cee Cee, and Melasan are talking. Bruni Sr. pulls his pants up in pride and nods his head in recognition of what he just said and continues talking, "Anyway, is tonight the night?"

Jeoff keeps on smiling. "I think I'm just gonna lay the ground-work tonight, Dad. I might be out of practice, but I still got some playa moves. I'm gonna—" Jeoff stops talking as Melasan walks up and smiles at everyone.

"What are y'all over here conspiring to do? You look like bad little kids over here." She smiles again.

"Yeah, they do," Mari says as she and Cee Cee walk up. "Hey, Jeoffrey," Mari says, kissing Jeoff on the cheek.

"Are you ready?" Jeoff looks at Melasan.

She nods. They head to the door with everyone on their heels.

"Don't rush back, son, okay?" Mari looks pleadingly at him. "Y'all kids take all the time you need."

"This is an important night," Cee Cee says, winking.

Jeoff gives her a look as Mel looks confused. Just as Jeoff and Mel open the front door, they hear a loud thump and a noise as though a sack of potatoes is tumbling down the stairs. All the adults run back down the entryway to the stairs to see Duran and Jeoff lying on top of each other at the foot of the stairs.

"What is goin' on here?" Jeoff demands.

Mari and Ni Ni run down the stairs, wide eyed. "Daddy, we were playin', and Jeoff and Duran fell down the stairs." As she is talking, Jeoff and Duran moan and groan.

Jeoff frowns at the four children. "Playin' what?"

Mari and Ni Ni get silent, still looking at Jeoff wide eyed.

"Playin' what, girls?" He gives them a look of severity.

"Football," Mari says quietly, and Ni Ni looks down.

"Football!" Jeoff yells.

"You know you're not supposed to play football in the house," Rev. Simpson says.

Jeoff looks at Duran and Jeoff. "Get up. Why're you still lyin' there?"

"Jeoff, I think they're hurt for real," Cee Cee says.

"Yeah, Jeoff, I think they might've broken somethin'," Mel says, grabbing his arm as if to calm him.

Jeoff takes a deep breath and looks around at the adults and then back at Jeoff and Duran. "Duran, can you get up?"

"Dad, I don't think so. My leg hurts real bad."

Jeoff rolls his eyes as Bruni Jr. and Rev. Simpson lean down to help Duran up.

"Son, I think we need to go to the hospital." Jeoff frowns and helps Jeoff Jr. up. "Come on." He looks at Melasan. "We'll take them in the Suburban."

"Jeoff, no. We can take them," everybody seems to say at the same time. "Jeoff, why don't y'all enjoy your evening, and we'll take the boys to the emergency room."

Jeoff shakes his head. "We can go after they get taken care of, huh, Mel?"

Melasan looks disappointed but nods. They pile the boys in the Suburban, and Rev. and Mrs. Simpson follow in their car.

Jeoff looks at Melasan as they sit in the truck. "I'm sorry, Mel. This isn't how I wanted this evening to go." He licks his lips and looks at the road.

"It's not your fault, Jeoff. You didn't push them down the stairs," she says quietly.

"Sit tight," Jeoff tells the boys. "I'm gonna have them bring y'all in."

He walks in the hospital and comes out in a few minutes with orderlies. The orderlies put the boys on stretchers and head into the hospital.

"I have to fill out the paperwork," Jeoff tells Melasan.

"They taken care of the boys yet?" Rev. Simpson asks Melasan.

"No, Jeoff went to fill out the paperwork," Mel says.

"Now that the boys are here, y'all can go on and go, baby," Mari says to her, looking concerned.

"Oh, it's okay. I don't think Jeoff's gonna leave 'em, and there'll be other nights, right?" Melasan looks at Mari, sensing something is going on.

Mari nods. They all walk to the waiting room and sit down.

"Everybody's been acting so strange tonight," Melasan says. "Is there something I don't know?" she asks.

"Only that I need some coffee," Rev. Simpson answers, smiling. "I'll wait for Jeoff though."

68

As if on cue, Jeoff walks into the waiting room, looks around for them, and then comes their direction.

"Well, they think Duran has a broken leg, but they're checking them both right now." He sighs, looking at Melasan. "These emergency rooms take forever. Are you hungry?"

She shakes her head, and he looks at his parents.

"Y'all didn't have to come, ya know?" he comments.

"Well, we were thinking that we could sit here with the boys and y'all could go ahead and go," Mari says, looking at Jeoff with desperation in her eyes.

"It'll be all right, Momma," Jeoff answers her distractedly. He stands up, grabbing Melasan's hand. "We're gonna go to the cafeteria to get a candy bar or somethin'. I owe you some kind of meal, woman."

He smiles at Mel, and they walk away.

Mari looks at Bruni Sr. "I want him to ask her before we tell him about the letter. It's killin' me to know this and not be able to tell him or not even know how to tell him." She grabs Bruni Sr.'s hand.

"I know. I wanted him to ask too so that he would have a bright spot in all of this." He sighs and leans back. "I've been prayin' on how to tell him, but that kind of information is just hard. I know he wasn't expectin' this."

"Expectin' what?" Jeoff walks up. "Have they said anything about the boys?"

Rev. and Mrs. Simpson look shocked.

"I didn't know you were there, son," Rev. Simpson says.

"I came to get Mel's phone. She left it over here by y'all." He looks at them as they look uncomfortable. "You know, tonight y'all have been acting as if this is my last chance to ask Mel to marry me. What's up?"

"Nothin' that we can't talk about later, son," Rev. Simpson says softly as Mari reaches for his hand, interlocking her fingers with his.

"Dad, you said it was somethin' you were praying about? What's up?" Jeoff sits down.

Rev. Simpson looks at his wife. "You go on and enjoy Melasan, and we'll talk later."

Jeoff looks like he wants to say more, but he consents and takes the phone back to the cafeteria.

As he rounds the corner, the nurse comes out to Rev. and Mrs. Simpson. "Are you the parents?"

"No. We're the grandparents. The parents are in the cafeteria. Are the boys all right?" they ask.

"They're fine. We put the older one in a cast, and the other just has a sprain. They both have bruises, but they should be fine. If you could tell Mom and Dad that they can take them home, then you can be on your way."

"Momma, I'll go get 'em." Rev. Simpson heads down the hall and sees Melasan and Jeoff leaned in close to one another talking. "I hate to break this up, but the boys are ready. Duran broke his leg, and Jeoff sprained his wrist. They can go home now." He looks at his watch. "It's already ten o'clock. Emergency rooms sure are fast, huh?" He smiles at them, looking a little stressed.

"Well, let's go get 'em." Melasan stands up and smooths her dress.

"You go on ahead, Mel. I'm gonna talk to Dad," Jeoff says to her. He watches her go and then turns to Rev. Simpson. "What's going on? Everybody at the house is actin' strange, and I know y'all are already strange, but there's somethin' up, isn't it?" he asks.

"Why don't you ride with me, and I'll have Melasan take your mom to the house with the boys?"

Jeoff nods, and they head to get the boys.

Jeoff and his dad get into his dad's car and ride silently for a while.

Rev. Simpson sighs. "Jeoff?"

Jeoff nods, waiting.

"The other day, we got a letter about Rookie."

Jeoff looks confused but says nothing.

"She's been in Arizona for the past three years and God only knows where else for the other three." He looks at Jeoff and clears his throat. "Look, son—"

"Is she dead?" Jeoff asks, fuming.

"No. She wants to return to Montgomery and see you and the kids." Rev. Simpson pulls over at a gas station and turns to look at Jeoff. "What are you thinkin'?"

"Is this why y'all wanted me to propose so bad tonight?"

Rev. Simpson nods. "I just wanted you to have some bright spot before I told you this."

Jeoff nods. "I don't know what comin' here is supposed to do for her." He rubs his head. "I've gotta tell the kids," he says half to himself. "Why now?" He looks at Rev. Simpson as he pulls the car back out into traffic.

"I don't know what to tell you, son. I was hopin' somethin' profound would come to mind before we had this conversation, but all I can tell you is pray."

Jeoff nods, feeling his face tighten. "So when is she planning to return?" he asks.

"I'm assuming a month. You can read the letter and take in all of this before you tell the kids. I know it's a lot." Rev. Simpson looks over at him. "You need to digest this before you tell the kids."

"Oh, I've digested it." Jeoff looks out the window.

Chapter 12

ROOKIE WALKS IN HER ROOM with attitude and sees a young lady sitting on the bed adjacent to hers.

She stops, looks at her, and says, "Who're you?"

"Oh, hey, girl. I'm your new roommate, Ranelle."

The young lady stands and offers Rookie her hand. She shakes it, still looking confused.

"Hey." Rookie sits on her bed and looks at Ranelle. "I didn't ask for a roommate," she says angrily.

"I didn't know that you had a choice," Ranelle says, on guard. "Look, homegirl. You need to talk to the powers that be 'cause they moved me in here."

"I'm not your homegirl, but I sure will talk to them 'cause I don't appreciate this. They got plenty empty rooms." She glares in the distance, sitting on her bed.

Ranelle raises her eyebrows and looks at Rookie sideways. "I don't know what's up with you, but you need to calm all that down 'cause I ain't done nothin' to you, but if you need it to, that can change." She calmly starts putting up her clothes.

Rookie scans Ranelle before answering. She sees an average brown-skinned sista girl with pouty lips and large doe eyes that appear to have once been innocent but now have seen too much. She's about five feet, six inches tall and oddly shaped with two spare tires around her waist, giving her a tough Michelin Man look. Her thinning hair hits the bottom of her shoulder blades and looks shiny and fresh as though it had just been freshly cut into its asymmetrical hairstyle. Her look is clean and meticulous, down to her well-manicured nails painted the same light blue with yellow and white accents as her Denver Nuggets basketball outfit. She has a light mustache, which merely enhances her hard "street" exterior. She puts Rookie in the mind of a dopeman's girl.

"Look, I've had a bad day. You do what you need to do."

"So what's your name since you say it ain't homegirl?" Ranelle asks.

"It's Rookie," Rookie answers as she watches Ranelle tape up a child's picture of three people holding hands under a rainbow. "You got kids?"

"Yeah, Rookie, I do." Ranelle looks at Rookie as though the conversation is closed.

The day progresses with no more talk between the ladies. The next morning, Rookie gets ready for her job. As she pulls her hair into a ponytail holder, she notices Ranelle sitting on her bed writing.

Ranelle looks her direction and asks, "So you Mexican or what?"

"My daddy was Mexican, and my momma is Black," Rookie answers.

Ranelle nods as though she understands and continues writing. "You speak Spanish?"

"A little, not as much as I used to."

"Me too. A little, that is." As Rookie heads to the door, Ranelle looks up again and asks, "So you got kids?"

"What?" Rookie, taken by surprise, stops short of the door without turning.

"Well, you asked if I got kids. Do you got kids?" Ranelle's eyes probe Rookie's back.

Rookie turns, her face burning. "I've got kids and a husband," she says, moving her head arrogantly.

"A husband?" Ranelle says, shocked.

"What you doin', writin' a book about me?" Rookie leans toward her roommate's paper.

She pulls it toward her chest.

"What's up with all the questions?"

"Chill out. I'm writin' my babies at home."

Rookie snorts and walks out the door. As she gets down the hall, she sits on a bench breathing heavily.

What's wrong with me? she thinks. *I am married with six kids. There's nothin' wrong with anybody knowin' that.*

She puts her head in her hands for a few moments, rises up, and goes to work.

"You don't love me, Jeoff. Don't lie and say you do," nineteen-year-old Rookie told Jeoff.

"Why do you say stuff like that? Of course I love you. Why else would I ask you to marry me?" Jeoff looked into Rookie's eyes, and she thought she saw a hint of sincerity.

"I love you too, Jeoff. I don't think I wanna be married though. Can't we just live together?" she asked.

He shook his head, looking frustrated. "Nope. I'm not goin' for that, and you know it." He scratched his head, thinking. "What's the problem? Is it 'cause we're young? 'Cause I got a job already, and it won't be three years 'til I get my architectural degree?" He looked at her in confusion.

"No, it's not that. Sometimes I forget I got you by a couple years." She licked her lips. "Babylove, there's a lot of difference between you 'n' me. I ain't even graduated from high school."

"But you could," he interjected.

"But I haven't," she shot back, and then she sighed. "You remember the song 'Little Red Corvette'?"

"Yeah, what about it?" he asked, looking like he was losing his patience.

"That's me." She looked down sadly.

"That's what you used to be," Jeoff told her, grabbing her hand. "Look, Rook, I know you've been around the way"—he smiled—"a few times, but this is you 'n' me. You know I don't bit more care 'bout none a that." He kissed her hand.

Rookie gets agitated.

"My momma says I'm always gonna be that person." She looked at Jeoff. "What if she's right?"

"What do you wanna be?" he asked.

"Well…I don't wanna be that person. Look, babylove, if we're gonna get married, then I wanna get my GED. I won't marry you until I get it." She turned and looked at him excitedly. "I keep startin' the classes and stoppin', but you're smart, and if you help me, then I can get my certificate, right?" She smiled at him, her pretty eyes gleamed in anticipation.

"Yeah, I'll help you, baby, and then we'll get married."

Rookie wipes her eyes quickly to rid them of the tears that have formed. She stares at the books as she quickly puts them away as though entranced.

"I am so proud of you for getting your GED!" Jeoff hugged her.

"It's no big deal. I don't know why you keep gushin' all about it."

She frowned at him, but he remained excited.

"With this step, there's nothin' you can't do, girl." He hugged her again.

She pulled back, still frowning. "Don't think this means I'm goin' to no college." She snorted. "That's for sidditty peoples like you and your peoples."

"Number one, my peoples ain't sidditty, and number two, you know you're just bein' mean."

As he finished his statement, Mrs. Simpson walked up and gave her a big hug. "This is a big step, baby. I'm proud of you." She kissed Rookie's cheek.

Rookie walked away angrily.

"You know you ruined dinner with your stank attitude," Jeoff told her.

"I didn't ruin nothin'!" she yelled back. "Can I help it if I don't like you and your peoples' sidditty ways? All that kissin' and huggin' on peoples ain't even called for!" She mocked Mrs. Simpson, "Oh, baby, we so proud of you." She smacked her lips and made kissing noises and then rolled her eyes, crossing her arms across her chest.

"What's wrong with affection, huh, Poo Poo?" He kissed her cheek. "I thought you told me you like affection." He kissed her neck. "Huh, baby? Is this sidditty? Huh, Rookie?"

"Rookie? Rookie?"

Rookie jumps as the head librarian touches her shoulder.

"I didn't mean to startle you, love, but it's one o'clock. I think you've almost worked completely through lunch. You better run to the cafeteria and grab yourself a bite."

"Yes, ma'am," Rookie answers.

"Duran, you remind me of your Pa Pa." Rookie had a two-year-old Duran sitting in her lap, rocking him.

"Pa Pa?" he asked innocently.

"Yeah, Pa Pa. He left when I was five, but I remember him."

She ran her fingers through Duran's silky hair, and he grabbed one to suck on.

"That's why I named you after him 'cause I remember him." She kissed his forehead. "I'll never leave you like he left me."

The words of the promise Rookie made to her oldest child echo in Rookie's mind.

"Where you goin', Momma?" Duran asked.

"I'm goin' to the mailbox." She remembers stopping as she opened the door. "You wanna come with Mommy?"

Duran, who was trailing a couple of steps behind her, stopped and stepped back, wide eyed.

"Do ya, Ranny?" she called him her nickname for him. "You wanna walk with Momma?"

Eyes wide as though he sensed something wrong, he shook his head no.

Rookie finishes her sandwich and returns to work. *I said I'd never leave him*, she thinks. *I didn't promise the others. I promised him.*

"Ranny, you're Mommy's baby. You'll always be my baby."

Four-year-old Duran smiled at her, his chubby fingers linked around hers.

She remembers telling her momma that she was pregnant.

"I knew it!" she screamed. "I knew you'd be a waste!" She put her hands on her hips and stared at her crying daughter. "Ain't no use in cryin' now. What you gon' do?"

Rookie shook her head, oblivious.

"We gon' get you a project 'cause you gonna get outta my house. After this one, you'll be big with another one. You too fast to be good for nothin' else." She started to scoot away in her dirty purple house shoes but turned around. "You just as triflin' as yo' daddy. He got a million kids, and you gon' have a million too." She scooted away, yelling behind her, "In the mornin', we'll get you your own project, so get packin'!"

Rookie packed what little stuff she had, hoping her momma was just drunk when she said Rookie had to leave.

But sure enough, her momma signed her paperwork, stating, "She's too much for me to handle. She needs to be outta my house. If y'all don't get her a project, I'll send her to a kid's home."

"Our program will allow for you to finish school, still work, and take care of your baby," the school counselor told a still-pregnant Rookie. "It's a strict program, so if you miss over three days, you will be expelled and will have to find another way to finish your high school career."

The program took her from her regular high school, so Rookie skipped to catch the bus across town to return to her old school.

I know Jamie'll be there for me, she thought.

She and Jamie had skipped numerous times to be together, and Rookie was positive he was the father of her baby. When she got to her former school, she found the father of her baby hugged up with a new girl.

"You betta get off my man!" She yanked the girl from lanky basketball star Jamie Durbin's grasp.

"Your man?" the girl exclaimed angrily.

"Yeah, this is his baby." She poked out her belly.

The girl looked at Jamie for an explanation.

He shook his head. "That ain't my baby. I don't even know that gal."

The two walked away laughing.

The girl turned around only to say, "You heard my man. Get ta steppin'!"

Rookie spent so much time chasing Jamie and begging him to be a good father to her child that she finally got expelled from the school program.

"Young lady, I'm trying to help you with your future, but you have to have a hand in that too. This boy doesn't skip school to beg you to be the mother of his child, does he?"

Rookie shook her head as the counselor chastised her.

"The only one who has to deal with this pregnancy is you. He ain't big with a baby, so he's free, ain't he?"

She nodded her head, devastated.

"I'll help you find employment and make sure you get your prenatal care, but you are no longer in this high school program. I hope one day you'll take your future as serious as I do and as serious as your baby needs you to."

When Rookie went into labor, only the nurse and doctor were there to help. Momma came by once.

As she held Duran, Rookie asked, "Momma, can I come home now? Please?"

She shook her head.

Rookie continued, "Momma, I don't know how to take care of a baby by myself."

Momma handed Duran back. "No, you can't come back to my house to live." She stood and looked at Rookie. "You look just like your daddy." She turned up her lips in distaste. "What a shame."

With that statement, she walked out the door. After they left the hospital, Rookie and Duran lay on a pallet near the front window of her project, and she cried. She made up her mind after that night she wouldn't cry anymore.

The day ends with Rookie trying to will herself not to mull over her life. The minute she walks in her room, that plan quickly dissipates.

"What's up?" Ranelle asks.

Rookie turns up her lips distastefully. "Don't you ever go any-where?" She looks her up and down. "Like a job?"

Ranelle stands up aggressively and walks toward Rookie. "I don't know what you got goin', but I'm not gonna warn you too many times, boss. You need to redirect"—she makes a hand motion as though redirecting—"your anger."

Rookie tries to walk past her, and Ranelle moves to stand in front of her.

"What's up?"

"What's up," Rookie says.

Ranelle moves out of her way. "That's better. I know your momma taught you some manners." She sits on her bed.

Rookie sits on her own bed and snaps back. "My momma didn't teach me nothin'! What'd yours teach you?" she asks.

Ranelle nods her head slowly, hearing Rookie's answer. She sits back against the wall, and Rookie smirks a little at how ridiculous Ranelle looks when her feet don't touch the ground.

Ranelle turns her head to the side. "You say what'd my momma teach me? She taught me plenty. I just didn't listen 'til it was too late." She drifts away in thought and then says to Rookie, "It's dinnertime, so I'm gonna go get somethin' to eat. You?" She looks at Rookie.

Rookie nods, and the two stand. As they walk down the hall, Miss Justine comes out of her office.

"Rookie, could I have a word with you?"

Rookie rolls her eyes, and Ranelle gives her a nod and walks away. Rookie drags in the door, and Miss Justine follows her into her office.

"How's the job going?"

"Real good. It's better than any of the jobs I've had here, and it pays the best." Rookie smiles at her.

"Do you have a letter for me yet?" she asks.

"Oh, I see where this is goin'," Rookie mutters, frowning. "I'm workin' on it," Rookie answers.

"Well, I just wanted you to know that I've taken the liberty of writing the Simpsons for myself," Miss Justine says, crossing her legs to the side of her desk.

"You what?" Rookie yells. "You had no right!"

Miss Justine sighs. "When were you planning to write a letter? Were you planning to deliver it when you got there?"

Rookie rolls her eyes.

Miss Justine continues, "I told you that I wouldn't get you this job unless you wrote that letter, and you have not come to any sessions since that time, which I would call dodging me." She turns in her chair and uncrosses her legs. "Now I was born in the morning but not this morning. I feel taken advantage of." She looks at Rookie, waiting for a response. "If you don't want to write them, you can always resign from your position and find yourself a new job," Miss Justine says calmly, picking a piece of lint from her silk blouse.

"That's not fair!" Rookie says angrily.

"You knew the rules going into this, Rookie. I'm merely letting you know that I still know what we agreed to and that I expect you to keep your end of the bargain," she states, tossing the lint into the trash can beside her.

"I was gonna write it," she mumbles angrily. "Did they write you back?" she asks, suddenly curious.

Miss Justine shakes her head.

"Then what'd you want me to write for?"

"Because you don't disappear for six years and then just pop up again. I'm not quite sure how I'm failing you in my job because you don't seem to understand that." Miss Justine puts an elbow on her desk. "You have to think about the consequences of your actions and how the people you left behind are going to react to your desire to return to their lives."

"I'm tired of you tellin' me that," Rookie says.

"Well, I'm equally weary of your not listening."

Rookie stands up. "Are you finished?" She looks at Miss Justine.

"No, I'm not finished." Miss Justine stands as well, smoothing her skirt. "I still expect you to write a letter to them."

"What?" Rookie exclaims. "But you already wrote them. What could I have to say?"

"What do you plan to say when you get there?" Miss Justine asks.

Rookie smacks and rolls her eyes. "You know."

"No, I don't know, and they don't either. I imagine getting a letter from me threw them for a loop. Perhaps your letter will ease some of their tension." Miss Justine stands, adjusts her blinds, glances out the window for a moment, and sits back down.

Rookie sighs and chews her lips. "I don't have nothin' to say in no letter." She looks at Miss Justine. "Do you know what I should say?"

"No, I don't know." Miss Justine walks over and takes Rookie's hand. "If you love and miss them as you say you do, then respect them." She opens the door. "I'm finished, and I'll be looking for my letter. You have two days. No exceptions.

Chapter 13

"I DO LOVE YOU, JEOFF. Do you believe me?" Rookie's words invade the recesses of Jeoff's mind.

They had spoken the very night before she left. Jeoff shakes his head, remembering.

"Sometimes I believe you, but most times, I don't," Jeoff had answered her honestly.

She looked slightly confused.

"You do some horrible things when you're drunk, and you even have some mean words when you're not. You've been drunk or high most of our marriage and have put the kids' lives in jeopardy in your body and outside of your body due to the partying you do. I've blocked out all of the drugs you've used, but I'm sure you've never stopped."

"I don't need you to list all my faults. I..." Rookie paused and looked at Jeoff as though needing some help.

"Do you think this marriage can work?" he asked.

She nodded emphatically. "We can even get counselin' if you want," she stated.

At that moment, when he looked at her, he thought he saw the girl he used to love so much.

The phone rings, shaking Jeoff out of his reverie.

"Jeoff here."

"Hey, Pokey Butt." Mel's cheerful voice rings through the phone. "You wanna come to the Embassy for lunch?" She pauses. "I figured, since dinner wasn't dinner last night, we could try lunch today."

"Sunshine, I don't think I'm gonna be able to do lunch today." Jeoff catches himself sounding dejected and tries to change the tone. "Maybe we can get together tonight. I just got a lot to do."

"All right." Melasan voice sounds soft and fades slightly. "I wanted to talk to you about the menu for this weekend," she says.

"Oh, baby. I forgot all about it. So much is goin' on. I tell you what. I'll come over there, and you can run it past me."

"All right." She perks up. "I'll see you in about what? An hour?" she asks.

"Yeah. I have a meetin' first, and then I'll be over there. I love you." He hangs up.

Mel sits on the other end, not believing what she has just heard.

Jeoff turns to his computer and stares at it.

"Where's your mom?" Jeoff looked at the kids.

Duran looked at him, wide-eyed.

"Where's your momma!" He remembers getting loud and then getting his thoughts together, wiping his forehead.

"Momma went to get the mail," Duran stated this point-blank as though, at eleven o'clock at night, it could still be a possibility.

Through more conversation, he found out that Duran had taken care of the kids and felt his face flame like fire. He got the kids together. They had each fallen asleep on the floor in front of the television, so Jeoff put them in bed and then stood in the small kitchen, looking out the window. There was nobody left to help him. He had alienated Melasan, and she was gone to school anyway. He couldn't call his parents and hear the same song from his dad.

Jeoff punched the wall next to the cabinets in frustration, leaving a dent in the wall and blood on his hand.

"She better not come back!" he said out loud. "I'm sick of this!"

Day after day, he remembers getting more and more furious. He went through the motions of taking care of the kids and himself and stopped going to class because he couldn't find a sitter. It was better this way, he told himself.

One morning, he gave Duran instructions on watching the kids and left for work. That evening, as he pulled up to the apartment, he slowed and then continued driving. By the time he came to himself, he was on the outskirts of Mobile. He thought about the kids, and the tears began to fall.

"I don't have anything to give those kids! I mean it!"

He swerved as he thought about all the times he held a baby in his arms, the pudgy fingers that had linked around his. He heard the radio play as his mind saw the kids dancing around the living room.

"I thought, when I graduated, we had a chance, and now you do this!"

He hit the steering wheel. The tears were falling like a thunderstorm so that he can barely see, so he pulled off the road. He didn't know how long he sat there crying, but soon it turned to begging.

"I'm tired. I'm so tired. I gave this marriage all I had. I gave that woman all I had. I have to go home. God, just please let me get home. Let me be the best daddy I can be to them. Please? If we have to make it on our own, we can."

When he got home, the kids were still asleep. He hugged each one and quietly apologized for even thinking of leaving them in that apartment.

"Jeoff, this is Professor Sapp. I notice you haven't been to class for quite a while. If you don't return soon, I'll have to give you a failing grade." He paused on the phone with Jeoff.

Jeoff twirled the phone cord on the other end, feeling his neck tighten.

"Is there something going on? Is there anything I can do to help?"

"Nope. Maybe I'll see you another time, Professor."

Jeoff hung up the phone and walked through the kids playing on the floor to the bathroom. He closed the lid to the toilet and sat on it.

What am I gonna do?

He looked up at the ceiling and then back at the floor. The apartment looked like a jail more and more every day. Sometimes he just slept; and other times, when he was awake, his body was tight and hurt. His arms ached as though he'd been lifting weights. No matter how much he slept, when he woke, the situation was the exact same.

Just then, he heard a knock on the door and then saw the shadow of young feet under the door.

"Daddy, are you in there?"

"Mr. Simpson, are you in there?" simultaneously the voice of his secretary is speaking through the intercom. "Mr. Simpson? I thought I saw him go in there."

Jeoff shakes out of his memories to wonder whom she is talking to.

"Mrs. Marilyn, I'm here. I'm sorry. I was in a daze," he calls into the intercom.

"Mr. Simpson, your eleven o'clock appointment is here."

Jeoff stands from his desk as his appointment walks in. Forty-five minutes later, Jeoff isn't even sure what happened in the appointment.

"I hate her!" Jeoff flinches as he remembers those words come from Duran's twelve-year-old mouth.

The months following Rookie's disappearance were hard for the kids. Some of them may not remember it, but Jeoff will never forget when Duran's birthday came and he thought for sure Rookie would return.

The night before his birthday, he had told Jeoff, "Momma's comin' home! It's gonna be a great birthday!"

He spent the whole party looking at the door for Rookie. After the party, when he said he hated her, Jeoff didn't know what to tell him because he hated her too.

Jeoff sits up in his chair as the phone rings again.

"Hey, boss!" He hears the familiar voice of Bruni Jr. "You wanna go play some ball after you get off work?"

Jeoff is sure Bruni has heard the news.

"Naw, man. I've gotta get to Embassy Suites and then catch up on some work." He's relieved he has something to do to keep his family off his back about this new information.

"Embassy Suites? What's over there? Another meeting?" Bruni prods.

"Mel works there, remember? We're havin' lunch, and I think I might even be late," Jeoff says, standing and grabbing his briefcase.

"Well, I'm here if you change your mind. You know I won't be here much longer."

"Yeah, I know," Jeoff answers.

"I'm serious, man. I'm here," Bruni repeats himself.

"And I hear ya," Jeoff answers and gets off the phone. "I'm not in the mood for everybody tryin' to make me feel better."

The phone rings again, and Jeoff ignores it.

"They can leave a message," he says to no one in particular.

"Jeoffy, I feel like you hate me." Rookie looked at him with wide eyes. "I know I've made some mistakes, but it's like you punish me every day."

Jeoff glared at her, his eyes brimmed with red from lack of sleep. "You've gotta be kiddin' me! What do you think I should treat you like?" He walked close to her, his body almost pushing her backward. "You've taken every ounce of manhood I have! Everybody thinks I'm a fool!" He stood so close the velocity of his breath made her close her eyes. "You're a drunk! A nonfunctioning drunk who only stops drinking to have more and more babies! You're a ho! A ho that never comes home! You don't cook. You don't clean. You just kick it! You make me sick! I used to adore you, now I could spit on you!"

Jeoff stares out the window in his office as tears roll down his face.

"You do hate me!" Rookie screamed at him.

Jeoff sat on their tattered couch, deflated. "No, I don't hate you. I hate myself…for loving you."

With his hands pressed against the warm glass of the window, he thinks about how he blamed himself for Rookie leaving. "If I'd only tried harder." After that feeling passed, he remembered feeling intense anger. So much was going on that he couldn't handle, and finally he allowed God to step in and show him he wasn't a failure. Year after year, he waited for news she had died, only to receive word that she wanted to scramble his life and the kids' lives up again.

Jeoff walks over to his phone and checks the messages.

"Where you at, son?"

The familiar voice of his dad made him smile.

"We all wanna barbecue tonight. Bring Melasan with you and meet us at the house around six." Rev. Simpson pauses. "Go on and ask her, son."

"Bruni, who are you talkin' to?" Mari's voice calls.

"I'm tryin' to leave a message, woman!" Bruni Sr. calls back, "Okay, your mom's botherin' me, so I'll talk to you when you get here with Melasan."

Chapter 14

"JEOFF?"

Jeoff looks up to see Melasan standing in his office.

"Why didn't you call me?" She looks concerned. "Is there something wrong?"

"Wrong like what, Mel?" Jeoff catches his own sarcastic tone and sighs. "I just have some things on my mind."

"Well, you missed lunch with me," she states, trying not to look upset as she walks to his chair and sits down. She smiles playfully. "I'll forgive you if you take me to dinner."

"No, I can't do dinner. Who sent you over here?" he snaps.

Melasan's smile fades. "What do you mean who sent me over here? I go where I wanna go!" She snaps back at him. "Jeoff, I don't know what your problem is, but I'm just tryin' to figure you out."

"Why do you need to figure me out? What's wrong with me that you need to figure me out?" Jeoff asks, frustrated.

"Look, Jeoff, I'm hungry. I didn't eat because I was waitin' on you. It's two o'clock. Let's just go to an early dinner or late lunch, and you can get some air." Mel stands up from her chair and walks over to him. "I wanted to discuss something you said earlier," she says softly.

"I don't need any air!" Jeoff turns away from her.

Melasan's face changes to a look of confusion and then to anger. "I just need space. Tons of it!"

"Here's your space, Jeoff!" Melasan storms out the door.

Jeoff thinks about what just happened and contemplates calling her on her cell phone when the phone rings.

"Jeoff Simpson's office," he answers.

"What's goin' on tonight, son? We decided we've had enough barbecue and wanna try that Super Buffet over by the airport. Whatcha think?" Rev. Simpson's voice invades Jeoff's thoughts.

"What do you mean, Dad?" Jeoff says tiredly.

"You got my message, right? We're all goin' out tonight, and then we'll go bowlin'," Rev. Simpson says. "I know you're not the best, but you can handle it, huh?"

Jeoff sits silently.

Suddenly Rev. Simpson says, "I'm on my way over to your office."

Before Jeoff can answer him, he hangs up. Jeoff lays his head on his desk and then contemplates leaving the office, but as he's packing up his stuff, Rev. Simpson walks in the door.

"Hey." He looks at Jeoff quizzically.

"Hey." Jeoff sits down at his desk.

Rev. Simpson sits down in front of him, just looking at him.

"I don't really wanna talk, Dad."

"Good 'cause I just want you to listen." He puts his elbow on the desk. "Jeoff, has God been good to you?"

Jeoff nods.

"Real good to you?"

Jeoff nods again, not sure where he's going with this line of questioning.

Rev. Simpson sits back as though pleased with himself. "Then you know that, no matter what Rookie decides to do, you're blessed in all of this."

Jeoff nods again, understanding.

"This is just a stepping-stone in your life. God has given you a brand-new beginning with a beautiful woman and seven beautiful children." He looks deeply into Jeoff's eyes. "I personally got blessed when Rookie left. Do you know how?" He continues as Jeoff looks confused, "I got to rebuild my relationship with my baby son."

Jeoff smiles tiredly as Rev. Simpson stands up.

"Remember, in all of this, God *will* get the glory."

"Thanks, Dad," Jeoff says, hugging him.

"You need to go to your prayer closet and talk to the Lord. He understands what you're feeling right now, but you need to talk to Him so that you can get things back in place." He holds Jeoff's face. "Okay?"

"Okay."

"Good! I gotta go. I'd like to see ya tonight." He doesn't wait for an answer, just walks out. As he reaches the door, he stops and turns around. "Love you, Jeoff."

"Love you too, Pappy," Jeoff replies.

After his dad leaves, Jeoff grabs his briefcase and heads out the door himself. "Mrs. Marilyn, I'm going to the construction site for a couple hours. You can catch me on my cell if anybody needs me." Jeoff walks to the parking garage and sighs as he sees his brother leaning against his Suburban. "What's goin' on?"

"I came to see about you." He looks at Jeoff.

Jeoff sighs. "Man, can a brotha get a break?" He grabs his keys and unlocks the doors.

"Where ya headed?" Bruni asks. "I'll go with you."

He opens the passenger side door as Jeoff says, "I really wanted to go alone…but I guess you're welcome." He goes to the driver's side and gets in, starting the ignition. "I guess you're wondering if I'm all right?"

Bruni nods.

"I am. I just got a lot on my mind." He looks at Bruni as they pull out of the parking lot.

They drive in silence for a while.

Then Bruni asks, "Did you ever think she'd be in touch?"

Jeoff shakes his head.

"I did. I figured it was just a matter of time. I figured she'd show up when you got Architect of the Year or somethin'."

Jeoff smiles at him. "I feel stupid, man," he says, hearing his CD changer playing one of Ben Tankard's soothing melodies.

Bruni looks a little confused.

Jeoff continues, leaning one hand on the steering wheel, "I don't have any of my friends from school 'cause nobody's dumb enough to get into the mess I'd made of my life."

"Believe me, there's plenty people dumb enough," Bruni assures him.

Jeoff rolls his eyes as they hit the highway.

"Where're we goin'?" he questions.

"I'm gonna show you part of my vision for the future," he says as the changer changes to the Winans' "It's been a long time comin' / But a change is gonna come." "You know, this song kept me going many a day and night. I watched many of my homeboys get them a good wife and move forward with their lives, but here I was steady havin' kids with a girl who didn't want nothin' out of life but her drink, drugs, and to leave me with more babies to take care of!" He lightly pounds the steering wheel just thinking about it. "I always wondered what it would be like to not be the fool in a relationship, to have somebody who loved me for me, who would be there no matter what. I know you know what I mean." He looked over at Bruni and then back at the road.

"You know, Jeoff, I haven't been through what you've been through, but everybody's somebody's fool, and there are way more brothas out there that have gone through what you're goin' through. Most people do what you did and don't talk about it, believe that. Look, I know you think I'm this big playa that kept Celeste waiting forever, but what y'all don't know is that she left me for about a year and a half."

Jeoff looks at him, incredulous. "You're just lyin' to make me feel better," he says.

"Nope. I couldn't stop cheatin', Jeoff." He scratches his inner ear and looks out the window. "She knew, but she just kept waitin' on me to grow up and get it together, but finally she got tired and left me"—he sighs—"for somebody else. Man, I did so much beggin' and pleadin'. He had so much of her attention, and she seemed like her mind was made up, and it wasn't to keep me." He looks at Jeoff again. "I became her fool. I didn't care where she had been or who she had been with, I just wanted her. When I got her back, I asked her to marry me and she said she wanted to wait. That scared me half to death." As Jeoff pulls into Prattville, Bruni thinks and then continues talking, "I always admired you for being more responsible than I ever have been. I think Rookie's leavin' was the best thing that could've ever happened to you and the kids."

Jeoff looks at him.

"I also think that her thinkin' about returnin' is the best thing that could ever happen to y'all as well."

Jeoff looks confused as he drives through town.

"I don't mean for a reunion. I mean for y'all to get on with your lives. I don't think you'd be where you are right now if she hadn't left."

They drive through a subdivision, and at the very back on a large piece of property, they stop.

Jeoff cuts off the engine. "This is where I was headed."

Bruni sits in the truck, looking at an expansive house with a long porch in the front, dormer windows on the second floor, and dazzling architectural effects. It has Jeoff's personality written all over it.

"What's this, Baby J?" He smiles.

"This is the house I had built for my family." He stares at the house and smiles. "I wanna propose to Mel in this house and live the rest of my life with her in this house." He gets out and opens Bruni's door. "I've been workin' on this house a long time," he says.

"You are one secretive brotha." He hits him on the shoulder. "I'd marry you if you built me this house, that's for sho." He shakes his head in amazement. "I'm gonna walk around for a while. I know you didn't come out here to talk to me." He walks away.

Jeoff nods, thinking of the simple yet full words his dad spoke to him.

He stands in the yard and listens to the trees blow in the breeze and then goes to the porch and sits in the porch swing. As the wind lightly drifts through the porch, he closes his eyes.

"It's been a long walk, Lord, but I'd be a lie to You if I said I'd rather let go of my journey now. You've brought me and these kids too far to give up just 'cause that woman says she's comin' back." He grits his teeth and continues to talk, rocking in the swing, "I ask that You give me the strength to move forward with my life. I thank You for my kids each and every one of them, and I thank You for the time that me and Rookie had together. It helped me grow in You. I thank

You for Mel, and I ask that You allow her to forgive me for forgettin'
how special all of our time has been together. I understand what
Daddy was sayin' and that You have taken care of me."

A tear falls from his eye, and he wipes it away, still keeping his
eyes closed.

"I thank You. I thank You. I thank You. I thank You for opening
my eyes and my heart. In the name of Jesus, let me be a blessing."

He opens his eyes and walks toward the Suburban more peaceful, his steps fluid and purposeful. Soon after, Bruni comes, and they
head back toward Montgomery.

As Jeoff heads back into Montgomery, he finds himself heading
to Embassy Suites. "Hey, Bru, you mind if we make anotha stop?"

Bruni shrugs his broad shoulders. "I'm a stowaway. Do what
you gotta do."

They stop at Embassy Suites, and Jeoff gets out and walks in
the hotel.

"Good afternoon," he says to the front desk clerk. "Could I
speak with Melasan St. Cyr?"

"Certainly, sir." The front desk clerk gets on the phone and calls
for Melasan.

As she walks out and sees Jeoff, her smile disintegrates.

"Thank you, Todd," she says to the clerk. "What can I do for
you, Mr. Simpson?" Her eyes cloud over with hurt as she looks at
Jeoff.

Jeoff reaches out for her hand, and she pulls back.

"I need to talk to you," he says.

"Oh, you talked plenty earlier. Now unless you came to talk
about the food for the party, we don't have anything else to talk
about." She looks at him impatiently.

"Look, just come into the courtyard with me. Can you do that?
I just need to tell you somethin' real quick, and then I'll leave, okay?"

Melasan sighs, and they head into the courtyard together. Jeoff
sits and motions for her to sit as well.

"I've been horrible this past couple of days, and one thing I have
to learn is not to take my problems out on other people."

He looks at Melasan, and she says nothing.

He sighs. "I found out that Rookie is coming back to Montgomery." Melasan raises her eyebrows as Jeoff continues, "It's amazing how you think you've gotten over something until it gets put in your face again. I thought all of my anger was gone, but the minute I heard she was coming here, I got so mad I couldn't take it." He looks at his hands. "It took me until today to understand that our relationship wasn't a waste of time. It helped me grow into the man I've been blessed to become. I'm sorry for snappin' at you and pushin' you away. That's not what our relationship is about."

"It's okay, Jeoff. That's quite a bit of information in a short amount of time." She smiles at him sheepishly.

"I had no right to hurt my sunshine though." He looks at her and smiles. "I have somethin' in my truck that I need to give you."

They both stand up, and he grabs her hand.

"You are one of the most important people in my life, and—"

"Melasan St. Cyr, you have a phone call on line 2."

The desk clerk's voice can be heard on the loudspeaker, and Jeoff looks disappointed.

"Jeoff, I've gotta go," Melasan says to Jeoff as he looks at her like a lost puppy.

"We'll talk tonight?" he asks.

"I've gotta get everything ready for your parents' party, so I probably won't see you until Saturday at the party," she answers.

"Okay, I'll see you then." He starts to walk away.

"Oh, and, Jeoff?"

He turns around.

"I won't be staying for the whole party," she says sadly. "I've got a date."

"A date?" Jeoff exclaims and then tries to regain his composure. "I thought that would be our night to talk," he remarks.

"Well, we can talk. I just have to leave early." She turns and walks away as her heart beats erratically.

Chapter 15

ROOKIE MOVES SLOWLY TO HER room and sits on her bed.

"What could I possibly say to these people?"

She reaches under her bed and grabs a notebook. She flips through pages of letters written over the years to the kids and to Jeoff that have never been mailed and puts the notebook back under the bed, flopping anxiously on her back.

"Mommy, are you okay? Rookie opened one heavy eyelid to look at a six-year-old Duran.

"Whaddaya want?" she asked groggily.

"Mommy, you been sleep since this mornin', and I'm hungry."

Rookie tried to sit up and lay back down quickly as the room began to spin. "Fix yourself somethin'. Mommy worked hard last night, and she's tryin' to rest," she told him and instantly went back to sleep.

In what seemed like seconds, she was awakened again by the landlord.

"What!" she yelled.

She remembers thinking her headache must have gotten worse because she heard screaming and a constant honking noise.

"Mrs. Simpson?" The angry and concerned face of Mr. Scarborough looked down at her. "Mrs. Simpson, while you were sleeping—" He drew back from the stench of liquor as Rookie stood to her feet. "While you were sleeping, the kitchen stove was on fire."

"On fire?" she said, confused, and then looked around as everything started to come into focus.

The wall behind the stove was black and charred, and Duran was sitting on the floor wide eyed with his thumb in his mouth and dirty tear tracks on his cheeks. Rookie looked at the landlord, feeling fear enter her body. How long had she been asleep? Did he try to wake her?

"Yes, on fire." He looked at Duran. "Why isn't that child at school?"

"I...I...overslept." Rookie's face burned.

Mr. Scarborough's severe look softened for a moment. "Look, I know your husband is in school and you're trying to watch these children alone, but you're gonna have to do better, or I will be forced to call Children Services."

"Mr. Scarborough, I..." Rookie fumbled clumsily with her clothes, trying to think of something to say.

"I mean what I say, Mrs. Simpson." Mr. Scarborough headed for the door and paused, turning around. "Oh, and the charge for fixing the wall will be on next month's rent." He slammed the door as he went out.

Rookie looked around the apartment as though seeing it for the first time. The loud noises were the children crying, the smoke alarm, and God only knows what else. Slowly she walked to the kitchen and opened the cabinet and closed the door quickly, remembering she had never gone to the grocery store as Jeoff had requested. They had food stamps; but she sold quite a few of them for drink, weed, and a little taste of stronger drugs to mix in. Jeoff never suspected. Opening the cabinet again, she took out a jar of peanut butter and jelly and got some bread from the top of the refrigerator. She fixed Duran some sandwiches and a glass of water and sat on the couch, watching him.

His grubby little hands pawed at his food, and he asked, "When you gonna get the babies?"

When you gonna get the babies? Rookie shakes her head, still hearing his statement, and it seems to get louder. *When you gonna get the babies?*

Her eyes open, and she looks at her roommate talking to another girl.

"Sorry, dog. I'm tryin' to get my homegirl here to sell me some of them sugar babies she got." She looks at the girl and Ranelle for a moment, then sits up again, gathering her notebook, extra paper, and pens.

Dear Duran,

I don't really know what to say to you. What are you now, seventeen?

The next day, Rookie tosses seven letters onto Miss Justine's desk.

"What's all this?" she asks, looking shocked.

"You asked for a letter, and I felt like they all need something to be said to them, so that's what that is." Rookie looks pleased with herself. "We gonna mail 'em or what?"

Miss Justine nods, touching the letters. "Do you want me to read them?"

"They're personal!" Rookie almost yells and then calms down. "You can read 'em, but you can't change a word."

"Please sit." Miss Justine waves toward a chair in her office.

"I gotta get to work. See you later." Rookie walks toward the door.

"Rookie?" Miss Justine calls to her.

Rookie turns around and looks at her defiantly.

"Good job."

Rookie turns her lips up in disgust and leaves. As she walks in the door to the expansive law library, she finds herself automatically drawn back into her memories.

"You're the most beautiful girl I've ever seen."

Jeoff looked into her eyes, and she smiled.

"I'm not beautiful. I'm just what all the guys want, including you." She pinched his cheek and smiled again, leaning back in her chair.

"Why do you always put yourself down?" Jeoff asks, fuming. "You're beautiful, not just because you're pretty, but because you have a beautiful heart, and I love you." He touches her shoulder. "It's so hard for you to believe that you're worth anything."

She touched Jeoff's face, gazing at him with devotion. "I guess I'm just not used to so much love. I mean, I love you, but it seems like your love is so much better 'n mine." She shook her head, trying to find the right words. "I mean, your love keeps me high like a hot air balloon, know what I mean?" She looked at him, anxious for him to understand. "I can't even understand why you'd marry a girl like me."

She sighs in her memory and also out loud.

The first few months of their marriage were like a dream. She seemed to float on a cloud every day.

"This is too much." They sat close together, and she said to him, "I gotta get out. I don't know what you want from me!"

Four months in was her first day of walking out.

Rookie shakes her head as she walks back to the halfway house. She pauses as she gets ready to head into her room, knowing that she's liable to see Ranelle.

"Hey," she says as she walks in the room.

"Hey back," Ranelle says distractedly.

She's leaning over a letter, holding the fuchsia paper delicately, her hands shaking. Rookie heads to her bed and sits down gazing at her, trying not to stare. Ranelle's harsh features seem to have softened, and her eyes scan the words on the paper as though trying to drink them in. She finishes the last page, gently folds the letter, and replaces it in its envelope.

"What's up?" she asks.

"What's up? I spoke to you when I came in," Rookie says. She scoots up on her bed. "What's got you so messed up?" she asks, curious.

"Not messed up, Boo. Happy." She smiles, lying back on her bed. "For the first time in a long time, happy." She stares at the ceiling thinking and, after a few minutes, turns over to lean on her elbow to look at Rookie. "Your people ever write you?"

Rookie shakes her head, not meeting Ranelle's gaze.

"I understand. Mine didn't used to." She stares into the distance. "Hmm, until today." She looks at Rookie again. "I got a letter from my girls and my old pastor."

"Your old pastor?" Rookie asks.

Ranelle gives her a warning glance. "I wasn't always like this. Anyway, I got letters from them, and I hope I hear from my boy too." She sighs. "You know, I never asked you how you got here. You gonna tell me?"

Rookie puts her hand in front of her mouth, lightly stroking her top lip. "I guess there's no reason why I can't. You know, I ain't here for bein' good, huh?" She takes her pillows and puts them behind her back, crossing her legs in front of her. "When I left home, my husband didn't know it, but I had tried a lot of drugs, but that weed mixed with crack got me, sometimes." She looks at Ranelle, her eyes getting red with memory.

"Ah, yeah, the primos." She nods with recognition.

"Well, after I left, I got mixed up real tight gettin' it all the time. I finally tried straight crack and wound up stayin' at the dope house most days. I was still in the same city for a while." She looks a little surprised at her own confession. "Well, either way, we wound up in Tallahassee. I stole some stuff, took it back to the dope house to sell, and while I was there, they got kicked in, and I went to jail too." She puts her head back on the pillows and breathes out loudly. "That time, they only got me for theft and sent me to rehab." She bites the inside of her lip. "I been to rehab a lot. Sometimes it's better 'n jail." She smiles wistfully. "Either way, I ended up here for sales and distribution." She closes her eyes for a moment and then opens them. "I wasn't really sellin' or anythin'. I was carrying a bird for my boyfriend."

"A bird? That's a key!"

"I know what it is," Rookie answers, almost embarrassed.

"That's some serious time, girl. So how long were you up?" she asks.

"Oh, I got three months in rehab," Rookie says.

"Three months!" An incredulous Ranelle sits up, flopping her feet on the floor.

"I told 'em it was his stuff and where the rest of his stuff was."

Ranelle leans her head back and looks at Rookie.

"It was his stuff," she says.

"Man, you ain't got no loyalty," Ranelle says, turning up her lips and smacking. "I thought he was your man?"

"He was, but he wasn't none of my husband or nothin'," Rookie says flippantly.

"Your husband? You ain't got no loyalty to him either. You left him to be with this dude and who knows else!" Ranelle retorts indignantly.

"You don't know nothin'! You can't judge me! You in here too!" Rookie says savagely. She calms a little as she vindictively asks, "Well, what you in here fo', Motha' of the Year?"

Ranelle sucks her teeth and nods her head at Rookie before she begins talking. "I was sellin' dope." She looks at Rookie pointedly. "My man was from Kansas City. I met him while I was going to school at Mizzou. I thought he was a student, but he was just a perpetrator. He knew about sellin' and knew about goin' to school, but he was mostly interested in sellin'." She sighs. "Yeah, I ain't perfect either." She sticks her tongue on her front teeth, closes her mouth, and makes a smacking noise. "Well, he was sellin' to the frats there, and when I got close to graduation, he asked me to move to KC and finish. I finished in KC, and then we just both went into the family business together. We had my son and our oldest daughter the first time he went to jail, and then we had our baby girl when he got out.

"I got used to that type of lifestyle, and even though I'd work a job as a front, we'd still sell, and eventually when our youngest was five, we came to Arizona to take the kids to the Grand Canyon and to make a buy. The buyer turned out to be an undercover." She turns her lips up. "He's supposed to be some born-again Christian and might get out on probation. Me"—she lowers her eyes—"I been gone a while and could get outta here if I had a home plan." She picks up the small notebook paper droppings and then sits up. "That's the end of my Motha' of the Year story." She stands. "I'm goin' to dinner."

Rookie stands too. "I'm goin' too." She looks over at Ranelle as they close the door. "So you tellin' me that you never used?"

Ranelle gives her a look of annoyance. "No, I left that to the hypes, like you."

Chapter 16

"What happened?" Bruni asks as Jeoff slowly climbs into the Surburban and sits staring blindly in the distance. "Man, what's wrong?"

Jeoff puts his head in his hands and mumbles inaudibly.

"What? Come on, J. You gotta tell me somethin'. You want me to drive?"

Jeoff nods his head and gets out. The two trade places, and as Bruni pulls out of the parking space, Jeoff just stares out the window.

"Man! Man! Man!" Jeoff hits his head with his hand and then sits quietly again, shaking his head. "She's got a date for Saturday night, Bru."

"The night of the party?" Bruni asks. "She's not comin'?" He looks over at Jeoff, surprised. "I didn't know she was seein' somebody. I told you she wasn't no good."

Jeoff looks at his brother incredulously as Bruni continues to pointedly stare at the road. When Bruni finally looks at his brother, the two bust out laughing.

"You're stupid," Jeoff tells him, still smiling.

"Man, I told you not to wait too long." He pulls in at Jeoff's job. "You sure she's got a date?"

"That's what she said," Jeoff answers.

Bruni taps the steering wheel, thinking. "So is she goin' bowlin' tonight?"

Jeoff shakes his head.

"No, huh? Well, don't tell the peoples you lost your almost woman." He smirks at Jeoff.

"I ain't lost her. I gotta tighten up my game for Saturday." He rubs his chin. "She's goin' shoppin' with Cee, Celeste, Momma, and Daddy for the party, so I know she's not outta the family, plus she's gotta take the kids shoppin' Saturday before the party too." He pauses with his thumb on his lower lip. "Where'd this dude come from though?" he asks no one in particular.

"I don't know, but you better show and prove 'cause who knows how long he's been on the scene." Bruni opens the door. "I'll meet you at the house so you can catch you a beatdown, and don't blame your losin' on your sad love life either." He laughs and goes to his car.

Rookie coming back? Mel thinks to herself as she walks back to the kitchen.

Her mind wanders back to Jeoff's graduation from Tuskegee. She had gone because Jeoff had invited her, and she wanted to wish him well. After the graduation, she saw him, Rookie, and the kids standing near the wall and went to congratulate him. As she approached, Rookie frowned at her.

"Congratulations, Jeoff." She reached up and hugged him.

Rookie snapped out, "Uh-uh, Jeoff! I don't believe you just gonna disrespect me like this. This ain't even cool!"

Mel stepped back and looked at her. "I wasn't tryin' to be disrespectful. I just wanted to congratulate your husband," she said to Rookie.

As she looked at her, she noticed that she was dressed in a red dress with thin spaghetti straps and red-and-black flower accents on it. She really filled it out, and the sour look on her face was so intimidating that it made Melasan feel like a ten-year-old.

"Well, you was disrespectful," she said, smacking for emphasis. "You might wanna think about yo' actions before you rub your body up against somebody else's husband 'cause I don't"—she rolled her neck and moved her hands—"appreciate it, missy."

Jeoff put his hand on her arm, looking embarrassed and stating, "That's not even necessary, Rook—"

She cut him off midsentence and got loud, "Do you wanna be with our babysitter? Huh, Jeoff?"

He looked green, and Melasan walked away, letting Rookie's words continue to hit her back. She knew she and Jeoff had kissed, but she didn't think Rookie knew anything about that. It didn't mean anything—at least not to him.

"I really appreciate your lettin' me use our secondary kitchen for the party Saturday," she says to her boss, coming out of her reverie.

"No problem. I love Rev. Simpson just as much as everybody else. He baptized all four of my babies. Plus we're not using this kitchen now," Nancy Mae, culinary director of Embassy Suites, states to Melasan.

Nancy Mae is a slender older lady in her sixties but appearing to be in her fifties. She's almost bony, rust-colored complexion with Indian-like features. Her long, wavy hair hangs to her shoulders, accentuating her high cheekbones and full lips. She tends to be candidly comedic yet abrasive. Melasan is just one step below her as culinary manager and has much respect for Mrs. Nancy, who has been a wonderful mentor to her.

"When are you gonna deliver the food?" she asks Mel.

"I was thinkin' that mornin', and then it could be warmed up there, but I have to get the key from Jeoff. Plus I don't wanna boil the shrimp until closer to the party." She frowns as she remembers that she just dropped a bomb on Jeoff. "Maybe I can call and have him leave it with Cee Cee," she says distractedly.

"Why would he have to leave it with Cee Cee? You two have a tiff?" Mrs. Nancy smooths her skirt, looking at Melasan. "I always thought you'd get it from him this evening. You two are always together. I just love your blended family." She smiles, and her dimples deepen in her cheeks. "What have you two been doing since he got his divorce anyway? Any plans?"

"I won't see him this evenin'," Mel says dejectedly. "And we don't have any plans, especially since I told him I have a date for Saturday. I'm not sure if he even wants to talk to me." She puts peeled potatoes into a stock pot for the potato salad and starts mashing yams. "He's been actin' so different lately." She looks over at Mrs. Nancy.

"Why'd you tell him you had a date, baby?" she asks.

"I had to. I didn't want him to be surprised when I showed up with somebody," Melasan answers, looking anxious and confused. "He's been actin' strange anyway," she says, putting the mashed yams

103

into a large mixing bowl. "Yesterday he broke a date with me." She puts in the cream and the rest of her ingredients for her sweet potato pies and starts the mixer.

Mrs. Nancy smiles, with her eyes dancing. "You told him you had a date because he missed your date, didn't you? That man loves you."

Melasan shakes her head in disbelief.

"He does. His nose is wide enough to drive a train through. I wouldn't be surprised one bit if he asked you to marry him."

"Mrs. Nancy! We can't even get a date together, let alone get married." Melasan feels her face get warm and turns to the mixer.

"Well, either way, you sure got him hot around the collar about this date." She puts her finger in the bowl with the sweet potato filling and tastes it, nodding her head that she likes it. "A fine man like that don't hang around the same woman for three years like he's her baby daddy and don't have no feelings." She looks at Melasan knowingly. "That man was in the delivery room with you if I remember correctly." She gazes down her nose at Melasan, not waiting for an answer. "Look, baby, you two have a pure and sweet love. I always tell my husband"—she smiles as though just thinking about him makes her happy—"'Herbert Mae, we have a pure sweet love, so you better act right 'cause a good woman like me won't be around forever.'" She smiles again and then looks at Mel. "Anyway, don't play games with Jeoff with a date that doesn't matter. Somebody might be waiting for you to make a mistake like this. If I wasn't so in love with Herbert Mae, I'd give you a run for your money." She winks at Melasan, her dimples deepening in her face again. "And who is this mystery person anyway?"

"Arika set me up with him. He's her cousin."

Mrs. Nancy rolls her eyes and makes a face. "Arika, huh? The hairdresser?" As Melasan nods, Mrs. Nancy makes another face. "She's not a good one to make relationship referrals. I hope you know that. You have far greater things in store for you, love." She leans over and pinches Melasan's cheek. "Like Pastor always says, 'Get ready for your blessin'.' You two are due for somethin' big and wonderful to happen in your lives. Besides, how you think them kids'll feel if y'all split up?" She pauses and says to Melasan, "Just out of curiosity, what would you say if he asked you?" She leans in toward Melasan again.

Melasan just stares at her with her mouth gaping.

Mrs. Nancy laughs and heads out the door. She stops at the door and turns back around. "Don't be a fool now. You don't need an extra man in this. Jeoff is all the man you need. That's what I tell Herbert Mae. He's all the man I need." With that said, she heads out the door.

Melasan stops the mixer and pours her mixture into pie shells with her mind distracted. *Should I go through with this date? What if it's a mistake?*

She places the pies in the oven and goes to her office, which is adjacent to the kitchen area. She pulls the phone from her desk and begins to dial.

As the phone connects, she says quickly, "May I speak to Arika?"

"She's on a head right now. You want me to have her call you back?"

Melasan thinks about all of the things that Arika's gonna say regarding her cousin who is all ready for this date and says, "No, that's all right. I'll talk to her later." She hangs up, feeling trapped, and then scoffs.

Mrs. Nancy may not know what she's talkin' about, she thinks to herself, drumming her desk, stopping only to play with her pen, capping and recapping it. *All this time and he still thinks of me as just a friend.* She scoffs to herself and turns her head slowly to loosen her neck muscles.

I love you, she hears Jeoff's gentle, deep voice in her mind.

She shakes her head as if not believing herself.

I'm not gonna let him get to me like this only to set me up for the big drop. I've gotta wean him outta my system. Melasan drops the pen and leans on her desk with her thumbnail in her mouth and sighs.

The phone rings, sounding shrill in the silent room. She picks it up and hears a deep commanding voice.

"Melasan St. Cyr?"

"Yes, my name is Aubrey Redmond. I'm Arika's cousin."

Melasan takes in a breath, wondering why Arika gave out her work number. *Probably tryin' to make sure I don't back out*, she thinks and then smiles, remembering just trying to call and back out.

"I returned from my business trip a little sooner than I expected, and"—he pauses, and Melasan notices that his voice is also velvety and peaceful—"I'm a little embarrassed to admit this, but I remembered Arika saying you work at Embassy Suites, so I looked up the number and called."

Melasan smiles, flattered.

"I hope I didn't overstep my bounds?"

The caressing voice lulls Melasan into silence. Just listening to him, she wonders what type of face fits with that voice.

"Hello?"

"I'm sorry." Melasan shifts the phone. "No, I don't think you overstepped your bounds. I'm intrigued and flattered by your curiosity." She blushes at her candor.

"Well, that's good. That's good for sure."

She can't help but notice that he sounds like a well-spoken man.

"Are you originally from Montgomery?" she asks.

Aubrey chuckles. "No. I'm Arika's Northern, more educated cousin from Richmond, Virginia. I moved here to provide engineering consultation for a firm on a three-year-contract."

"I just know you don't sound like Alabama."

They both laugh.

"My mother was very strict on grammar and diction," he says.

Melasan laughs again at how cute the statement sounds.

"Believe me, Arika gives me a very hard time about how I talk."

The laughing subsides, and the phone gets quiet.

"Well, I didn't call to tie up your day. I was just wondering if you'd like to get together tonight to kind of break the ice before tomorrow?"

Melasan pauses, thinking about Jeoff.

"I realize I could be shooting myself in the foot because you may decide you don't want to see me tomorrow, but I really would like to spend some time with you."

Melasan nervously speaks, "I have to cook for a function that we are stoppin' at tomorrow briefly. I'll be here almost all night gettin' ready." Her voice trails off, and her eyes focus on the blinking light on her phone to signal she has another call. "I have another call, so—"

"Just a little time together. Maybe for an ice-cream cone?" Aubrey gently prods.

"All right. I should have a small window from seven to seven forty-five. Does that work?" Melasan's stomach feels queasy, hoping he says no.

"That's fine. Should I pick you up at the Embassy Suites?"

"Yes," she answers.

As they both hang up, Melasan lets out a deep breath and answers the other line.

"Melasan St. Cyr."

"Mel?"

Her heartbeat increases as she hears Jeoff's familiar voice.

"Hey, I wanted to know if you'd have any time to get together this evenin'."

She hears papers rustling.

"I know you're busy gettin' ready for the party, but I just wanted to see you. If you could just take an hour break where we could talk…"

She feels her hand sweating as his husky voice touches her soul.

"I have too much to do, J," she says softly, mentally kicking herself. *This is how it's got to be*, she rationalizes.

"You tryin' to tell me that you can't even take a break, huh?" Jeoff's deep voice grows deeper in frustration.

"Well, I just have stuff that has to be done, and—"

Jeoff cuts her off, "All right then."

"J," Melasan tries to calm him as she notices he's upset.

"I'll holla, Mel," he says.

Next she hears the hum of the dial tone. She places the phone on the cradle upside down and grabs a Kleenex to wipe the sweat off the phone.

Later that night, Melasan places her cut vegetables to the side and walks out to the front lobby to wait for Aubrey. She doesn't have long to wait as a medium-height man—about five feet ten, muscular build, and cream complexion with brown freckles sprinkled across his cheeks and nose—walks up.

"Hi, Melasan, I'm Aubrey."

She looks a little shocked that he recognizes her and then remembers that he has seen her before. She has never seen him, only heard about him from Arika. Another surprise to her is that his hair is in short dreadlocks and faded on the side with his beard neatly manicured and faded into his sideburns with a small mustache that complements his sparkling coffee-colored eyes.

"Nice to meet you," she says, standing.

He leans in and gives her a light peck on the cheek, and the sweet, masculine scent of his cologne fills her nostrils.

As he leans back, she says shyly, "I like your cologne. That's a wonderful scent."

Still standing, he states, "When the company sent me to Paris, there was a shop where you could have your own scent made, so I took advantage of the opportunity." His eyes swim like pools as they gaze deeply into her own. "Maybe one day I can take you to get your own made." His eyes crinkle at the corners, showing his flirtation.

"Maybe," she flirts back, smiling.

Aubrey puts out his hand. "I promised you an ice-cream cone, and I don't have much time, so my chariot awaits."

As they head to the parking lot, Melasan scans Aubrey. His Polo jeans must've been sent to the cleaners because his crease is impeccably straight. His matching Polo shirt and leather yachting shoes pull the look together, letting her know that he is a man who is either very meticulous about his appearance or he wants to impress. Melasan feels a little self-conscious in her plain blue sundress with light sprinkles of flour and beads of sweet potato despite the cooking jacket she removed in the kitchen.

The two stop at a sleek black Mercedes-Benz sedan, and Aubrey politely opens the door for her. As Melasan settles in the car, she feels the gray leather interior gently caress her body. Aubrey opens his own door and climbs in.

"Now where's a good ice-cream spot close to here?" he asks, looking at her.

"There's Skippy's. It's a little spot not too far from here," Melasan answers.

As Aubrey starts the car, she thinks, *Why'd Jeoff wanna see me so badly?*

She shakes the thought off and listens to the hum of car.

"Are you chilly? I can turn the air down," Aubrey asks, his hand already reaching for the controls.

"No, I'm fine. I've been admirin' your ride here. I don't think I've ever ridden in a Mercedes." She smiles shyly.

"They're all right. I'm somewhat of a car buff, but I always wanted a Mercedes-Benz out of college, and once I achieved that, I try to maintain that standard. Plus this CLS55 really caught my eye." He licks his lips in thought and turns his head to look at Mel. "What captures your interest? I know you're a chef, but what would you do with your life if you could?"

She rubs her nose as it itches and then looks at Aubrey curiously. "That sounds like an interview question, don't cha think?"

Aubrey chuckles, his deep voice vibrating in the interior of the car. "I guess this is like an interview. We're interviewing each other to find out our likes and dislikes."

He smiles at her appreciatively, and she blushes.

"I mean, I've seen you around before, but I'd like to get to know you as thoroughly as possible to see if the brains match the overwhelming beauty."

Melasan raises her eyebrows and smooths her hands on the skirt of her dress. "Well, I don't know what to say to that." She smiles, and her eyes sparkle.

I am really enjoying myself, she thinks.

"A perfect return would be to let me know how extremely and immediately entranced you were by my strikingly handsome appearance."

He grins, and Melasan giggles.

"Well"—she looks over at Aubrey pointedly—"I'd open a school for so-called last-chance and second-chance students." She grins as he makes the motions of sticking a knife in his heart. "You know, teach them so they can get their GED and then teach them the cooking skills I know so they can cook on a cruise ship or in a hotel or wherever their dreams take them. Just at least lend a hand in some financial independence." She smiles, reminiscent. "My friend and I share our dreams all the time."

"Are her goals similar to yours?"

Melasan nods, not correcting him that the friend is Jeoff.

"What does she want?" he asks.

Melasan swallows and folds her hands in her lap. "To teach those same and others construction and architectural skills and then purchase at least one hundred acres to design and build houses for low—to moderate-income families. We'd call it Peace Subdivision, meaning Peace because you now have peace because you have a piece of the American Dream."

Aubrey raises his eyebrows, impressed. "None of that is unachievable, you know?"

"Turn left here," Melasan says. "Do you know how it can be achieved?" she asks.

Aubrey puts the car in park and turns to look at Melasan. He slowly leans seductively across to her side of the car and opens the glovebox, still gazing at Mel. He reaches in and grabs his wallet and then slowly moves back to his side of the vehicle.

Melasan quietly breathes a sigh of relief, thinking, *Thank God he didn't try to kiss me.*

Aubrey quickly gets out of the car and opens Melasan's door, reaching out his hand for her. "My lady?"

"Thank you," she says, accepting his hand and stepping out onto the concrete.

They order their ice cream, and after the clerk gives the cones to them, they sit at a table with a brightly colored umbrella.

"Now, to answer your question, yes, I do know how such a dream can be achieved."

Mel takes in a breath.

"I can sit down with you and discuss some grant options that are open for such ventures. You may need to form an organization that is 501(c)(3) categorized," he says, stretching his legs and smoothing his pants.

"Too much starch?" Mel asks, smiling playfully.

Aubrey smiles too, and his eyes lower thoughtfully and raise again. "You have a beautiful smile." He grunts softly. "And no, not too much starch. Well, maybe." He chuckles.

"Well," Mel begins, "I could run this idea by my pastor. I believe that my church may be the perfect organization." She looks in the distance, thinking. "Even the home building?" she asks.

Aubrey nods, scooting closer to her. "Yes. I'd be more than willing to sit down with you and your friend. At my home church back in Richmond, we take advantage of as many grants as possible," he answers.

"Your church?" Melasan raises her eyebrows.

"Yes, I am a Christian man. I'm not surprised my cousin never mentioned that."

Melasan shakes her head, impressed.

"There are a large number of grants that are faith based. I wish more churches were aware," Aubrey says, finishing his cone. "That was refreshing." He places his hands on the table and looks at Mel. "So are both you and your friend single?"

She nods, licking her cone.

"Do the two of you think about the future? What kind of person you'll marry, and if you want more children—" He stops for a moment. "Does she have children?"

"Yes," Mel answers, drawn into the questions as though he's asking specifically about her and Jeoff.

"Well, the both of you have to think about that, about finding a godly man to spend your present and future with, who will be accepting and loving to your children as well as open to adding more to the brood." As Melasan finishes her cone, Aubrey gently grabs her hands and smiles slightly, staring into her eyes. "I talk to my friends about finding the type of woman God would be pleased with."

She blinks her eyes listening to Aubrey's conversation, uncomfortable at the turn it has taken, and jumps as, out of the corner of her eye, she sees a little girl who looks just like Cha Cha. Aubrey is still talking, but she barely hears him as her eyes follow the girl ordering a cone. Then a man and a teenage boy on crutches approach. Mel shakes her head in disbelief.

"I know this might be unbelievable and forward of me, but I want you to know what my intentions are in dating any woman," Aubrey says, thinking that she's shaking her head at him.

His voice goes inaudible as Melasan's breathing grows shallow, realizing that Jeoff is at the counter ordering a cone.

He never comes to Skippy's! she thinks frustratedly.

"Mimi!" the voice of Cha Cha yells out the children's nickname for Mel, and to Mel's horror, she innocently skips her direction. "Hey, Mimi! We went bowling tonight, and Daddy did awful." She glances the direction of Aubrey and utters a distracted hello. She looks a little confused but knows better than to ask any questions. "Are we still goin' shoppin' tomorrow?"

"Of course, baby."

As Melasan answers Cha Cha, she can feel Jeoff's eyes burning craters in her chest cavity. She chooses instead to look at Aubrey.

"Aubrey, this is Cha Cha."

"Duran's got his crutches, and he's been racing me in the yard. I won twice," Cha Cha says.

Melasan hopes for an end to the conversation.

"Oh, Daddy's waving for me. Come with me MiMi." Cha Cha pulls Melasan and, before she can protest, has her standing in front of Jeoff. "Hey, Daddy," she says, smiling.

"Go sit in the truck, puddin'," Jeoff says to Cha Cha, still looking at Melasan. "So you couldn't just tell me that you had a date?" he says, his eyes darkening.

"I didn't have a date, Jeoff," Melasan says, sounding to herself like she's squeaking. "I've been working for the party tomorrow, and…" She trails off as Jeoff breathes deeply and slowly.

He places his fist in front of his mouth with one hand wrapped around the other and breathes in again, closing his eyes. He opens his eyes and looks directly into hers, making all her muscles squirm.

"I guess your wanting to be away from me didn't have anything to do with my forgetting lunch." He looks Aubrey's direction. "You always had plans." He sucks his teeth and sighs. "So is that who you're bringin' to the party, or do you have other boyfriends?" he asks, blinking his eyes slowly as he looks at her.

She tries to look in his eyes, but he has shut down shop on her. There's no information to obtain in them.

"Jeoff, I don't have a whole buncha men, and he's not..." She trails off desperately as Jeoff sucks his teeth and nods his head.

"Hey, you two have a nice night, okay?" He takes long strides to the Suburban, gets in, and seems to turn the ignition and pull out of the parking lot all in the same motion.

Chapter 17

ROOKIE WAKES IN THE MORNING, feeling groggy, and notices Ranelle getting dressed.

"What time is it?" she asks, leaning on her elbows.

"Good morning," Ranelle responds.

Rookie sighs heavily. "Good morning."

"It's seven thirty. Why? What time you gotta be there?" Ranelle smiles at her own sarcasm.

"The question is what time do you gotta be there? It's Saturday." She rubs her headscarf.

Ranelle sits and ties her blue-and-white K-Swiss. Rookie can't help but notice that she looks nice in her white cotton hooded sweat suit with blue accents, gold hoop earrings, gold Figaro necklace, and hair pulled back with two blue-and-white ponytail holders.

"You'd think you'd be glad I'm going out today, all the lip service you give." She looks over at Rookie.

Rookie looks noncommittal.

"Well, I've been taking some college courses in my spare time." She stands and grabs a blue book bag.

"College?" she asks, incredulous.

"Yeah, college. I may talk like a tackhead, but I'm not." She swallows. "I have to have a plan for when I leave here." She grabs a gold ring from her dresser and puts it on her thumb.

Rookie nods. "I guess. What's your degree in?"

Ranelle, heading of the door, stops and turns. "Law."

Rookie laughs boisterously, and Ranelle giggles.

"Just playin'. It was art appreciation."

Rookie raises her eyebrows.

"It's useless, but I figure, if I take some fashion design classes combined with business, then I could maybe make the art appreciation play in there in another way." She turns back toward the door. "I gotta go. I don't have time to talk."

She walks out the door, and Rookie's left to her own thoughts. She lays on her stomach, pulling the flat pillow over her head in attempt to prevent thoughts of her former life. Saturdays are always the hardest.

Domininisierra was the prettiest baby Rookie had ever seen, next to Duran. She was born with a full head of thick, straight coal-black hair.

"She looks a little like Eddie Munster, doesn't she?" Jeoff joked.

When the doctor handed her to Rookie, she nestled her in the crook of her arm and stared at her adoringly. There was nothing more precious. Rookie loved to hold her and kiss her and would, at times, whisper in her ear, "You won't be a waste, will you?" Jeoff and his family nicknamed her Ni Ni, but Rookie called her by her full name or Sierra. After a few months, Sierra began to take more to Jeoff.

"She likes you better," she said softly to Jeoff as he changed her diaper, powdered her, and bantered playfully with her.

"That's because Mommy sits on her do nothin' while Daddy takes care of the baby," Jeoff said back.

"Duran doesn't like you better. That's my baby," she said childishly.

Rookie throws the pillow off of her head and jumps out of the bed. She gets her toiletries together, slips on her flip-flops, and races out the door as though being chased.

"Mommy loves you best," she told Duran.

"Don't do that," Jeoff snapped.

"Why not? You love Sierra best!" she shot back.

Jeoff looked at Duran. "I love both of our children and nobody more than the other."

He returned, and Duran smiled.

"Well, you love them more than you love me," she answered.

Somehow the day dwindles away with Rookie between the recreation room and her bedroom hour after hour. She drags to her bedroom for what seems like the hundredth time and flops on the bed, staring at the ceiling.

Years ago, a nine-year-old Rookie with two braids hanging down her back searched her momma' s belongings while her momma lay passed out on the couch. She smiled gleefully as she found a piece of paper that said "Duran Marevangepo" followed by a phone number.

"Can I speak to my daddy?" she asked.

"Who is this?" the deep Spanish accent asked.

"This is Rookie," she said.

"Well, Rookie, this is Daddy." He paused. "How'd you get my number?"

"I found it," she answered. "Daddy, will you come get me? I've lived with Momma long enough. Please?"

He paused on the other end.

"Please?"

"I'll come get you Friday."

She sighed angrily, for it was only Tuesday.

"I won't be able to get off work until Friday. Just be ready Friday, and then you can meet your brothers and sisters," he promised.

Rookie waited for Friday like a child anticipating the mouth-watering delight of Christmas.

"My daddy said he's comin' to get me Friday," she bragged.

"He's lyin'," her momma said.

"Na-uh!" Rookie countered.

Friday, however, came and went. She tried the phone number every day for two months, but it wasn't in service and never returned to service. Every so often, she'd try it when her momma really got on her nerves.

"Mail call!" Ranelle's throaty voice thunders in the room, shaking Rookie from her trance.

Before she can think of anything smart to say, a charcoal-gray envelope falls on her chest. Excitedly she tears it open while Reanelle sits with her own mail.

Dear Rookie,

We pray this letter finds you healthy and in good spirits. My family has received the letter from your counselor, and I felt compelled to send word to you. Congratulations on your many milestones, and may God bless you with many more. Your journey may not have been easy, but you have emerged victorious.

The family is well. The children are healthy and have thrived wonderfully in your absence. The news of your desire to return to Montgomery was, to say the least, a surprise. I commend you on your bravery in the decision to return. However, I must question your motives.

Rookie frowns.

It is my job to protect the interests of this family, and as a servant of God, it is also my job to aid in the guarding of your heart from foolish fantasies. Dr. Moira stated in her letter that you exhibit a stronger sense of responsibility, so I urge you to search your heart for the most appropriate and most considerate way to return. Life is not the same as it was in Montgomery six years ago, and I am encouraged that your life also has changed.

I believe that, when repairing and rebuilding relationships with the children, you will do so in patience and in love. There are things they don't understand, and only you and God can give answers to those questions. Please contact us with the date of your return, and we will make arrangements for you to spend time with the children. I pray your mind does not harp on a glorious homecoming yet a peaceful merging of lives once torn asunder.

God bless and keep you,
Rev. Bruni Simpson Sr.

Rookie furiously rips the letter in half and sits on the edge of her bed, fuming.

"Bad news?" Ranelle glances over.

"Yeah." Rookie glares, thinking of her letter. "That was from my father-in-law. I can't stand him!"

"He wrote you a mean letter?" Ranelle asks, neatly folding her letter and placing it back in its envelope.

"They don't want me with my husband or my kids!" she complains.

"Well, what's your husband say?" Ranelle asks.

Rookie breathes heavily and stares at the ceiling. "He hasn't said anything!"

Ranelle grabs two pillows from her bed, tosses one on the floor, and sits cross-legged on it; and with the other one, she puts her back against the bed.

"Girl, I gotta know. When's the last time you heard from your husband?"

"I haven't," Rookie says, biting her lower lip. "But they can't talk for him! They ain't never liked me!" She rolls her eyes, glancing at Ranelle.

"You haven't heard from him since you been in here?" Ranelle curiously asks. "He's mad 'cause you're in Arizona?"

"I haven't heard from him the whole time I been gone. He didn't know where I was," she answers sullenly.

"Wait a minute. You're gonna have to explain this to me like I'm three years old 'cause you're losin' me." She readjusts the pillow behind her back.

"He didn't know where you were?"

Rookie nods.

"So how'd your in-laws find out where you are?"

"Miss Justine told 'em."

Ranelle looks confused.

"I told her I wanted to go home, and she said they needed to know, and she wrote them a letter because I don't know where Jeoff lives now." She looks distressed.

"You weren't gonna tell 'em?" she asks.

"When I got there," Rookie states, sighing.

"When you got there? Girl, you been gone six years!" Ranelle states, amazed. "You haven't talked to that man in six years? No wonder your in-laws don't like you. Are you even still married?"

"Of course I'm married! Jeoff doesn't believe in divorce." She frowns. "Besides, they've never liked me and have always had it in for me." She rolls her eyes again, lowering her lids.

"Well, no offense, sista, but I think you're kinda bold for thinkin' you can go back," she says, uncrossing her legs and recrossing them.

"No offense? You can always go home. They should be glad I'm coming home! My daddy never came back. At least now, my babies'll know I love 'em," she retorted.

Ranelle nods thoughtfully. "You've got a point about the kids, but your husband, that's a whole 'nother story." She smacks, shaking her head.

"Jeoff loves me! He'll never stop lovin' me!" Rookie yells.

Ranelle shakes her head again. "You are absolutely crazy. I've met some crazy people, but you take the cake. You don't even realize how bold of a sista you are to think you can just up and go back like that. You've been with other men while you been gone—"

"He don't know that," she replies insolently.

Ranelle rolls her eyes, ignoring the comment. "I been gone two years keepin' constant contact, and it's been hard on my kids and the rest of the family. I ain't nowhere near delusional like you are." She looks Rookie up and down.

"That's 'cause your family don't want you!" Rookie jumps up and heads out the door.

The rest of the weekend brings nothing but uncomfortable silence in Rookie and Ranelle's room.

Chapter 18

MELASAN WAKES UP EARLY SATURDAY morning after a night-long wrestle with sleep. After the encounter with Jeoff, the rest of the time with Aubrey seems to be a blur.

"I don't understand him!" she fusses to herself, kicking at her comforter.

So you couldn't just tell me that you had a date? She remembers his statement and feels her stomach turn. *I guess your wanting to be away from me didn't have anything to do with my forgetting lunch. You always had plans.*

She feels weepy, yet no tears come. She kicks at her comforter again in frustration.

I don't know what he wants, she thinks to herself. *He has me in a tizzy over all of this.*

She holds her head as though in pain, and the phone rings.

"Hey, girl!" Cee Cee's familiar voice vibrates through the phone. "What time are you and Boo comin' by to go shoppin'? Celeste says she's ready to go now."

Celeste and Cee Cee can be heard laughing.

"Yeah, girl, Bruni gave me some money, and I gotta spend it before he comes to his senses!" Celeste yells in the background.

"I'm awake, and I know it won't take but a second to have my little sleeper ready," she says, sounding melancholy.

"Hey, you all right?" Cee Cee asks, sounding concerned.

"Oh, yeah, I'm cool. I'm just a little groggy from workin' late last night," Melasan answers.

"I forgot all about that. If you wanna beg off and stay and work some more, you can," Cee Cee says jokingly.

Melasan half laughs.

"You sure you're all right?" she asks again.

Melasan doesn't answer, only nods as a tear trickles down her face.

"I'm gonna let you get ready, and we'll meet you over here. We got all the girls, and we know we only got until one, so hurry up, okay?"

The phone clicks, and Melasan sits on her bed, crying silently.

So is that who you're bringin' to the party, or do you have other boyfriends? She remembers Jeoff's unresponsive, stony glare and can't remember his being so angry, not even at the kids.

Somehow Melasan makes it through the shopping expedition; and of course, Boo begs to stay with the other kids, which makes it easy for her to pick up the food for the party. She gets in her hunter-green Navigator and slowly takes her cell phone out of her purse. She starts the ignition and pulls up Jeoff's number and, as it dials, disconnects.

"Come on, Mel. Get it together," she pleads with herself.

Her cell phone rings, and she notices it is the ring programmed to Jeoff's cell number.

"Melasan?"

The soft huskiness of his voice takes her by surprise.

"Melasan?" he says again.

"Yes?" she finally answers, pulling into the Embassy Suites parking lot.

"Do you need any help loading the food?" he asks.

"What?" she asks as she begins to cry.

"Do you need help with the food? I know you have a lot of it, so I figured we could load up the Suburban and the Navigator and take it over there and set it up," he says, sounding detached.

"Um, yes, yes, I do need help," she says, wiping her face with a tissue. "There's a few people here that are gonna help too, so it shouldn't take too long," she answers, turning off her ignition.

"If your boyfriend's gonna be there, then you won't need my help," Jeoff says brusquely.

"Just some staff from work, J," she says softly. "Jeoff, he's not my boyfriend," she offers quickly before he can hang up.

"I'm not too far from Embassy Suites, so I'll meet you in about ten minutes."

He hangs up, and in a matter of five minutes, she sees his Suburban pull up.

He sees her and calmly says, "Hey, I woulda brought the boys, but they've been up all night."

She nods. "Thanks for your help."

"I wouldn't have it any other way," he says, looking at her briefly.

Her heart wrenches as she notices he won't look in her eyes. They finish loading up and get in their respective vehicles.

"If you follow me, then I'll get you to the house, and we can get everything unloaded," he says, getting into his truck.

As they approach the suburb, she looks around at the houses, impressed; and as they approach the house for the party, she is awestruck.

"I guess you chose this one for the party because it's the most impressive," she says to Jeoff, getting out of the truck. "You are truly gifted."

She tries to make small talk, but he makes her feel like a punished child for trying. So she finally consents to his silence, and they unload the food. As the other people she brought along set up the food, she watches Jeoff head for the door and follows.

"Jeoff?"

He turns. "Hey, don't worry about locking up. The alarm is set to come on as y'all head out," he says, getting in his truck. "I'll be here before anybody else gets here this evening, so that should take care of your arrival."

"Oh," she says sadly.

He scans her quickly before she looks at him again.

"Thanks for your help."

As Jeoff pulls up at his townhouse, he notices Bruni's rental in the driveway.

"What's up?" he asks, walking in the door.

"Man, I had to get away from all that estrogen in the house!" Bruni sits at Jeoff's breakfast bar looking like a younger version of their dad, minus the gray and with more muscles. "Them women'll drive you crazy," he says as Jeoff smiles distractedly, tossing the keys on the bar. "I asked the boys where you were, but they were out of it."

"I went to help Mel move the food into the house for the party," Jeoff says.

"So what, you spent some more time mackin' her down?" Bruni asks, the gold from his teeth gleaming in the light from the kitchen.

"Nah, man. I think I'm gonna leave all that alone," Jeoff answers sitting down dejectedly.

"What?" Bruni looks at Jeoff, confused. "All this work and now you say you gonna leave that alone? 'Cause of some dude?"

"We saw her last night with that dude. He was holdin' her hand, and she was soakin' it all in." Jeoff looks distressed and gets up to pour some juice. Without drinking, he says, "This may as well be Rookie all over again, and I don't need that. Me and my kids don't need that." He walked back to the bar and sat down, rubbing his head.

"Man, you're crazy. That girl ain't nothin' like Rookie. Stop sittin' around here on your rump roast feelin' sorry for yourself. You and I both know that girl's been drinkin' your bathwater for three years if not longer."

He looks sternly at Jeoff, and Jeoff looks away.

"Yeah, you know it. You even got the videos over there to prove it."

"Well, where'd this cat come from then? How long's he been sniffin' around?"

"I don't know where he came from, and I don't care," Bruni answers, grabbing Jeoff's glass and taking a swig from it himself. "You shouldn't either. Your job is to propose to the woman you love, tonight."

He stops talking as Duran hobbles into the kitchen.

"Mornin', Daddy. What's up, Uncle B?"

Bruni and Jeoff answer him.

"Gumba was tellin' me 'bout how Grinny was engaged to some dude, and he stole her right under his nose." He pulls the cereal from the cabinet. "Now that's a *real* playa." He winks at his dad and hops out of the kitchen with his cereal bowl to the living room.

She looked so pretty today, Jeoff thinks to himself, *and sad*.

Chapter 19

"Woman, I can't find my tie!" Bruni Sr. yells out to his wife. "I thought y'all laid out my fancy duds for tonight?"

Mari calmly steps out of their bathroom, leans down to the bed, picks up his tie, and hands it to him.

He smiles, closing one eye and looking at her suspiciously. "You probably brought that in from the bathroom.

She laughs and goes back to the bathroom.

Downstairs Bruni Jr. and John sit on the couch in the living room. Cee Cee and Celeste prance in as though on the catwalk. They both look stunning with Cee Cee in a gold halter dress with spaghetti straps that accent her graceful neckline. Celeste smiles at Bruni Jr., showing off in a taupe scoop-neck dress that hangs enchantingly on her shapely five-foot-two frame.

"You look good in my money, baby," Bruni tells her with a smile.

"Well, now that y'all look good, and we look good, where are the man and woman of the hour?" John asks, looking around.

As if on cue, Rev. and Mrs. Simpson appear on the stairs, giggling like two teenagers.

"You're still the love of my life," he whispers in her ear with a tiny nibble to her earlobe.

She smiles demurely, lowering her eyelids, and whispers, "I love you dearly, Bruni Simpson."

"Aw, man!" Bruni Jr. says. "Y'all shoulda been done with all that smoochin' years ago!" He playfully turns up his nose.

"I think my curls are falling form all the heat between you two." Cee Cee shakes her Shirley Temple curls, favoring both her dad and her mom with her five-foot-nine height, gazellelike grace, and slender build.

"Y'all are just jealous. One day, y'all might be as good as us." Mari smiles and then looks around. "Where're the babies?"

"Well, Jeoff picked up his so they could get dressed and head to the house early. Everybody else is in the cars, so we can leave," Celeste informs her. "We're hoping for somethin' great to happen tonight," she says with a sparkle in her eyes.

Everyone nods in agreement as they head to their respective vehicles.

At the house, Jeoff sits in the porch swing while the children are inside helping Melasan put some finishing touches on the decorations and setting up the food. More of the staff from Embassy Suites comes bringing in round tables and two long buffet tables. Some of the ladies from the church also are helping with the setup. The tables come together quickly with alternating white tablecloths and black centerpieces and black tablecloths with white centerpieces.

The army of white-jacketed chef clones and church ladies neatly place the food on the buffet tables. There's seafood gumbo and rice, boiled shrimp that was boiled with corn on the cob, baby scallions, and new potatoes. The corn on the cob is spread like rays of the sun around the shrimp, and the new potatoes are in beveled bowls beside them. There's also a delectable mixture of blue crab and Alaskan crab stuffed into the shells of the blue crabs included on the table with cool potato salad and a large octagonal clear bowl of green salad. The second table holds a sumptuous-looking two-tier white-pearl iced wedding cake with words of congratulations from the many members of the church and their auxiliaries. The lemonade is light and fluffy and looks almost white with shaved ice on top. There are also perfectly baked sweet potato pies, lemon meringue pies, pecan pies, and pineapple upside-down cakes. Melasan poured her heart into putting together a menu with the Simpsons' favorites.

The deacons of the church came by earlier in the day and strung elegant white lights with teardrop bulbs through the trees in the backyard and also on the front porch. The deejay was setup and playing music so softly that it wafts through naturally with the evening breeze, and the view of the river pulls the whole breathtaking scene together.

Melasan aids everyone in finishing up and getting all refills on hand and eases out the front door. She gazes at Jeoff with his long legs hanging off the porch swing and lightly grazing the porch.

"Hey," she says tenderly.

"Hey," he answers back. He stops the swing and asks, "Wanna sit?"

She sits on the swing beside him, and they sway gently until Jeoff breaks the silence.

"Mel, I'm sorry."

She looks at him with adoration gleaming in her eyes. "J, I need to get dressed, but can we talk later?"

He looks at her calmly.

"Tonight?"

He nods; and she rises and walks to her truck, pulls out a garment bag, and comes back to the porch.

"It's all right if I get dressed inside?"

He nods again.

As the door closes behind her, he closes his eyes and puts his hands together in a silent prayer. Upon finishing, he, too, rises and enters the house.

"Kids, it's our job to greet the guests and then take them to the backyard." He looks at the children—Duran, Ni Ni, Devon, Mari, Jeoff Jr., Cha Cha, and Boo—as they eagerly look back at him in anticipation. They seat family and numerous guests, and Jeoff smiles as he sees Melasan's parents walk in the door.

"Great to see you," he says to Mel's dad.

"Great to see you too, Jeoff. Since everybody's home, we don't get to see too much of y'all. I guess that'll change in a couple weeks, huh?"

Jeoff nods as Mrs. Pete admonishes him.

"Hello, my babies!" she calls out to the children, giving them each a hug. "Grandma misses y'all." She looks at Jeoff accusingly, shaking a finger at him.

Devon and Mari take them to sit with Rev. and Mrs. Simpson.

Jeoff watches them with a smile, and as he turns, his heart catches in his throat as Melasan strides in with Aubrey.

"Jeoff, this is Aubrey. Aubrey, this is Jeoff," she introduces them.

"Good to meet you, Jeoff," Aubrey says to Jeoff, putting out his hand.

Jeoff shakes his hand, eyeing him warily. "Aubrey."

He then turns to Melasan and looks her over in her amethyst sundress with small stones around the V neckline, her hair pulled up in a refined chignon with soft ringlets cascading around her face and her four-inch heels expanding her height to five feet ten, and quickly drinks in the womanly scent of the lotion sparkling on her skin.

"You look so beautiful, sunshine."

She smiles modestly and walks away with her arm through Aubrey's.

"Would you like to get something to eat?" he asks.

"If you don't mind, I'd like to sit alone for a moment," Melasan tells Aubrey.

They stroll through the people, noticing many people trying not to stare and some openly staring and whispering.

Sis Jones walks up, grabbing Melasan's hand boisterously. "Girl, you put your foot in this food! As a matter of fact, you put both feet in and just waded a while!" She shakes her head impressed, looking pointedly at Aubrey as though waiting for an introduction.

Melasan gives none, so she walks back to the buffet table.

Melasan blushes, and the two make their way to a table. Aubrey pulls out a chair for Melasan and one for himself.

He looks at her with remorse in his eyes. "I could continue to play dumb this evening, but I'd be remiss if I weren't to point out the obvious from last night. Jeoff is the friend you were speaking of, isn't he?"

She nods, clasping her hands in her lap.

He smiles wistfully. "You are a remarkable lady, Melasan. However, I do know that I have gotten to you too late." He smiles again, his eyes crinkling at the corners. "I'm happy for you."

"I'm sorry," Melasan says, apologetic. "God has someone for you too. I'm sure of it. You're too good a catch."

"Well, go get your man before he combusts," Aubrey states, showing his white teeth. "I'm fine here. I think I may even mingle."

She pats his hand and stands to see Jeoff standing a few feet away watching. She sighs as he turns on his heel and quickly heads inside the patio's French doors. She, too, walks briskly and heads into the house; however, she doesn't see him.

"Have you seen Jeoff?" she asks one of the ladies in the kitchen.

"No. But I do need more potato salad," Sis Greta states.

"It's in the refrigerator on the third shelf," Melasan answers, walking away. "Devon, have you seen your dad?"

"Mimi, I saw him a minute ago, but I'm not sure where he went."

She sighs in frustration and heads down the hall. She opens door after door until finally, Jeoff emerges from one, oblivious to her search.

"Hey, Mel, you lookin' for the bathroom?" he asks innocently.

Mel's breathing heavily now, and her hair is damp as small dots of sweat line her forehead. "No, I'm lookin' for you," she states bravely.

"Oh." He closes the door and steps into the hallway. "Do you wanna tour of the house?" he asks.

"Well…I guess so," a confused Mel answers.

They walk through the hallway, and he shows her bedroom after bedroom.

What do I care about this house? she thinks to herself.

The tour seems complete when Jeoff turns her direction, drawing her into his eyes.

"Do you remember my tellin' you about this house?" he asks.

"This the one for the young couple?" she questions.

He nods and reaches for her hand. "Do you wanna see the bedroom that you helped me design?"

She nods as though in a trance. The sounds of people gaily talking and laughing as well as muffled music can be heard distantly as she and Jeoff walk to the front steps that lead to a loft area in the house. He opens the door, and Melasan takes in her breath. The room is romantically decorated in what she would guess to be at least three different blues, white, and lace. The room is fit for a very regal couple.

"It's exactly as I imagined," she says excitedly to Jeoff.

She turns to the vanity and runs her hand across it, eyeing the tubular curling iron stands and large circular mirror. She turns and walks over to the window seat and gazes out, catching the view of the river while the moon shimmers through the sheer curtains.

Jeoff makes it to her in two strides and says, "Here, let's sit."

He reaches for her hand, and she gives it to him, sitting.

"Now, in order for this to work, I'm gonna need you to be quiet and let me talk, okay?"

She nods.

He turns, and his engaging eyes make her shiver nervously in spite of herself. She feels anxious, yet she's not quite sure why.

"Melasan."

He sighs and reaches in his pocket, and she almost stops breathing. His hand conceals what he has, and then he hands it to her. She looks at him confused as her fingers detect the familiarity of crisp bills of money.

"That's for all the years that you babysat and sometimes didn't get paid. I owe you," he says softly.

"Jeoff, you don't have to—"

He puts his finger to his lips, and her eyes lower almost drowsily.

"Shh." He removes his finger, still holding her gaze. "This is also for you." He reaches into the opposite pocket and pulls out a blue velvet ring box.

Melasan gasps, her eyes widening. He opens it, and inside is a gold ring with a single solitaire diamond on it. Mel puts her hands over her mouth.

"Take it," he says.

She reaches for the ring, thinking it odd he'd have her get it out of the box. She has to tug sharply; and when it comes, the velvet piece holding it comes out too, revealing that the ring is merely a key ring resembling a ring. The key ring holds two gold-tone keys.

A little frustrated, she says, "Jeoff, what is this?"

He leans closer to her, and his eyes lower as though preparing to kiss her. Embarrassed, she feels her lips move toward his.

Instead of kissing her, he continues talking, "These are the keys to your house."

Again, she looks confused. "My house?"

"This is the house I designed and had built for you, for us, and for our family."

Her mouth gapes open, and she blinks her eyes quickly as though in a dream.

"Can I talk now?" she asks, childlike.

"No, not yet." He lets out a breath. "Listen close 'cause you may never hear this again." He rubs his palms on his slacks. "Do you remember when I kissed you almost nine years ago in my apartment?"

She nods, amazed that he remembers.

"I fell in love with you that night. Maybe sooner, but I knew it then for sure. It's you that helped me get my degree. If you hadn't kept pushin' me and lettin' me know that you believed in me, I don't know what I would have done." He sniffs and continues, "I wanted all of this to be right"—he waves his hand—"the divorce, the house, the direction of the wind, the kind of soap I used in the mornin', know what I mean?"

She nods again, rubbing her fingers across the house keys.

"When I saw you with that guy—"

"I—"

She tries to speak, and he gives her a stern look.

"When I saw you laughing with him and him holding your hands—"

"You saw all that?" she asks, incredulous.

"I was there longer than you think," he answers. "I'm always watchin'." He raises an eyebrow. "Either way, Mel, I saw my whole world fall apart that night."

"I shouldn't have went out with him," she says, looking at him with her head cocked to the side and longing to touch him.

"Your goin' out with him made me react and realize that there's a whole world out there that knows you're beautiful and won't take you for granted like I have been doin'."

He touches her face, and she leans into his hand, closing her eyes for a moment.

"I owe you this house and so much more. I love you, Melasan."

Jeoff removes his hand from her face, getting off of the bench and down on one knee. He reaches into the top pocket of his shirt and pulls out a stunning ring.

"Melasan, will you please marry me?"

Her mouth drops again, and he takes her left hand.

"Please?"

"Yes."

She hears herself croak and wipes her eyes as tears have begun to fall. Jeoff stands, pulling her to her feet. He gently grabs her face and searches her eyes; and at the end of the search, he gives her a long, yearning, passionate kiss. His long arms pull her waist into him and hold her weakened body. Finally, the two stand back and reflect on the last few minutes of their lives.

It is Jeoff that speaks, saying, "Let's go outside and tell everybody the good news."

Hand in hand, they glide down the stairs and outside to the backyard like two victorious eagles. Rev. Simpson looks up from devouring his boiled shrimp to see them sauntering the direction of his table and nudges Melasan's dad. They both stand as the couple approaches the table.

"Attention, everybody, Melasan and Jeoff are *finally* gettin' married!"

Chapter 20

Rookie sits outside Miss Justine's office, her eyes narrowed and her face curled into angry contortions. She stares at the door as though burning it with fire.

"All right, I'll see you Friday." Miss Justine walks out the door, and as the young lady walks away, she turns Rookie's direction. "Since when do you come so early?"

Rookie frowns in answer, and the two walk into Miss Justine's office. Rookie flounces into a chair, sighing dramatically.

Miss Justine sits in a chair beside her desk, looking thoughtful. "Clearly there is something on your mind?"

"Yes, there *is* somethin' on my mind." Rookie smacks, pulling her knees up to sit cross-legged in the chair. "I got a letter"—she elongates and accentuates the word *letter* and rolls her eyes—"from my husband's father."

Miss Justine leans forward in interest. "Oh, really? Did you bring it with you?"

Rookie cocks her head to the side angrily to look at Miss Justine and smacks again. "Please let me remind you, Dr. Moira"—she pulls her lips together, primly mocking Miss Justine, and Miss Justine frowns—"that our agreement was only that I write the family, not that I let you see everything they write back!" She flops against the back of her seat.

Miss Justine nods her head knowingly. "So the letter wasn't to your satisfaction?"

"Of course it wasn't! My in-laws hate me! Always have. They didn't even tell Jeoff I was comin' home!" Her lips quiver in frustration, and she bows her head, snatching a tear from her cheek.

"How do you perceive that they haven't told him?" Miss Justine asks, still leaning forward.

Rookie rolls her eyes, licking her lips. "It's obvious, ain't it?" She sighs, placing her hand on one hip in the chair. "He ain't contacted me."

Miss Justine smiles slightly.

"My baby's been waitin' all this time for me, and the waitin's been makin' the wantin' stronger."

Miss Justine moves to her desk and sits behind it in her own chair. "What kind of books have you been reading lately?" she asks.

"I don't read," Rookie indignantly says.

Miss Justine scratches her head, looking at Rookie. "I just thought that perhaps there are romance novels in the rec room library that you have been perusing," she answers.

Rookie rolls her eyes again.

"Has the thought ever crossed your mind that your husband did not make contact of his own volition?" she asks.

"Own what?" Rookie asks.

Miss Justine presses her lips together and thinks of a better way to explain. "Perhaps he did not write because he desires not to write," she states calmly.

Rookie shakes her head determinedly. "His daddy said some-thin' like it's his job to talk to me for the whole family." Rookie chews at the polish on her nail and then spits. "I don't know why he wants to be the talker now. He ain't never talked to me in the past. It was always Mrs. Mari that talked to me."

Miss Justine listens and leans forward on her elbows. "So do you want me to read the letter and perhaps aid in unclear state-ments?" She blinks her vibrantly sand-colored eyes and focuses them on Rookie. "Could you explain why you felt the need to rush to your appointment today?"

Rookie scratches a knee. "'Cause his letter made me sound stupid and"—she pauses, resting the scratching hand on the same knee—"like a monster." She looks sad and reflective and then snaps back, saying, "I'm not a monster, and no, I don't wanna discuss it."

Miss Justine blinks her keen eyes and brushes back a strand of black hair that has fallen from its bun. "I'm trying to give you choices, Rookie. You'll be leaving soon, so I'd really like to know what's on your mind."

The room grows quiet, and Rookie silently stares at the ceiling and then looks again at Miss Justine.

"You know, you kinda remind me of Mrs. Mari, how that you're such a smart, professional Black woman." She rubs the back of her neck under her hair. "She's all business like a sergeant too," she finishes. She puts an elbow on one of her legs and leans her face on her hand. "That bed in the room is a killa! I wonder if I'll have a more comfortable bed in Montgomery. Of course I will. I'm sure Jeoff is doin' good for himself and the kids."

Miss Justine clears her throat. "I believe that you are exhibiting a very dangerous thought pattern. It isn't healthy that you continue to assume life will be peaches and cream when you return. You should strongly consider thinking realistic thoughts about your return."

Rookie looks deflated. "I'm not goin'."

"What are you talking about, Rookie?"

"Well, you don't want me to go. His daddy'n'em have probably been workin' all this time to poison him and the kids against me, so what's the point?"

"The point is that, a while back, you said you wanted to right this wrong," she answers.

"So just right my wrong and know that it might take some time for me and Jeoff 'n' the kids to be right?"

Miss Justine nods, looking minorly encouraged. "Now our hour is over, but I believe we should speak again Wednesday since you have such a short time left."

"All right," Rookie agrees, almost pleasantly.

"Um, Rookie?"

Rookie stands out of her chair and stretches her legs. "Yes, ma'am?" she asks guardedly.

"What mode of transportation are you taking to Montgomery? Plane? Bus?" she asks.

"Plane. I wanna get there as soon as possible," Rookie replies.

"Well, if you're willing to consider taking the train, I can procure you a ticket for far cheaper than a plane ticket. The trip will take a couple days longer, but it is a journey with numerous sights to see." She waits for Rookie's answer.

"I guess I could do it that way. What do I have to do for you now, give a kidney to your husband?" Rookie asks sardonically.

"No. This is my gift to you. Just be sure to have a safe trip and use the time to reflect on life and the possibilities," she remarks.

Rookie frowns, catching what she's getting at.

She marches down the hall, looking forward to rubbing it in Ranelle's face that, in just a few short weeks, she'd be leaving.

I hear Miss Justine and all, that it might take some time for life to be right with Jeoff and the kids, but Jeoff has never been able to wait more than a few weeks to be back with me in the past, so this won't be much different. I may have to work a little harder. That's all."

She smirks at the look she imagines will be on her face, and her look changes as she enters the room. All of Ranelle's things have been packed and are sitting by the door. Ranelle is nowhere in sight. Rookie walks back down the hall to the parole officer's office.

"Where's my roommate?" She breathlessly pushes out.

"And that would be…"

His snide tone is enough to make her want to turn around and leave, but she wants to know if Ranelle is returning back to prison.

"Her name is Ranelle. I'm not sure about the last name," she answers.

He raises his eyebrows. "Your roommate has a home plan."

"A what?" Rookie says, not believing.

"A home plan. She's goin' home to finish out her parole with her family. I probably shouldn't share that information with you since she didn't, but you don't have any impact on her life, do ya now?"

Rookie shakes her head, dragging out of the office and back to her room. Ranelle's luggage is no longer there, and Rookie flops on the bed feeling dismal. She does have family—family that, without a doubt, wants her. What does Rookie have? She doesn't have any guarantees and is beginning to wonder if she is making the right choice.

The air conditioner kicks on, and Rookie spies a piece of paper flying off of her dresser. She stands, stops it with her foot, and reads it.

Rookie,

> Sorry to leave without saying goodbye, but my family had my home plan in the works, and I didn't know it. I know we didn't become close or the best of friends, but if you need to talk to somebody when you get to Montgomery, give me a call. (573) 586-2484.

> Ranelle

Rookie smiles slightly and stuffs the piece of paper in her things.

Chapter 21

"I REALLY WISH YOU'D GIVE us more time to plan this weddin'," Evelyn Pete says to Melasan.

"Momma, I've been waitin' a long time for this day," Mel answers. "I know we can work magic with the time we have. All that matters is that my groom and my peoples are there, right?"

Mrs. Pete nods, still looking disappointed. "I'm glad y'all are gettin' married. Y'all been pinin' over each other for a while now." She pats her daughter's arm affectionately. "Well, no time to talk. We've only got 'til Saturday, and it's already Tuesday. I gotta meet Mari at the bakery, so I'm not tryin' to run you off, but Momma's gotta go." She quickly kisses Mel and heads out the door.

Melasan grabs her purse and keys and reaches for the doorknob when her cell phone rings and vibrates.

"Hello?"

"Melly? This is Aunt Florese," her deceased husband's aunt's voice rings through the other end.

"Well, hello! How y'all doin'?" she asks.

"Doin' just fine. Your momma tells me you're gettin' married?" she asks.

"Yes, ma'am."

"I wanted to have the honor of makin' your weddin' dress.

"Oh my!" Melasan says, shocked. "You don't have to do that, Aunt Florese."

"I know I don't, but you've always made sure we get to spend time with our little bug Adrienne even though Henry's long gone. And I talked with my sister and his daddy, and they're gonna call you too, but we wanna do this," she finishes. "Oh, and we won't take no for an answer. Now you know I'm a seamstress by trade, but we don't have much time. I need you today to choose the pattern you want, figure out what kind and color material you want and your measurements, and call Aunt Florese back *today* so I can get done by Thursday, okay?"

"Yes, ma'am."

"Me and your family here'll drive it to you and be at your weddin' to wish you well. I always felt badly about how Henry died so early in your marriage and prayed that you'd find someone to share your life with. Now call me *today*, and I'll see you soon. Love you, baby doll."

She hangs up, and Melasan locks the door and floats out on cloud nine.

"I ain't never seen such excitement when we come home!" Cee Cee exclaims; sits at the kitchen table with John, Celeste, Bruni Jr., and Bruni Sr.; and marvels.

Bruni Sr. takes a bite of toast. "That means you oughta come home more often so we can have excitement all the time." He smiles.

"Well, Daddy, I know this time has been mostly monopolized by my baby brother."

She grins, and John snickers.

"But me and John have news."

Bruni Sr. raises his eyebrows. "Well, tell it, baby girl."

"John's gettin' transferred to Mobile, so we'll only be two hours away instead of all the way in Atlanta."

"Now ain't that a blessin'!" he shouts. "So, my boy, you got any movin' plans you need to tell me about?" He turns to his namesake.

"Nope. I ain't no baby like Cee and Baby J."

At that exact moment, Jeoff pops in the kitchen door.

"What's up, kinfolk?"

Everybody starts laughing and says hey back.

He waves their laughter off with a hand and focuses on John and Bruni Jr. "Big boy, you'll be my best man?"

"You shoulda asked me that before you proposed," he fake fusses.

Jeoff ignores him. "Johnny, groomsman?"

"What are we s'posed to wear? Not tuxes?" John asks.

"I was thinkin' more like basketball shorts and tank tops," Bruni teases.

Jeoff gives them both a crazy look. "Tuxes all day long. Y'all got time right now to go to the shop? Mel wants blue and silver."

He holds up his watch, glancing at it, then back at the two of them; but they're already standing. John leans down and kisses Cee Cee, and Bruni likewise kisses his wife.

"What about me?" Bruni Sr. asks.

Bruni Jr. leans over and kisses his forehead affectionately, and he wipes it off.

"Ain't you wearin' some fancy marryin' robe?" Jeoff nudges his brother, grinning.

"I guess I am, but it won't be blue or silver," he says dejectedly. "I had a good idea though," he offers, cheering up. "Why don't we get a couple more tickets, and you and Melasan go on the same cruise me and your momma are goin' on?" He winks jokingly.

"Hmm, nope, don't think so, Pop. I want Mel all to myself."

Everybody in the kitchen falls out laughing and talks all at once.

"You *know* they wanna be alone!"

They laugh again.

Jeoff blushes. "Com' on, y'all. Let's go." He grabs his brothers and ducks out the door, laughter following him.

"Girl, I can't believe you!" Arika screeches as Melasan walks into the beauty salon. "If I'd known lover boy was gonna go all crazy and propose, I'd have told you to date long ago."

Mel ignores her comments.

"So when's the wedding date? Three years from now?"

"Saturday," Mel comments dryly.

"Saturday? As in this Saturday?" She looks shocked.

Mel nods and then looks concerned. "How's your cousin? Is he all right?"

"Yeah, he's fine. Now, about this wedding—"

"I'd like for you to be a bridesmaid," Melasan cuts in. "I'm sorry for cuttin' you off, but I've got so much to do. I need to get measured and call Aunt Florese and get the girls' dresses. We're tryin' to get them to wear somethin' they already have."

"You're gonna let me do their hair, right? It's part of my wedding gift."

Melasan nods and then snaps her fingers. "If you already have a blue dress, that'll do. I've still gotta catch Celeste and Cee to ask them." She thinks. "But nothin' fancy, girl, just family and a few friends in the backyard of our house."

"House?" Arika's eye bulge.

"I'll tell you about it later, but he had a house built for us!" She almost swoons. "Meet me at my place after you get off, okay?" Melasan bounds back out the door.

"Okay, ladies." Melasan looks at Ni Ni, Mari, Cha Cha, and Boo. "Are y'all ready for Saturday?"

"Yeah, Momma," Mari says, looking in Melasan's eyes happily.

"I love you, my babies, and I look forward to many more beautiful years with you." She kisses and hugs each one.

Then they all start talking at once.

"Hold on. Hold on. I gotta make a phone call." She makes her phone call, clicks the phone off, and looks at her girls. "I think y'all could get away with wearing your Easter dresses for the wedding. What do y'all think?"

"Momma," Ni Ni pleads, "I thought Daddy said y'all wanted silver and blue. None of our dresses are either of those colors." Her pleading eyes focus on Melasan.

Mari and Cha Cha chime in simultaneously, "Our grandmas said they'll take us shoppin' tomorrow!"

Mel shakes her head incredulously. "So that's that, huh? They're really spoilin' us."

"My mommy and daddy are gettin' married!" Boo shouts.

"Hey, girls!" Mel shouts her greetings to Cee Cee and Celeste. "Thanks for agreein' to be in the weddin'. Have a seat. Arika'll be here in a minute."

Just then, Arika bursts in the door with a dress. "Hey, y'all."

They all greet her.

"Where are y'all's dresses?" she asks.

"We have to go shoppin' again." Celeste grins. "Nothin' we have'll do."

"If y'all are gettin' somethin' new, I am too! So shoppin' tomorrow?" Arika asks.

"Of course!" Cee and Celeste agree together.

"Oh, yeah, before I forget," Cee Cee says, "Daddy's got your boys tomorrow. They're goin' to the tux shop."

"Yeah, they heard your girls were gettin' dresses, and they revolted. I think Daddy was gonna take 'em anyway," Celeste tells her. "Cee, we better get goin' 'cause Momma and your mom have us doin' a few things at the house."

"Yeah, girl, see you tomorrow," Cee Cee says, rising. "What time?"

"Two," Arika answers. "I gotta run too. Need to get a wedding gift."

Cee Cee and Celeste leave.

Arika stands and kisses Melasan on the cheek. "Congratulations, girl. I am so happy for you." She heads to the door. "Oh, and since you ditched Aubrey, do I still gotta go to church?" She scoots out laughing as Mel throws a pillow at the door.

As she picks up the pillow, the phone rings.

"Hey, sunshine." Jeoff's sultry voice sends goose bumps up her spine. "You miss me?"

"Yeah." Sitting down on her couch, Melasan hugs the pillow to her chest. "What about you?"

"No doubt. I haven't seen you all week." He groans. "I think we're gonna be so busy on opposite ends of the world that we may not see each other 'til Saturday."

"I might not make it that long. I'm havin' withdrawals," she teases, twisting a corner of the pillow.

"Oh, you've got to. I need a lot more years with you. I love you, and I'll try to see you sooner than the wedding, Mrs. Simpson."

She says goodbye, and the phone clicks.

Wednesday and Thursday go by in a whirlwind, and although Melasan and Jeoff talk during the day and every night as they drift off to sleep, they still don't see each other.

"Have you seen, Jeoff?" Mrs. Pete asks, pouring lemonade for herself, Melasan, and Mrs. Simpson.

"No, Momma," Melasan whines testily. "I was hopin' I'd see him tonight."

Mrs. Pete glances at Mrs. Simpson conspiratorially. "Sorry, Punkinhead, but Florese dropped your dress off, and we need to make sure it fits right, matches your flowers, and get accessories."

"They're here?" Mel asks.

"Yes, but you don't have time to socialize," Mrs. Pete admonishes.

"She needs shoes, Evelyn," Mrs. Simpson offers.

"Oh, yeah, and shoes. I almost forgot."

They grin as Melasan groans, holding her head.

"I can't take anymore shoppin'!" She lays her head on the kitchen counter, mumbling into it. "I never thought I'd say that."

"You sound like one of the grandbabies, all the fussin' you doin'." Mrs. Pete takes a drink of her lemonade. "Mari, ain't rehearsal this evenin'?"

Mrs. Simpson nods.

Mrs. Pete clicks her teeth on her glass. "See, you'll see him this evenin' before the boys snatch him away and we snatch you away." She cackles merrily, high-fivin' Mrs. Simpson.

"Hey, babycakes," Jeoff whispers to Melasan, "rehearsal went quick, so I'll see you tomorrow at four?" He winks. "Wanna sit on the porch while they talk about their weddin'?"

She nods, and Jeoff already has her in motion. They sit on the swing and stare off into the night sky.

"I wanna just sit out here and kiss you all night," he utters softly.

She obliges him with a soft kiss and then leans back, tracing his jawline with her finger. "Thank you for this beautiful house and completing my family with my children. You really had me fooled." She leans her head on his shoulder, trying to ignore the sound of footsteps approaching.

"All right, lover boy, Pops said he thought he saw the two of you sneak away," John says. "We're ready to go. The men are stayin' together, and the women are goin' their own way."

"Our own way?" Mel asks.

"Y'all are goin' with each other, away from us," he asserts, poking out his chest.

"See you tomorrow, baby. God willin'." Jeoff kisses her lips swiftly as John tugs on his arm.

"I love you."

She watches him walk away, and then he disappears as the men converge around him.

"I am so tired! I can't believe y'all kept me up all night!" Melasan sits in the stylin' chair with her girls to either side of her getting their hair done too.

"Mommy, we're gonna be princesses," Adrienne says.

Arika puts finishing touches on Ni Ni's hair and then comes back to curl Melasan's hair. "Well, like you, I've never heard of an all-night shower." She clicks the iron. "But it was fun." She turn's Mel's chair to face her. "The girls should be done soon, and I know I'm cuttin' it close, but I wanted everybody's hair to be fresh, especially yours." She looks approvingly and then cuts off the irons. "All right, let's go get everybody dressed."

They crowd into Mel's truck and pull up at the Pete household at three o'clock, where Mr. Pete is sunken into the couch.

"Hey, muffin, you ready?" The corners of his eyes crinkle as he gazes lovingly at his daughter.

"I will be soon, and you look sharp, Daddy." She blows him a kiss and goes down the hall to her old bedroom.

She can hear the children—Cee Cee, Celeste, and Arika—talking loudly and laughing. She opens the door to her room, closes the door behind her, and leans against the door for a moment. She walks across the floor and touches the plastic covering the dress. As it crinkles, she begins to cry.

"Thank you, God. You've been so good to me." She gets on her knees and raises her hands toward heaven. "Will I ever be able to thank you enough? I thought you'd left me when Henry died, and I thought I was alone when I found out I was pregnant…" She wipes her face, smiling. "But I've never been alone. I've got seven beautiful children, a new house, and a wonderful husband that I love and will love for the rest of my life. Thank you." She stands, lifting the plastic off the dress.

The white satin overlaid with blue organza falls out silkily. Melasan marvels to herself at how Aunt Florese took a simple pattern and turned it into an elegant gown. She carefully unzips the dress and steps into it. Finishing with her accessories, she steps into the hallway.

"You look like a queen!" Mari says.

"Yes, don't you look gorgeous!" Mr. Pete exclaims, standing from the couch. He grabs her hand and pats it with his other one. "Let's go, baby. Everybody's waitin' on you." He squeezes her hand again. "Love you, Melpoo."

He kisses her cheek and then her hand, and they head outside and then to the wedding.

The bridesmaids talk excitedly as they approach the driveway to the house. But Melasan stays silent, and their voices drone on. They all get out of the Navigator and walk into the house.

"Bridesmaids, we need you," someone says.

They each leave for their respective partners. Arika's with Duran, and he beams, proud that his dad chose him as a groomsman. Melasan winks at him as they head out the patio door. The wedding flourishes by, and Melasan suppresses the desire to pinch herself to make sure she's not dreaming. Jeoff takes her breath away in his silver tux and blue vest.

He is so handsome! she says to herself as her heart pounds wildly.

Jeoff gazes directly into her eyes and she into his as they recite their vows, and she feels as though she may pass out from sheer ecstasy. After the wedding, Jeoff holds her hand the rest of the evening.

"You get more and more stunning every day." He kisses her lips and then her forehead, smoothing her hair back.

He messes up more hairstyles like that, she muses to herself. Out loud, she asks, "Stunninger?"

"Every day."

They laugh and then stand as it's announced that it's time for their dance together. The song "At Last" plays, and she melts into his arms. The song ends too quickly for her, and then she winds up dancing with her daddy and a myriad of other people as they pin dollars onto her dress for dances.

She finally falls into her chair beside Jeoff, stating, "I can't believe they pulled this elaborate weddin' together in a week!"

The blue-and-silver alternating napkins lined the buffet table. There are finger sandwiches, tastefully done leftovers from the anniversary dinner, and a gorgeous three-tiered wedding cake with silver sugar pearls on the sides and silver-and-blue flowers on top. The part of the yard for the reception is decorated with tiki torches and balloon bouquets. Jeoff and Melasan have stood under a balloon arch, and the doorway of the patio is lined with a balloon garland. The lights are still in the trees from the party and glisten festively against the night sky.

They cut the first piece of cake and drink their foaming blue punch from the silver fountain out of plastic champagne flutes. They greet guest after guest with hugs and kisses and everyone saying, "It's about time!" The family even hired Brother Tebbitts to take all the pictures. The children made a fake beach near a plastic pool, so they take several pictures near that. The boys look handsome in their silver tuxes with blue ties, and the girls are so pretty in their shimmery blue dresses. Melasan had no idea how the moms found the dresses that looked so much alike. The kids even surprise them with a three-day hotel stay in Mobile. The day is just too glorious, and the newlyweds' evening is breathtaking.

Chapter 22

"WAKE UP, SLEEPYHEAD." JEOFF NUDGES Melasan.

"I am so spoiled." She stretches and leans over to give him a kiss. "These first couple of nights in our own house have been heavenly!" She yawns, tosses back the covers, and pads to the bathroom without her house shoes.

When she emerges scratching her head, she notices Jeoff is already dressed.

"Hurry up, slowpoke. We gotta get Daddy and Momma to the airport." He heads down the stairs.

"Wait for me, baby," she calls, quickly pulling on a pair of jeans.

He comes back smiling. "What, you miss me already?"

Melasan sticks her head through a T-shirt and wraps her arms around his neck. "Yeah."

He holds her waist, and they kiss slow and lingeringly.

"Okay, woman, now we gotta go." He pulls away, grabbing her hand.

They race to the living room. Mel grabs her purse, and they get in the Navigator with Jeoff in the driver's seat.

"I need some keys, poopsie."

"You must not pay attention 'cause I put my extra set on your keyring the day after you proposed." She bats her eyelashes at him playfully.

Reaching into his front jeans pocket, Jeoff says, "I saw somethin' different, but I just thought them kids were playin' with my keys."

He starts the truck, and they head for Montgomery.

"I feel cheated." He reaches for her hand and plays with her fingers.

"Why?" she asks with concern in her voice.

"Because I gave you keys to the Surburban more than a year ago." He fake pouts.

"Oh, my poor baby." She touches his face. "That was because you lose your keys all the time." She sits back in her seat, chuckling.

"After we take the old peoples to the airport, we'll get breakfast and get on the road, okay?"

She nods.

"I can't believe your parents took all the kids, and"—he turns off an exit—"I'm surprised and proud of our kids for paying for our honeymoon."

"I am too. Apparently they had their own money, and your daddy used his credit card to take care of everything," Melasan informs him.

"Well, I'm blown away, absolutely blown away." He pulls into his parents' driveway and toots the horn, jumping out of the truck. "Sit tight, baby. I'm gonna get their bags."

Rev. Simpson greets him as he comes in the door. "I knew that was you honkin' like we're in the projects."

The two hug.

"So where's your Mrs. Simpson?"

"She's in the truck waitin' on y'all. I came in to help with the bags." He stands back and looks at his dad. "Ooh-wee! Ain't you clean!"

Rev. Simpson poses, showing off a red crushed-linen short-sleeved shirt with white pinstripes and matching pants. He also sports a red Dobbs hat with a white ribbon on the band and red-and-white huarache men's sandals.

"I just clean up good, that's all."

Rev. Simpson grabs a couple of suitcases, and Jeoff likewise grabs the other two.

"So you enjoyin' married life?" His gold teeth sparkle, matching the insignia on the luggage.

Jeoff almost swallows his face with joy. "It's so much better than the first time." He lays his hand on the doorknob.

"Speaking of the first time, I haven't heard anything from Rookie since I sent that letter. You gonna talk to the kids about that?" He nods for Jeoff to open the door, and as Jeoff heads out, Rev. Simpson turns around. "Love, could you put some pepper in it?"

"Coming!" Mrs. Simpson's steps can be heard as the two head out the door.

They load up the bags and sit in the truck.

"Good mornin', Mrs. Simpson." Rev. Simpson tips his hat to her.

"Good mornin'."

Rev. Simpson taps Jeoff on the shoulder. "So what you gonna do about that girl comin'?"

"I remember us thinkin' before she was comin', and when it didn't happen, everything was turned upside down for at least a month. That was a few years ago, so if—and I do mean *if*—she turns up, then we'll cross that bridge when we come to it."

Fifteen minutes later, Mrs. Simpson opens the kitchen door wearing a white sundress with red polka dots, her hair hanging down under a white rattan wide-brim sunbrim and white sandals accented with a red flower on their tops. On both arms, she has carry-ons. Rev. Simpson gets out, opens the door for her, and gently holds her hand as she gets in, intentionally not looking at him.

"How do you do, Mrs. Simpson?" she greets Melasan.

"I do just fine, Mrs. Simpson. Y'all are mighty sharp. You gonna put everybody else on that cruise to shame."

"This is forty years' worth of coordinatin' with my honey." She pats Rev. Simpson's leg.

He leans over and whispers in her ear, "I'm gon' find out what's in them bags. You know you don't need 'em."

She looks out the window, smiling demurely.

"Okay, peoples, here's the airport."

Jeoff parks, and they unload and put everything on a baggage stroller.

After everyone hugs, he tells them, "We'll pick you up Saturday. Have fun."

"Y'all have fun too. We love you," Mrs. Simpson calls out, chasing Rev. Simpson's disappearing form into the airport.

"Well, love, our bags are already in the truck, so I'll take you to breakfast since it's only seven thirty," Jeoff says to Mel, pulling off.

"Yeah, 'cause I'm starving! Feed me please!"

They eat at a Waffle House and hit the highway to Mobile. Three hours later, they are heading into Gulf Shores.

"Oh, Jeoff! Have you ever been here?"

He shakes his head, staring at the sandy sun-drenched oasis in Alabama, the very state they live in. Amazingly enough, the children purchased them three nights in a Gulf Shores condominium on the beach of the Gulf Coast. They check in and are led to a secluded condominium nestled into the beach, with the Gulf of Mexico exotically swaying in the distance of a fabulous view from their balcony. Jeoff tips the bellhop; and he and Melasan survey their sophisticated surroundings—a generous arrangement of wildflowers sitting in a clear vase on the dining table for two, bubble bath, and matching thirsty robes and oils for massages in a basket by the Jacuzzi tub. They take off their shoes and run their toes through the thick carpet like small children.

"Jeoff! There are chocolate-covered strawberries in the refrigerator!"

"Jeoff walks quietly up and wraps his arms around her waist. "Unforgettable."

The three days skate by quickly as the two enjoy the charm and romantic atmosphere. The first day, they shop at the tourist spots and relax on the balcony, savoring the Southern sunset. The climate stays mellow and balmy, so Jeoff suggests they visit Alligator Alley.

"Alligator Alley?" Mel's eyes enlarge. "Ain't that where they feed you to the alligators?" she asks.

"Nah. They've got the meat of other tourists ready for us to feed them gators." His eyes sparkle. "Come on, sunshine. I wanna feed the gators."

They leave the second morning to view over 150 alligators, with Jeoff feeding five and Melasan ducking and squealing every time she attempts to feed one.

"Now that's over, let's go to the gardens," she sweetly says to Jeoff.

"The ones on the grounds by the condo?" he asks suspiciously.

"Yeah, silly. They've got bikes and a trail. No animals."

Wednesday whisks by; and on Thursday, the final evening, they decide to indulge in the romantic cruise for two included in their package. The peaceful pull of the boat lends to the unparalleled excellence of the ride. Jeoff and Melasan stand on the deck, fingers interlaced and bodies leaning toward one another. The stars sparkle overhead as Jeoff places little sweet kisses ever so gently on Mel's hair. Melasan feels her heart ache with boundless love, and she sighs.

"You happy?" he questions, staring into the night.

"My cup runneth over."

Chapter 23

"HEY, MOMMA," ROOKIE GREETS HER mom.

"Rookie?" Miss Phyllis hazily focuses. "Well, it is you! I thought you was a ghost!" Her eyes narrow. "What you doin' here?" she harshly asks and pushes open the screen, stepping out onto her wooden porch with Rookie.

"I'm not tryin' to stay," Rookie states, sounding intimidated as she looks at the woman who once put her out of her home.

Miss Phyllis is older, haggard with her once beautiful, smooth cocoa skin now grayish brown, her eyes still bloodshot either from just drinking or just the years of drinking weathered on her. Her hair lies flat on her head in ear-length jagged cuts in a style that she is planning to only curl for Saturday nights.

She looks like an old hag, Rookie thinks. Out loud, she says, "I just wanna know 'bout Jeoff and the kids."

"What you want with them?"

"Momma, I'm goin' home." Rookie juts her chin out defiantly.

"Well, just where is this home?" Miss Phyllis puts her hand on her hip, her yellow flowered housecoat slightly rising.

"Wherever they are, I mean..." she stammers.

Miss Phyllis reaches into the pocket of the homely dress doubling as her housecoat, pulling out a pack of Kools and a lighter. She taps the new pack, eyeing Rookie; pulls off the plastic barrier; lights one; and blows out some smoke almost offensively before answering.

"Why don't you just leave them peoples alone?" She puts the pack and lighter back in her pocket. "You ain't had no problem leavin' them alone for the past six and some years. Why now, girl?" Her eyes get a deeper red from the smoke, and she flicks some ashes into her hand.

"I see you still get your nails done," Rookie observes.

"Don't you worry 'bout me," Miss Phyllis snaps, flicking more ashes into her hand. "You just tryin' to make nice to get some information. And I gots information, believe you me."

The ashes on her cigarette grow long as she concentrates on her long-lost daughter.

"I love Jeoff, Momma, and I need to know where to find him, please!" Rookie's eyes swell with impatience.

Miss Phyllis turns up her lips. "So you love him, huh?"

She nods.

Miss Phyllis snorts. "Well, he don't love you." She turns to head back into the house.

"You hateful old woman!" Rookie screams at her back. "You just don't want me to be happy. You never have! Just tell me where they are. I know you know!"

Miss Phyllis stops walking and turns around angrily, flicking the cigarette off the porch. "You just like ya selfish daddy! You know, I used to cry over that dog, and I asked him why he left us, and you know what he said? He said he didn't know."

She advances toward Rookie, and Rookie holds her breath.

"Your husband got married Saturday."

Rookie's face turns ashen. Her knees begin to shake, and she looks at her mother disbelievingly.

Miss Phyllis bursts out into hysterical laughter. "So you still think you can go home?" She walks into the house, slamming the screen behind her and turns and locks the screen.

Rookie sits on the steps of the house she once lived in to steady her emotions. She finally stands and makes her way to the bus stop.

Is that mean old woman lying?

Her Momma's laughter pounds in her head, and she almost misses the city bus.

"You gettin' on?" the bus driver asks.

Rookie nods, stumbling on.

"Hey, if you been drinkin', I don't allow that mess," he snaps.

She can't even argue, just sits in the first seat she can find.

Married? We're still married! Ain't we? Rookie comes to herself slightly, pays for a transfer, and rides to Rev. and Mrs. Simpson's house.

She takes a breath, boldly walks to the door, and rings the doorbell several times with no answer.

Maybe they don't live here anymore. She rubs her forehead. *Maybe I don't remember streets that good anymore.*

She looks around seeing no one on the street defeated and returns to the bus stop.

I can't find 'em.

The bus appears, and she drags to the back, eyes tired and bloodshot and cheeks tear streaked.

"Are you?" A tall dark-complexioned woman with short hair shaved in the back and slicked to her head with much gel stops in front of her. "Rookie Simpson?"

"Yeah," defiantly Rookie answers, and then a flicker of recognition enters her mind. She scans her recesses, coming up with "Danielle?"

"Yeah, girl. Where you been? I ain't seen you in a month of Sundays."

She sits beside her, talking nonstop, and Rookie listens intently, trying to drink in the life of old.

"Well, here's my stop. Here's my number." She hands Rookie a half a piece of paper. "Call me sometimes." She stands.

"Hey, Danielle, is Rev. Simpson still at that same church on Redmond?"

"Yep. A girlfriend of mine got married there last month. They charged her for using the church! Somethin' 'bout she and him wasn't members. Churches are s'posed to be free to everybody!" She rolls her neck. "That's what the Bible says. The churches are free. Anyway, I can't stand church folk. What you been doin' with yourself since the divorce?"

"What?" Rookie asks.

"Lady, you getting' off or what?" the bus driver impatiently asks.

"Call me, girl."

154

She gets off, and Rookie lays her head on the seat in front of her, feeling her heart touch her feet. She lets the bus take her to the boarding house she checked into and goes to her room.

"We've got to take the kids back to pet the alligators." Melasan leans back in the leather of the passenger seat and, before Jeoff has a chance to answer, falls back asleep. She rouses again when they enter Montgomery.

"You've gotten mighty attached to that passenger seat, ain't ya?" Jeoff looks at his wife with a grin.

She dons a guilty look. "I'm sorry, baby. All this pamperin' makes a girl tired."

He pats her leg. "It's all good. You got plenty time to drive."

"You wanna switch when we get to Momma'n'em's?" she asks as he pulls onto her parents' street.

"Why? You don't want them to see what a lazy bum you've turned into?"

She playfully swats at his leg, and they laugh as he pulls into the drive.

"Daddy and Momma are here!" Devon and Jeoff are climbing trees in the front yard and jump down running to Jeoff and Mel.

"Hey! I missed you!" Melasan hugs and kisses them.

They approach the house talking at the same time. Mel and Jeoff are only able to pick up on bits and pieces of conversation.

"Went to the new snowball stand—"

"Packed some stuff to move—"

Snippets of Devon and Jeoff talking run on together.

Then Jeoff said, "Pa Pa split his pants."

"What?" Jeoff Sr. asks.

They all laugh as Mr. Pete rounds the corner limping.

"Don't even ask. I'm too old to play ball with these kids even with Duran on crutches."

They get all seven of the kids rounded up and in the Navigator, talking wildly among themselves.

"Momma and Daddy, thank y'all so much!" Melasan embraces her parents.

Jeoff gives them a hug.

"Thank you too," Mrs. Pete says as her husband nods in agreement.

"Thank us?" Jeoff gives them a confused look.

"Yeah, thank you! For giving us lots of grandbabies. Mel's an only child, and we always wanted lots of grandbabies to spoil. They're such a joy!" gushes Mrs. Pete, snatching Jeoff up for a second hug.

"We're glad to oblige," he tells her.

"Daddy, are we stayin' at our house tonight?" Ni Ni and Mari ask.

"The only bed there is me and your momma's. I haven't had a chance to move everything else."

"We can sleep on the floor!" Duran yells. "A man needs his space."

"A man!" they all yell.

"We'll sleep there tonight and start bringing stuff over tomorrow. Maybe we'll be close to settle in by the time we pick up Daddy and Momma," Jeoff answers.

Chapter 24

FOUR O'CLOCK IN THE MORNING, Rev. Simpson rises abruptly, looks over at his wife sleeping soundly, and slips from the covers. He heads to his study as though in a trance and gets on his knees. After some time, he rises, putting his hand on his desk for support, and opens his Bible with a contemplative look on his face.

At seven, Mrs. Simpson's voice calls out to him. "Bruni?"

"In the study, lover," he calls back.

She comes in, noticing his open Bible. "I felt you leave this mornin'. I thought you were goin' to the bathroom." She sits on his desk and reaches to rub his beard. "The Lord changed your sermon, huh?"

He nods, closing his eyes at the caressing touch.

She silently hums, and then she tells her husband, "I'll be prayin' with you, love." She rises and heads upstairs for a shower.

Forty minutes later, the couple enters the church, with Mrs. Simpson in a green dress ruffled at the bottom with thick gold vertical stripes and Rev. Simpson in a green double-breasted suit with gold pinstripes and a green tie with John 3:16 scripted in gold lettering.

At the conclusion of Sunday school, the church begins to fill quickly. Jeoff and Melasan enter from the Sunday school wing with the children. They sit together as the children disperse to their numerous posts: Duran, on his crutches, to usher; Mari to one of the keyboards; Cha Cha to the drums; and the rest to the choir room to prepare to march in with the Mass choir.

As they near sermon time, the soloist stands and begins to sing, "A change, a change has come o-o-over me."

Rev. Simpson strokes his mustache with his eyes closed and opens them to notice Rookie walking in the doors of the sanctuary.

It is Duran and Brother Jaquan that open the double doors for her, and although Duran looks at her, he seems to hold no recognition. Rev. Simpson's eyes close again as the song continues, and he feels the peace of the Holy Spirit like a cool breeze flowing gently through the building.

"He washed away all my sins, and He made made me whole…"

The congregation claps and gives much clamor at the beauteous climax of the song. Rev. Simpson stands and waits silently for a moment and then prays.

Rookie fidgets uncomfortably in her seat and leans to her neighbor, asking, "How long does this last?"

"As long as the Lord lets it, love," the lady answers.

"Romans chapter eight, thirty-fifth through thirty-ninth verses. I'll be reading from the King James Version."

Pages are heard turning, and then the congregation stands with the pastor.

"Stand up, baby," the lady prompts Rookie.

She stands. *I don't remember this when me and Jeoff came,* she thinks.

"Who shall separate us from the love of Christ? Shall tribulation, or distress, or persecution, or famine, or nakedness, or peril, or sword? As it is written, for thy sake, we are killed all the day long. We are accounted as sheep for the slaughter. Nay in all these things we are more than conquerors through him that loved us. For I am persuaded that neither death, nor life, nor angels, nor principalities, nor powers, nor things present, nor things to come, nor height nor depth, nor any other creature shall be able to separate us from the love of God, which is in Christ Jesus our Lord."

Rev. Simpson looks up with a peaceful glow about himself and says, "May the Lord add a blessing to the reading, hearing, and doing of His Word. You may be seated." He looks around the congregation. "The topic of the sermon is confessions."

Why is he staring at me? Rookie thinks.

She scoots in her seat again, not liking the uncomfortable feeling in her gut. As the sermon progresses, she contemplates leaving.

But the pew is considerably full, and it will be hard to leave without attention.

Duran stares at the Black woman with Hispanic features he seated.

She looks like my—he mentally shakes his head. *A lotta times, you thought you saw her, fool!* he chastises himself yet continues to stare.

"How come we don't have a momma, Duran?" ten-year-old Ni Ni asked. "Why'd she leave?"

"She didn't leave," Duran told her. He held her hand, wiping her tears with his other hand, and said, "The day she went to the mailbox, she was in a hit-and-run accident. The car that hit her took her to the hospital right away, and she went into a coma. They didn't know what apartment she lived in, and everybody they asked said they didn't know her 'cause, you know, Momma was gone a lot."

Ni Ni nodded, listening intently.

"When she woke from her coma, she had amnesia."

"What's that?" she asked, sitting up to hear more of this wonderful explanation.

"It means she lost her memory. She forgot she had kids, so when she woke up, she just started traveling, hoping something would help her remember. And when she gets back here, she'll remember and come home, and we'll all be happy."

Ni Ni leaned against him, content with the description of their estranged mother. At first, Duran understood that he was trying to make his younger sister feel better; but after some time, he began to believe it—wanted desperately to believe it. More years passed, and he grew angry and knew in his heart that she left them because she wanted to.

"Before accepting my calling to preach, I committed some of the worst sins I thought any man could ever commit. Nobody would ever forgive me for this, or that, I thought," Rev. Simpson said.

Rookie has been moving throughout the whole sermon, and he seems to be coming to some type of close. She smooths her hands again, trying to avert her gaze, yet finds herself locked into those eyes in spite of herself and begins to cry silently.

The lady beside her looks over empathetically and pats her hand. "You feel it huh, baby?"

"Feel what?"

"God is the forgiver of your sins. Whatever you've done, bring it all to Jesus."

The choir begins to sing, and everybody stands. Two chairs mysteriously appear at the front of the church, and Rookie's nemesis stands in between them, welcomingly holding out his arms. Somehow, Rookie finds herself past all of those people she previously did not want to pass, to leave, in the aisle and in those arms, openly weeping. Although Rookie never liked Rev. Simpson in the past, she discovers being enveloped in his embrace a safe place of refuge. She feels protected from the schisms of life—the disappointments and heartaches. When he lets her go, she slumps into a seat, feeling physically tired and a little letdown that the safe haven is gone yet like a release has taken place. Then the air goes out of her bubble as her eyes focus on Jeoff. His eyes are frozen on her, and his arm is around a woman whose eyes are also scanning her as though she's an alien.

Who is she? Rookie's mind swirls. *She looks familiar…like—*

"Young lady, do you have a statement you'd like to make?

"The babysitter!"

"Excuse me?" the older lady says to Rookie.

"Yes, ma'am. I'd like to make a statement." Rookie grabs the microphone and stands. "I have done a lot of things wrong in my life. Six years ago, I just walked away and left my family behind."

The congregation listens intently.

Rookie wipes away more tears. "My name is Mrs. Rookie Simpson. I have come home to reclaim my family that I have been away from." She looks at Jeoff sheepishly. "I'm sure you all know my family. I have six children here, and my husband is sitting right over there." She points at Jeoff.

Several people take in dramatic breaths. Rev. Simpson calmly nods at Sis Morris, and she takes Rookie's arm and leads her toward a side door.

"I'm not through!"

Before she gets to say another word, she is quickly whisked out of the sanctuary into a quiet room. Mrs. Simpson and several older ushers gather the children together, along with Jeoff and Melasan, and take them to a classroom. Rev. Simpson can be heard having prayer in the sanctuary, and the children are all looking at Jeoff.

"What's she doin' here!" Duran angrily yells.

"Yeah, Daddy, how'd she get here?" Devin asks.

"Where's she been?" Mari's voice can be heard.

"Why's she tryin' to ruin our lives and embarrass us?" Ni Ni says woefully.

Jeoff Jr. and Cha Cha say nothing.

"Sit down, children, and I'll try to fill you in as much as possible," Jeoff says.

Melasan sits between Ni Ni and Devin.

"I should have told you when I found out."

"You knew she was comin'?" Duran says accusingly. "How long has she been keepin' in touch with you, Dad?" he asks furiously.

"It's nothin' as elaborate as that, son. A few weeks ago, a letter came to your Gumba and Grinny's house from your mother's therapist."

The children look at each other and then back at Jeoff.

"She stated that Rookie was thinkin' of returnin' to Montgomery but had no interest in tellin' us, so she wanted to make us aware."

He stands next to Duran and touches his arm. Duran yanks it away.

"I got pretty mad when I heard about the letter too, and then I prayed about it. Gumba wrote a letter to her, askin' her to let us know when she was comin' so that we could prepare y'all, and she never answered, so I thought it was just like all the times before when we thought she was comin' home."

He looks around at the children, and Rev. and Mrs. Simpson come in the door.

"I understand, Daddy," Mari says softly.

"I don't understand!" Duran turns swiftly toward the door.

Rev. Simpson stops him. "Calm down, son. We all have to work through this together, as a family."

Mrs. Simpson reaches out and holds Duran's hand.

"Daddy," Jeoff Jr. speaks, "why'd she wait so long"—he swallows, eyes large—"to come back?"

"I don't know. Those are questions you'll have to ask her." He looks at Rev. Simpson. "Is she still here?"

Rev. Simpson nods. "Brother Tebbitts is drivin' her to our house, and we'll meet them there. We, your mother and I, figured this conversation would take a while, so we need the children to be as comfortable as possible."

The ushers that helped them into the room help them take the children to the Surburban and kiss Melasan and Jeoff, disappearing back into the church.

On the way to the house, Mari Simpson asks her husband, "You knew she was comin', didn't you?"

"I knew this mornin' at four when God woke me up," he answers.

"I could feel it too. I just didn't want it to be."

The ride to the house is silent, and Jeoff reaches over and grabs Melasan's hand. As they pull up, Rev. and Mrs. Simpson have somehow gotten there ahead of them and have already taken Brother Tebbitts and Rookie inside. The children file out of the truck silently, with the exception of Duran and Ni Ni, who stay inside the truck.

"Hold on a minute, baby," Jeoff says to Melasan.

She keeps the children outside, and Jeoff leans in the door.

"You're not goin' in, children?" he asks.

"What do we have to say to her?" Duran asks, holding his sister's hand. "She left us! Like we were trash, she left us!"

Jeoff climbs into the truck. "I know you have questions for her, and I know you may even have questions for yourself, but you are by no means trash. She lost by leavin', and we got better, the best even!"

Duran looks at him skeptically as tears escape his eyes.

"Son, God gave you a momma that won't ever leave you."

Duran peeks out the truck at Melasan and nods, sighing.

"I remember when she left," he says.

"I do too, son." He grabs Duran's other hand. "But we have to face this so we can move forward. You can get some questions answered and find peace."

They get out of the truck together, and all nine of them enter the house together. Mrs. Simpson meets them in the foyer; and they all walk into the living room where Rookie, Brother Tebbitts, and Rev. Simpson sit. Rookie blinks slowly as each child walks into the room and sits in the living room. She eyes Adrienne suspiciously and realizes that Duran was at the door. All of the children were active participants of the service in some facet. They all sit and wait, looking at her.

"Hello," she says shyly. "Duran," she says to Duran, "you're so handsome."

He frowns slightly.

"I'm not sure about the rest of you because you're so close in age. I'm...sorry."

"Yeah, you're sorry." Jeoff Jr. gets up and leaves.

Duran follows behind him. Mari, their grandma, goes out to check on them.

"I dreamed you'd come back," Li'l Mari says to her.

"You did?" Rookie asks, pleased.

"Yes, ma'am. I don't understand why."

Rookie gets silent.

"Why'd you leave in the first place?" she asks.

"I...uh..." She remembers her momma's words, how that her daddy said he didn't know, and she somehow knows she can't say that. "It wasn't anything you did," she says softly, biting a nail and looking around the room.

"You didn't wanna be our momma?" Cha Cha asks.

"I wanna be your momma now, Mari?" she guesses at the name, embarrassed.

"I'm Cha Cha. She's Mari." Cha Cha points at Mari. "I already got a momma." She rises and goes to sit beside Melasan and Jeoff.

"Her?" She looks at Jeoff, rage filling her body. "I know who you are!" she says, standing. "You're nothin' but that babysitter! You always wanted my husband!"

She runs across the room, and Melasan stands. Rookie jumps, her arms reaching toward Melasan, and Brother Tebbitts snatches her backward before anything can happen. Melasan never flinches; however, Ni Ni screams and begins to hyperventilate. Jeoff leaves the room and returns with a paper bag. He sits next to Ni Ni in one of the recliners in the room and has her breathe into the bag.

"Young lady, you need to get yourself together!" Brother Tebbitts bursts out. "This family has gone through enough without all of this, this drama from you! You come in the church and ask if we remember you. I don't remember you, but I remember all this young man went through, and I done seen these kids come up." Brother Tebbitts rubs his bald head. "I won't have all of this. I love this family, and I just won't have it." He sits, holding Rookie's arm. "I'm sorry, Rev. Simpson, but this is just uncalled for."

"Is this what you came for?" Jeoff asks, stroking Ni Ni's hair as her breathing stabilizes.

"Finally he speaks," she says evilly. "So what is she?" She nods toward Melasan. "Your fill-in until I return?"

"Melasan is my wife," Jeoff says coolly.

"She can't be your wife. That would make you a bigot!" Rookie screams.

Jeoff looks at Brother Tebbitts; and without him having to say a word, Brother Tebbitts lets go of Rookie's arm and ushers Ni Ni, Adrienne, Mari, Devon, and Cha Cha out with him. The children look back longingly at Jeoff and Melasan.

"We'll be there shortly, babies," Mel says.

Rookie glares at her.

Jeoff can't help but smile at her misuse of the word. "You mean bigamist, and no, I am not. Our divorce was final a week or so before the wedding," he continues as Rookie struggles with her emotions.

Her face contorts, and she looks like she may cry and scream in rage all in the same.

"You...you..." she struggles, taking a breath, "you said you didn't believe in divorce. I..." She takes another breath. "I believed you." She looks over at Melasan again with knives in her eyes.

"I don't believe in my children gettin' deserted without a mother either," Jeoff speaks calmly with no malice in his voice.

"I…" Rookie struggles again. "Can I talk to you alone, Jeoff?" She looks at Melasan.

"There's nothin' that you and me need to discuss, but you do need to figure out what you're gonna do with yourself. Do you want a relationship with these children?" he asks.

"I want all of you," she says straight-faced. "I want my family back, Jeoffy."

She pauses, and Jeoff looks at her, noticing that she looks nothing like the Rookie of old. Her hair is still long; but she's missing a couple teeth—one in the very front, giving a very large gap, and the other to the side. Her figure is skinny, sunken even, and her face has large wrinkles with steel eyes.

"You've never been able to say no to me, Jeoff, not for long."

She looks pointedly at Melasan, and Jeoff smirks.

"He'll return to me." She rolls her neck. "I'll talk to the kids when you return to me."

"Then you may as well leave," Jeoff tells her. "You don't have any parental rights. I had those revoked at the divorce. So when you get yourself to some part of the real world, you can contact me, and I'll see if the children want to spend any time gettin' to know the woman who left them to have a good time."

He grabs Melasan's hand, and they exit the room, finding the children in the basement with their grandmother. Rev. Simpson stays behind with Rookie.

"What do you have to say!" She turns on him.

Rev. Simpson stands and gently ushers her to the door. He hands her a piece of paper. "This is me and Mama's number," he says, referring to Mrs. Simpson. "You are welcome to call our home to get in touch with the children. I'll be praying for you."

Before she realizes it, she is out the door, and it is closed.

In the basement, Mrs. Simpson is talking with the children about their mother, and they look up as Jeoff and Melasan come in the room.

"How's everybody feelin'? Anything y'all wanna talk about?" He looks around.

They make no motions.

"Let me tell you this then, the woman who carried y'all in her body has problems, serious problems and had problems before that I just didn't wanna face. She didn't know how to be a momma, which is why God sent you this momma to love you." He holds Mel's hand. "I assume she'll be in Montgomery, and no matter where she is, I won't stop you from gettin' to know her and formin' a relationship with her."

"I don't want a relationship with her," Duran says quietly.

"I don't wanna relationship with her either," Adrienne innocently says.

Everybody laughs.

"Well, you may still wanna get some questions answered," Jeoff tells him. "I know that, even though we've all been happy, it's been hard not knowing what happened, why she left, and if she ever planned to return."

Everybody except Jeoff and Cha Cha nod. Jeoff picks at something on the carpet, pretending not to listen.

"Daddy, I don't think I remember her." Cha Cha looks distressed and begins to cry.

"It's all right, baby. It was a long time ago."

"Maybe it's better that you don't remember her," Devon says sympathetically.

"Yeah, 'cause she sure don't remember us!" Jeoff scoffs. "Y'all are too close in age. I only remember Duran!"

Mrs. Simpson looks at Jeoff Sr. "That's what she said."

"Baby, what are you gonna do about Jeoff?" Melasan asks him later that night.

"We're just gonna have to pray for him. He has to work through this in his own way. We're here, and I know he knows that."

She nods.

"This is a lot for them to take in right now."

She kisses Jeoff, pulling back the covers on their bed.

"I haven't checked the voice mail on the phone, but I'm sure that everybody and their momma has called."

Chapter 25

"Hello?" Jeoff sits at the desk in his office, trying to get back into the swing of normal life after three exciting weeks.

"Hey, Dad," Duran's boyish heavy voice greets him on the phone.

"Hey, Dude," Jeoff greets him with his nickname for him.

"I wanted to apologize for yesterday." His voice cracks with emotion.

"Son, you don't have anything to apologize for. Yesterday was a shock to everybody." He pauses, hearing Duran's breathing.

"You didn't seem shocked," he almost whispers.

"Well, Dude, it's my job to not act shocked. I gotta take care of y'all. I'm the daddy." He smiles to himself as he thinks of Duran's innocence.

"I always thought she'd come back all apologetic and stuff"—he swallows, and Jeoff can hear him shuffling the phone—"not actin' like we owe it to her to take her back."

"Yeah, your mom's always been bold like that," Jeoff observes.

"She's not my mom. She birthed me, but my momma, Melasan Simpson, raised me."

The phone shuffles again.

Jeoff almost laughs. "I'm sorry. No offense to your momma, you know I know who raised you." He smiles again. "I think I had *some* part in that."

"Yep." Duran's smile can be heard. "Dad?"

"Yes, sir?" Jeoff watches his other line blink persistently, then disappear as it goes to voice mail.

"I think I wanna talk to Miss Rookie."

"Oh yeah?" Jeoff says nonchalantly, feeling his pulse race nervously.

"I've got them questions you were talkin' about, and I need her to answer them so my heart won't ache," Duran says, shuffling the phone again.

"I got a question, if you don't mind, Dude."

Silence is heard on Duran's end as though consenting to the request.

"When did your heart start achin'?"

More shuffling, and then Duran's muffled voice is heard. "When she said she was goin' to get the mail."

"I'll set it up, son."

"Thanks. I gotta go. I'll see you when you get home."

"I love you, Dude."

"Love you too."

The phone clicks, and Jeoff does some searching around and finds out what boarding house Rookie's in and calls.

"Rookie Simpson please?"

He hears lots of yelling and knocking on doors; and finally, after several minutes, Rookie answers.

"Hello?'

"Rookie?"

"I knew in my heart you'd call," she says breathlessly.

"Don't trip. I called because Duran would like to spend some time with you," Jeoff states.

"What about you?" she asks.

"I think the two of you could meet at the Waffle House near the airport," he states, ignoring her statement.

"Are you comin'? Are you?"

"I'll bring Duran to see you," Jeoff forcefully says, finding himself getting warm with anger. "Look." His other line blinks again. "I've got another call, so—"

"I'm leavin' in a few days," Rookie interjects. "There's no point in me seein' any of the kids."

"What?"

The light on the phone stops.

169

"You heard me. I said I'm leavin'. I'll see Duran, but you need to explain to him that I'm leavin'. There's nothin' for me here. I don't even know those kids. They got nicknames I don't know, and I don't recognize 'em," she says dejectedly. "They sure don't wanna remember me."

"You know"—Jeoff sighs and holds his breath, counting to ten—"this really ain't bit more about you, and I wish you'd grow up and stop runnin' from anythin' and everythin' that is the least bit challengin'!"

"What do you expect me to do? Sit and hold each one of 'em's hand? Take 'em to the zoo? What? I don't have nothin' to give 'em without you! I love you, Jeoff." Rookie sniffles on the other end.

Jeoff, unfazed, answers, "I see what this is about. You came back because of me."

"That's right." Her voice sounds as though her mouth is pressed against the phone's mouthpiece. "Our love is too powerful to lose."

"What love, Rookie? You don't love me. I'm a security blanket, always have been. How come you didn't have any kids after you left?"

Silence.

"How come you didn't leave with the kids?"

More silence.

"'Cause you knew I'd take care of everythin'."

"This ain't a fair conversation. You're still mad at me!" She sniffles again.

"Answer me. I'm not mad anymore. Just answer me," he implores her.

"I didn't have any kids. I had abortions, two abortions. I didn't take the kids because I knew you'd look for 'em."

He snorts.

"I knew you'd take care of 'em. I didn't expect to be gone so long, Jeoff. But I do love you."

"Do you want a relationship with the kids?" he asks, ignoring her again.

"Tell me you love me too," she asks.

"Rookie, do you wanna work on a relationship with the kids?" Jeoff asks again.

"Tell me you love me!" she begs and hears silence on the other end. "No. No, I don't want nothin' with them kids!"

He sits silently for a moment.

"Do you—"

He hangs up.

"—love me?"

Jeoff gets up and goes to a meeting, After the meeting, he calls Melasan.

"Hey, you ain't called me all day," he teases.

"I been tryin' to catch up. How 'bout you?" she asks.

"Same. I talked to Rookie."

"Oh yeah? Did she wanna see the kids?" she asks.

"No, but Duran said he wants to see her and that he has questions. He said he knows who his momma is."

"I'm glad he does. I'd hate to have to clear that up for him," she teases and then gets serious. "I thought she might have returned as a grown-up, ya know?"

"Yeah. I just want God to do what He's gonna do with this situation and, most of all, protect my babies," he anxiously says.

"He is protecting them," she says back. "I gotta get back to work, lovey. Are you pickin' me up?" she asks.

"Yeah. I don't understand why I had to take you to work in the first place," he answers.

"We're conservin' gas." She giggles. "I don't have time to explain it all to you. I love you. Don't worry. Keep prayin', and I'll keep prayin' too."

Jeoff finally checks his voice mail; and the voice of Melasan's momma, Mrs. Pete, can be heard on the first message.

"Jeoff, I'm sorry to be callin' you at work, but I called you and Mel's cell phones with no answer." She pauses for effect. "Anyway, after all the drama yesterday, I didn't get a chance to check on my babies at church, and I didn't wanna call y'all at home 'cause I know they had so much to deal with, but y'all call me and let me know that everythin's all right. I love y'all."

The second message is from his secretary informing him of the meeting he just attended. He erases both, making a mental note to call his new momma. After work, he picks up Melasan.

She jumps in, kisses him, and scans his face. "Did you talk to Rookie again?"

He shakes his head.

"What are you gonna tell Duran?"

He shrugs his shoulders.

"I talked to Momma," she informs him.

He smiles, knowing some fussing is coming.

"She wanted to know why she hadn't been called, and I calmed her down. She was pretty upset about Sunday. I'm sure quite a few people are. They don't want nobody hurtin' their babies since they think them kids are their personal possessions." She smiles.

Jeoff's cell phone rings.

"Hey, son!" Rev. Simpson's voice can be heard on the other end, loud enough for Melasan to hear him.

She laughs.

"Rookie called and asked if tomorrow evenin' would be a good time to meet with Duran and you at the Waffle House. She said she discussed it with you, and I told her all right. That is all right, ain't it?"

"Yeah, I'll make sure he's there."

When they get to their house, Duran and Jeoff are arguing loudly.

"You traitor!" Jeoff yells. "She ain't gonna do nothin' but leave again, and then you'll be lookin' stupid for even talkin' to her!"

"Hey, boys!" Jeoff Sr. grabs them both. "Jeoff, you can't stop Duran from goin' to see Miss Rookie. That's his right, just like it's your right not to see her."

"Well, she's just gonna…gonna…" Jeoff yells.

"Gonna what?" Jeoff Sr. asks him.

Jeoff doesn't answer.

Mari says, "Hurt him."

The next evening, Duran and Jeoff pull up at the Waffle House. They wait for thirty minutes.

Jeoff looks at his son and asks, "How long you wanna wait?"

"Just a few more minutes, Dad," he says, looking at the door.

They wait thirty more minutes and stand to walk out, and Rookie walks in the door.

"Sorry I'm late," she says, looking at Duran quickly and then at Jeoff longingly.

"I'll be at the next table," Jeoff says to Duran.

"Thanks for waitin'," Rookie says to Duran. "Your Dad says you wanted to talk to me."

Duran sits quietly, looking at Rookie for some time, and then he says, "You said you'd never leave me."

She coughs, not expecting the statement. "I...I don't know what you want me to say. I asked you if you wanted to come with me," she says defensively. "Do you remember that?"

He nods, looking upward to fight tears. "Why'd you drink so much?" he asks.

She just moves her mouth with no answer coming.

"I remember you sittin' in the bathroom smokin' somethin'. What was that?" he asks again. "Why'd you leave after Cha Cha? How come you didn't leave after anybody else? How come you don't know how old I am, and how come you can't tell the difference between any of the other kids? Where were you? Rehab? Jail? Where?" He stops, looking at her, anger and disappointment blazing in his eyes.

"You have a lotta questions. I don't think I have all the answers. I was in rehab for a while and jail for a while and a halfway house for a while," she answers. "I left a lot of times. I just didn't come back that last time, so your baby sister shouldn't take it personal," she says, and her eyes harden. "I was smokin' a lotta stuff in them days. You got a good memory." She stops as though finished answering his questions.

"How come you don't know how old I am?"

She shakes her head as though she can't answer his question.

"So you don't remember the other kids?"

"I remember 'em!" she snaps. "I've been gone a long time!"

"How come you think you should be able to come back and live in our house with us like we know you?"

She stares blankly at him.

"I remember when you left, and I took care of all of us until Dad came home. I remember. I remember a lotta stuff." He starts to cry and looks at his dad for assistance. "Dad?"

Jeoff stands and walks over to him. "You ready to go?"

He nods, still crying and wipes his face. "Did you ever love us?"

With that last question, they walk out the door, with Rookie staring after them.

A couple of evenings later, Ni Ni comes to Jeoff. "Daddy, I'd like to talk to Miss Rookie."

The next day, he calls the boarding house.

"Hello, Jeoff." She sounds somehow calmer.

"Ni Ni—uh, you know her as Domininisierra—wants to talk with you. Is that possible?" he asks.

"What does she want? To tell me off and ask crazy questions that I can't answer too?" she asks.

"I imagine she has questions, but I thought you'd want to talk to any of them who wanted to talk to you," he says.

She sighs.

He takes Ni Ni to the same Waffle House, and they sit down together.

"Hello, Miss Rookie."

Rookie flinches yet smiles slightly at the formality. "Hello, Domininisierra. What do they call you?" She relaxes a little, seeing that the conversation is milder than the one with Duran.

"They call me Ni Ni."

"I remember that. I used to call you Sierra," she says, looking into the past.

"I'm surprised you remember me," Ni Ni says softly, looking at her own shaking hands. She puts them under the table.

"I remember all of you," Rookie answers as a waitress walks up. "I'll have a cocoa, and you?" She looks at Ni Ni, who shakes her head.

It gets uncomfortably quiet, and Rookie looks around the room.

Finally, Ni Ni looks up, blinking her eyes quickly to keep the tears from falling. "Why'd you wait so long to come back?"

Rookie shakes her head. "I don't know."

"Why don't you know? Why'd you leave?" Her voice trembles with emotion.

Rookie again shakes her head.

"Why didn't you at least call? You never called."

"I don't know."

Ni Ni's eyes change from sorrow to anger. "You didn't even write."

"I wrote lots of letters. I just never sent them, Sierra." Rookie's tone begs for forgiveness.

"My name is Ni Ni." She stops to breathe. "People say I look like you."

Rookie smiles with pride. "Yes, you do."

"I hate that. I'd rather peel my face off than to look like you." She stands and walks away.

When she reaches the Surburban, she sits silently.

"How'd it go?" Jeoff asks.

"Fine," Ni Ni answers.

"What'd you talk about?"

"Nothing."

Jeoff looks at his oldest daughter sitting with the passenger seat hugging her. His heart breaks as he notices how grief-stricken she appears to be. Her eyes look heavy as though tears have been falling for hours, but from across the restaurant, he never saw her cry. He knows she doesn't like to cry. He wonders what he missed but considers how the conversation is already like pulling teeth and decides to take the rest of the ride home in silence. He waits for the others to request meetings, but they each have their own separate reactions. Pulling into the garage, he waits for Ni Ni to get out of the truck, and then they both go into the house.

I'll have a talk with her, he thinks to himself.

But before the thought gets time to sink in, he hears commotion.

"Boys, stop it!" The voice of Melasan carries from the living room.

"Traitor! You might as well go live with her!"

Jeoff walks into the living room to see Jeoff Jr. and Duran arguing.

"It's not my fault you won't even talk to her! You're just afraid you might like her!"

At that statement, Jeoff Jr. plunges headfirst at his brother, and the two wrestle on the floor. Melasan looks at him with frustration in her eyes, and Jeoff steps forward to pull the boys apart.

"I can't stand you, and I can't stand her!" Jeoff Jr. yells at Duran.

The two gravitate to each other again, pulling their father in.

"That's it! Get up, right now!"

The two boys come to themselves and sit on the floor, breathing heavily with Jeoff between them.

"Now what's goin' on here?" he asks.

"You know what's goin' on," Jeoff Jr. says saltily.

"Boy, don't you talk to me like that. Now what's goin' on?"

Jeoff Jr. says nothing, and when he looks at Duran, he shrugs.

"I tell you what. If you don't want to see Miss Rookie, like I told you before, then you don't, but you don't penalize your brother for wanting to get some questions answered."

He looks at Jeoff Jr., and still he says nothing. He sighs and stands, looking at Melasan helplessly.

At the conclusion of her next meeting with Duran, Rookie stops Jeoff before he can leave the library, their new meeting place.

"Can I talk to you?" she asks.

"Son, go get in the truck," Jeoff says to Duran, hitting the security button on his keychain. "What?" he says to Rookie.

"Can I come home now? Now that I have talked with Duran these past few times, I'm sure that I can get the others to come around. You can't tell me you just stopped loving me," she says, searching his eyes.

"I told you before. This ain't about you. It's about my kids and their peace of mind," Jeoff says, looking at her in confusion. "All the drugs you took must've fried your brain," he tells her, turning to walk away.

She grabs his arm. "If you won't love me, I'm leavin'." Her eyes are hollow with desperation.

"You said that before," Jeoff tells her.

"I mean it," she returns. "I'm not your kids' counselor. I'm not talkin' to nary another kid. I'm leavin'!" she screams.

Jeoff pries her hand off his arm and walks to the truck.

"I'm leavin'!" she screams.

Duran looks shocked.

Rookie takes two buses back to the boarding house and paces in her room like a caged animal.

"I gotta get outta here!"

She snatches a duffel bag and the slip of paper containing Ranelle's contact information twists and sways in the air, landing in her hand. She takes her phone and dials the number.

"Hello?"

"Um, yeah, I mean, uh, is Ranelle there? I mean, can I speak to Ranelle please?"

"Nel, telephone."

"Hello?"

"Hey, it's, uh, Rookie. I got your message."

"Hey, girl!" Ranelle's joyful voice brings tears to Rookie's eyes. "Are you in Alabama?"

"Uh-huh," Rookie mumbles.

"Are you—What's wrong?" Ranelle asks, sounding concerned.

"I guess you'd be happy to know that they don't want me!"

"Girl, you can play that tough game on somebody else."

Rookie cries silently.

"What happened?"

Rookie continues to cry.

"I've been praying for you."

"A lotta good that does," Rookie complains.

"It does do a lotta good," Ranelle answers. "No matter what happened, you've gotta fight for your family."

"How? I bought this cell phone just to talk to them, and—"

"Get to know them. Get some help with all of your issues, and no matter what, don't leave until you do."

"What do you know?" Rookie says sarcastically.

"I know plenty. You need somebody there with you to work through all of this. I have, and I feel so much better for it."

"I'm leavin'!" Rookie snaps.

"There are people who'll help you. Talk to a pastor or—"

"A pastor! A lotta help you are!" Rookie hangs up.

Chapter 26

THE DOORBELL AT REV. AND Mrs. Simpson's home rings.

Mrs. Simpson, in the midst of a mission meeting, looks confused and says, "Ladies, I'm not sure who that is, but I'll be right back."

She heads to the door and stops abruptly as she sees Rookie's face looking through the glass of their screen door. She smooths her pants, breathes deeply, and unlocks the door.

"I need to talk to you," she demands.

Mrs. Simpson stands silently for an extended amount of time, so Rookie becomes uncomfortable.

"Uh, can I talk to you?"

She looks at this young woman, who is much thinner—no longer shapely, rather gaunt with haunting features—and wants to strongly decline the conversation.

"Sure, I just need to finish my meeting. If you could return at—"

"I can't return," Rookie cuts off her midsentence.

As Mari gazes at her, she marvels at how she is so very different in appearance, except for the strikingly beautiful eyes, the same eyes she shares with Ni Ni. Her knuckles are skeletal, and the hair is no longer strong and flowing.

"I can't return. I don't have time."

She looks so stricken and distressed, and Mrs. Simpson thinks she sees the tracks of tears.

She shakes the thought off as imagination. "Wait in the living room while I end my meeting." Eyeing Rookie suspiciously, she returns to the dining room, where her mission circle anxiously awaits her return. "Well, ladies, as the Holy Ghost would have it, I have some pressing missionary work to attend to."

The ladies all look intrigued, yet knowing this is the most details they'll get from their pastor's wife, they adjourn and exit the Simpsons' home out the kitchen door.

Following their exit, Mari Simpson utters a prayer and heads for her living room.

"I guess you and your husband are the happiest you've been in years," Rookie says.

"I'm not sure I follow you," Mari answers, sitting in a chair adjacent her.

"Oh, you follow me all right. I come home, and my husband is married, and you've poisoned my children's minds against me!" Rookie screeches.

A cloud of disgust and rage passes over Mari's face, and she presses her palms against the chair as though to steady herself. "I believe you are severely delusional, young lady. First of all, I would never wish the unhappiness and confusion that you have brought upon our grandbabies. I cannot ever lie and say that I was pleased with you and Jeoff's marriage. However, I *never* wanted those children to be left with their lives in limbo for years upon years!" She loosens her hands and swallows. "Nobody pushed Jeoff to another woman but you after all these years of being gone and nobody knowing where you were, not calling, not contacting anybody, not checking on your children. You! And most certainly, nobody poisoned your children but you!" She looks around the room as if thinking and continues, "You have the mightiest nerve to come into my home and try to go off on me as though all of this is anybody's fault but your own. We asked you to think this through. We asked you—"

She stops as Rookie breaks down, resembling a crumpled blanket thrown to the floor, and her expression changes to one of empathy.

"They don't know me! They're not babies anymore!" She gulps in large sobs. "He doesn't love me anymore! Everybody hates me!" She stops sobbing and looks around the room as though not remembering where she is and then recollects. "I'm leaving. I'm leaving today. That's what I came to tell you. You need to tell your son and those kids that."

Mari's softened look returns to anger. "I will not."

Rookie looks shocked. "What?"

"You won't shirk your responsibilities off onto me. If you want to leave, then you'll tell them yourself."

Rookie's eyes widen with fear. "But you want this. You want me to leave!"

"No, love, you want to leave. You want to run. You need to stay and face this."

The emotion of their conversation deflates. Mari looks at Rookie with sharp eyes but softened emotions.

"Why should I face anything? They all hate me."

"Nobody hates you. Not understand you, yes, but hate, no. I believe you could have some type of relationship with the kids if you'd hang in there."

"You've gotta be kiddin' me." Rookie shakes her head in disbelief. "The only one who'll speak to me is Duran. I've talked to Sierra once but never again. How can that be any kind of a future? What about my future with Jeoff?"

"Well, to be honest with you, you have no future with Jeoff other than the future that you have with those children. Even if they never speak to you again, you have to put your best foot forward and stay. You have to let them know that you're not here to hurt them."

"I don't even know what to do. I thought I'd be..." She begins to tear up again.

"You really thought you'd be returning to Jeoff's open arms?" Mrs. Simpson asks.

"He told me he'd always love me and that he didn't believe in divorce," Rookie weakly answers.

"Oh, love." Mari Simpson looks at Rookie as though seeing her for the first time.

"What..." She struggles with her words and then shakes her head. "You don't know me. Nobody knows me." She sticks her chin out defiantly.

"So you came back so that they can know you?" Mari begins to get angry again at the arrogance.

"Well, yeah, and so that…" She looks at her hands. "When I was here, they were babies. They're too different for me to stay." She stands.

"I know you're sorry, and you need to tell them that." Mari marvels at the revelation that she herself doesn't even want to believe.

"I told you. You don't know me. I'm not sorry!"

"That's how you've been able to survive, but your heart feels differently, doesn't it?"

Mari looks deeply into Rookie's eyes and sees each and every one of her grandchildren in the pools of her eyes. She sees the fear of a young girl who walked away and then got too lost to return. She becomes overwhelmed at the onslaught of information the Lord is unloading on her but receives it, knowing that she already has questions. Why her? Why now?

"If that's true, who'll help me? Can you…help me? Can you help me stay?"

She looked like a small child with this question; but as the two women sat in that room together, Mari knew she had never seen this woman before, this child who wants help.

Chapter 27

"So what was she like?" Mari and Ni Ni sit cross-legged on the floor of their bedroom facing each other.

"Maybe you should find out for yourself," she answers sullenly.

Mari turns up her nose.

"She was all right. She said she wrote letters over the years to us." She looks at her sister.

"I didn't get any letters," she answers sarcastically.

She looks Mari in the eyes. "Why don't you want to see her?"

Mari shakes her head. "There's nothin' to see. What would we talk about anyway? She missed my whole life."

Ni Ni leans forward a little. "Your life's not over."

Mari frowns. "I don't know her, and I don't think I wanna know her."

"You're just saying that 'cause Jeoffy feels that way."

"No, I'm not, Ni. She scares me," Mari interjects.

"Daddy won't let her hurt you, and I don't think she uses drugs or drinks anymore. Do you remember any of that?" she asks.

"Some. I don't really like remembering her, and she doesn't really remember anybody except for you and Duran," Mari says sadly.

"That's not true. She remembers. She just doesn't know us."

"How come you haven't gone to see her anymore like Ran?" Mari asks, calling Duran by a nickname. "He seems like he really missed her." She looks at the carpet. *Maybe he wants to leave with her,* she thinks this thought to herself, not wanting her sister to know her fears.

"I don't think I wanna see her anymore," Ni Ni answers.

"Why not? Did she say somethin'? You better tell Daddy if she did!"

"No, I just—It just doesn't seem right."

Mari looks away. "She acts like we're supposed to be excited that she's back. I wish she'd go back where she came from."

Upstairs, in Melasan and Jeoff's bedroom, Adrienne sits in the window seat while Melasan sits on the bed with Cha Cha.

"Baby, how do you feel about your mom coming back to town?"

Cha Cha shrugs.

"Are you all right with everything?"

Cha Cha gives her a blank expression. "I don't know her. I have a momma." She hops down from the bed and goes to sit in the window seat with Adrienne. Then she turns and looks at Melasan. "I have a momma that wants me. She left 'cause she didn't want me."

"I don't think that's it, baby. She had a lot of problems," Mel explains.

"Everybody's got problems. Daddy never left us, and you wouldn't leave us either." She plays with the barrettes on the ends of her hair.

"I think we don't understand all of the problems she had then," Mel says. "I know it's hard to understand. I don't understand it myself, but we shouldn't be mad or not forgive her."

"I'm not mad." Cha Cha looks at Mel. "Carla Ginn wants me to come to her birthday party Saturday. Can I go?"

Melasan nods.

"Mommy, Cha's first mommy left when she was two. She is a bad person." Adrienne stuck out her lip for emphasis on this statement. "Devon says she left them like they were just trash."

Melasan draws in her breath at the emotions absorbed by her youngest.

Later that night, after the children are in their rooms and Jeoff and Melasan lie in their bed, she turned to him and leaned on an elbow.

"Jeoff, how do you think the kids are handling Rookie's return?"

"They're not, baby," Jeoff answers. "I've been praying about it, and I really don't know what else to do."

"I know what you mean. I feel helpless not being able to fix this for them."

Jeoff nods.

"When Jeoff and Duran fought, I didn't know what to do. I'm so glad you came home when you did. I thought they were gonna tear each other limb from limb."

"I knew it hurt them, and I guess they didn't have to deal with it as long as she was gone," he answers.

"You either," Mel says softly. "This hurts you too."

"It hurts me for the kids. I've gone through the brunt of the anger I had. I don't think I lost the same thing they lost. I lost a woman that wasn't good for me, but they lost a part of themselves. You know, how that Ni Ni looks like her and they each have different parts of her, and I know that hurts them." He leans up on his elbow facing his wife. "I never understood why she left that last time, and I don't think I ever understood her at all. You know I blamed myself for years because she told me when I first asked her to marry me that she wasn't the marrying type?"

Mel nods her head in understanding.

"It's hard to stomach when you marry the wrong person." He shakes his head. "I still don't know what to do about our kids though. Devon hasn't said a word about the whole thing. I think Jeoff is angry for himself and for his brother."

"What do you mean?" Melasan asks, confused.

"They met a drunk once on the way home from school that told them that he could be Devon's daddy. He got in a lot of fights after that, and it took some time to get a handle on."

"Those poor babies. I remember the fights, but you didn't tell me it was about that."

Jeoff shrugs. "Who wants to discuss that kind of stuff? I thought that would never come up, at least not for him. He's my son no matter what happened in the past." He sighs. "Either way, I know he's not talking because he's just that mad, and Jeoff's mad for him and for the others."

"I talked to Cha Cha today, and she didn't talk much either, basically changed the subject up on me. She's pretty slick that one. And…Adri said that Devon says that she just left them behind like trash."

Jeoff shakes his head. "He's really hurt a lot behind her leaving. Man, we all did, and then Duran's heart was so broken because he had the strongest memories of her. I wish she would think what she has done rather than worrying about being in some fantasy world."

"Well, either way, you and those children have a strong testimony, and once this is resolved, it'll get even stronger."

Chapter 28

"WHAT'S WRONG, LOVIE?"

"Baby, I feel like I'm betraying my family." Mari Simpson sits in her recliner, uncomfortably feeling on the verge of tears.

"What do you mean?" Rev. Simpson reaches for her hand.

"Rookie came to see me. At first, she was her old self."

Rev. Simpson nods for her to continue.

"Rude, belligerent, accusing of everybody but herself, and then right before my eyes, she…transformed into…this helpless child, and then God told me that I have to be the one to help her."

The tears silently fall from her eyes, and Rev. Simpson's eyes well up.

"Oh, Ri." He squeezes her hand.

"Why me? There's a million other people that should be able to help her. Why me? I don't even like her! Look at what she's done."

"God has a reason for choosing you, Ri. She needs you, nobody but you. You can do this."

She moves from her recliner to sit on his lap in his matching one. "How will I tell Jeoffy?" She puts her head in his chest. "Why didn't she come to you?"

Rev. Simpson laughs. "God chose you, baby." He rubs her back.

Chapter 29

"You know, Duran, I wonder why you still come to see me," Rookie states.

"I always wanted to get to know you."

"I didn't ruin that for you?"

He shakes his head. "I try not to let it."

Rookie sits at a library table across from Duran, their alternate meeting spot. "I wish I could talk to the others like I talk to you."

"The others think you left because you didn't love us," he states flatly.

"That's not true," she answers softly.

"What…what is the truth?" He rubs the table, trying not to meet her gaze.

"I was young and selfish."

He looks disappointed.

"You know my daddy left me?"

He stares at her without answer.

"He did. Maybe that's what made me leave my kids."

"You had a choice, just like you chose to come back." He looks distractedly at a magazine. "Why did you come back?"

"I wanted my family back."

"Why'd you think we wanted you back?" he says, suddenly upset. "Why didn't you come back on my twelfth birthday?" He thinks for a moment. "You know my baby sister used to scream when anybody would leave her sight? But she doesn't remember you. Strange." Duran turns the pages faster. "My dad kept goin' to school even though you weren't there, and then you come back just after everything gets better. Why?" He doesn't wait for an answer. "We all just kept waiting and waiting. We even thought you were dead." He looks at her.

"What's all this about? I thought we were past all of this." Rookie looks shocked and hurt.

"I'm sick of all of this. I'm not coming anymore." He stops turning the pages.

"What? Why?" She looks panicked.

"You think we owe you somethin'. Who cares that your daddy left you too. It shoulda taught you not to leave your kids! You were supposed to know how it felt. But you just came back like life stood still until you got here." His dark eyes darken deeper, and he stands. "Ni was right. You never even thought to write a letter!"

Rookie touches his hand, and he pulls away.

"Please, you're all I've got." She stands and grabs his hand again. "Duran, I'm sorry."

"You need to start tellin' everybody else that."

He looks through her and pulls his hand away, leaving the library.

"I'm not goin' to see her anymore," Duran tells his dad as they head home.

"Why not?"

"My brothers and sisters don't like it, and I don't want them hurt."

"Dude, you have a right to spend time with her if you want," Jeoff tells him.

"They're more important than she is."

Rookie lays her head on the cool wood of the library table. For once, she's too devastated to cry.

If you need me, I'll be here for you, the familiar words of Mari Simpson come back to her.

"Why? You don't even like me?" she had asked her.

"Because God loves you, and no matter what is happening in your life right now, you can make it through this."

Rookie has left the Simpsons' home that fateful night feeling motivated but not necessarily believing Mrs. Simpson in all of her words of help. She continues to press her face against the table, hoping to die or be transformed to a better time in life.

"You can't keep leaving like this, Rook!" Jeoff had told her. "One day, you're gonna come through those doors, and we won't be here anymore."

She had laughed when he said that, but how true those words turn out to be, how true. They aren't here anymore, and it is all her fault. She slowly rises from the table, reaches into her purse, and pulls out her cell phone.

"Can I speak to Ranelle please?" Her hands shake as she talks.

"It's me, girl. What's goin' on?"

"Man, you sound different every time I talk to you!" Rookie marvels.

"I'm happy, so, so happy. But back to you. What's goin' on? Last time we talked, you hung up on me."

"Sorry. You're the only friend I've got."

"You must be depressed. Now I'm your friend."

Rookie sighs.

"Go on. Tell me what's on your mind."

"I've seen the kids and my husband."

"So what's goin' on? Are you workin' on a relationship with any of them?"

"Jeoff has gone for good."

"That's the husband?" Ranelle asks.

"Yeah, that's him. He's somebody's husband now," Rookie sullenly answers.

"Somebody's husband? Girl, let me sit down. It sounds like you got a lot to say."

Rookie hears the sound of a chair.

"Tell it."

"All right. My husband divorced me and married somebody else!"

"Baby, Grandma's got your notebook," Ranelle speaks to a child in the background. "I'm sorry. I heard you."

"You heard me!" Rookie yells, walking out of the library. "He got divorced and married a few weeks ago. If I had taken a flight I could have stopped him. I should cuss Miss Justine out. She knew what she was doin'. They probably told her he was gettin' married and to stall me."

"Calm down. He had a right to get married. Probably shoulda done it years ago."

"Thanks." Rookie sits on a bench.

Ranelle sighs. "It's true. Just face it."

Rookie mumbles, "I do face it every day."

"What about the kids?" Ranelle asks.

"They hate me. My oldest was talkin' to me, but now he hates me too." Rookie shifts the phone to the opposite ear.

"They don't hate you. They're hurt," Ranelle asserts.

"I'm hurt too!"

"What are you hurt from?" Ranelle asks.

"Um..."

The two laugh.

"Do you have a job?"

"Yeah, I'm workin' at Subway. I want a better job like the one I had at the library."

"You gotta get your behind out and look for it. Make a résumé and use them as a reference," she answers.

"A what?"

"Look, go to a high school or college and ask these questions, or—"

"I know a church," Rookie finishes her sentence.

"You need Jesus," Ranelle says softly.

"My minutes are almost gone," Rookie ignores her statement. "I gotta go."

The two disconnect, and Rookie's phone rings immediately. She checks the caller ID and answers.

"Hello, Mrs. Simpson?"

"I'm going to take you to see a friend of mine," Mrs. Simpson says when she pulls up in her Ford Echo.

Rookie smiles.

Mrs. Simpson says, "What?"

Rookie laughs. "I'm surprised at the car. I can't believe Pastor Simpson's wife is driving a little bitty Ford Echo. I had you pegged as a Cadillac Fleetwood woman."

Mari Simpson smiles, unfeigned. "I leave the big cars to my family. I like fuel economy." She drives for a while and then turns to Rookie. "I guess you're wondering what made me call you today. I got the feeling when you left the other day that you didn't believe I'd help you." She looks at Rookie.

"I guess I didn't, but I really don't have anywhere else to turn."

"Sometimes that's where God wants us, where we have nowhere else to turn. For some reason, He wants me to help you, and I'm gonna be here to do it." She hums a little to the Mary Mary CD that's playing and then stops to look at Rookie. "I was telling you before about a friend I want you to meet. I think you will really enjoy her company."

In no time at all, the two pull into the driveway of a small white house with three front doors and a large green front porch. The yard is as large as the house is small with an expansive apple tree to the side, sporting several rotten apples. There's an old water pump protected by chicken wire close to the backyard and also near yet another door.

At the clanging of the doorbell, the friendly face of a small medium-complexion woman meets them at the door.

"Oh, it's wonderful to see you, Ma Ree!" She hugs Mrs. Simpson and then hugs Rookie without being introduced.

She holds Rookie tightly; and she feels safe, peaceful, and somehow known. She tries to pull back at first and then settles into her arms.

"Oh, baby, I know. I know."

Rookie's shoulders droop, and she feels as though she has passed out until the lady lets her go. She studies her features while Mrs. Simpson introduces them. The vibrant lady's name is Rev. Idella Banks. Her keen hazelnut eyes glance at Rookie, and she feels her face burn with embarrassment as though the lady already knows her.

"Come in. We're just beginnin' our meeting, and I'm sure y'all'd love to meet everybody. Now, Rookie, this is a meetin' where people come to heal and talk with God."

Her youthful eyes catch Rookie, and in spite of herself, Rookie smiles.

As they leave the front of the house, Rookie scans this Rev. Idella Banks. The lady is an unimpressive height with short, curly gray hair braided back into a French braid and a grandmotherly shape. She walks with authority and purpose, and although it is easy to tell that she is elderly, it's not so easy to guess the exact age. Her eyes are brown and youthful; and her weathered hands tell the story of plucking feathers, ironing, and canning.

"I hope you didn't think you had to dress up, child."

Rookie was concerned about being underdressed; but Rev. Banks wears a pair of purple flowered culottes, a white ruffled tank top, and a pair of pink flip-flops. She gives her that keen glance again as Rookie quickly looks away.

"There ain't nothin' God won't forgive you for. Remember that. These people here feel as though they have done the worst things, things that God Almighty won't let them return to His loving embrace for, and I, along with several other ministers in the fold, have been chosen to spread the good news that it's just not true."

They walk into the room, and immediately Rookie sees a muscular honey-complexioned man with a low-cut fade talking in soft tones.

"I used to...to beat my wife." He stops talking and breathes in deeply as though struggling. "She stayed with me and took the beatings, the cheating, and the drink until finally she couldn't take it anymore." He stops talking again.

The voice of Rev. Banks can be softly heard, "Go on, baby. Get your healing."

He looks upward to stop everyone from seeing his tears, but one falls to his cheek. "She took our twins and left." He begins to cry. "I...I saw her after I got out of rehab, and she saw me too, but...the fear in her eyes when she saw me...I just want a chance to make it right." He finally breaks down completely and has to sit down.

Rookie feels her own heart and conscience tug. In a progression of two hours, she hears many stories, many of them similar to her own, chances that were once there now gone.

As she and Mrs. Simpson head for the door, Rev. Banks stops Mari and talks with her for a bit. Rookie takes that moment to dodge this woman that makes her feel so uncomfortable.

"Hi, how are you? I'm Serena." A woman reaches out her hand to Rookie.

"I'm Rookie...Simpson."

"Are you here for the meetings?" Her gaze is friendly and holds Rookie's.

"I...I'm not—"

"Well, you should. We are all here to help each other. I don't know what we'd do without the help. It keeps us focused and moving upward."

Before Rookie can answer, she can feel the presence of Rev. Banks standing at her arm.

"How are you, Sis Serena?" She smiles widely and genuinely.

"I'm blessed, Rev. I wanna thank you and your husband for inviting us all to your home. I've got to run, but, Rookie, it was nice meeting you, and I hope to see you soon."

Rev. Banks turns to Rookie. "Ma Ree says that you're gonna need help with a ride to the meetin's to your job and just overall makin' it through this rough thing we call life."

Rookie nods.

"I'm prepared to be your friend just like Ma Ree, and between God and the two of us, we're gonna be here for you."

"Why?" Rookie heard herself slip.

"Because we all need each other. Now do you have a job?"

She nods again.

"Good. Do you have a place to stay?"

Rookie nods, feeling like a small child, and then finds herself writing down the address to the boarding house and taking Rev. Banks's phone number.

"Call me anytime. Me and the husband don't sleep unless it just can't be stopped." She smiles.

The weeks pass quickly as Rookie attends meetings, makes friends, and grows stronger. One meeting, Rev. Banks comes in with a camera fussing about, not being able to work it.

"Can anybody take pictures at the meetin'? I want y'all to see how wonderful y'all look, but I can't operate this thing."

"I'll do it," Rookie volunteers.

When the pictures get developed, Rev. Banks marvels.

"These are professional, I declare!" She beams at Rookie. "You should do this for a livin', not work at Subway. What you think?"

"I don't think those type of places would hire me," Rookie answers.

"I've got a friend that works at Olan Mills. I can vouch for you. How 'bout it?" She looks at her pictures again and shakes her head with joy. "It's closer to my end of town, so maybe you should move over here?"

Rookie nods, and the following week, she has a new job and a new residence.

At the end of a meeting, Rookie sits outside with Mari Simpson.

"What's wrong, love? You look worried."

"I have to speak next week. Rev. Idella has asked that I tell my story."

She stops talking, and the two ride in silence with only the CD player humming to hide total silence.

"I can't. I just can't."

"Why can't you?" Mrs. Simpson asks.

"Nobody's story is as bad as mine. Nobody left their marriage and six kids behind." She looks at Mrs. Simpson. "I been listenin', and nobody's done that." She stares in the distance like a small child. "I can't."

Rookie sits down at her job, knowing that she doesn't need to be there but more than prepared to miss the meeting Rev. Banks asked that she tell her story. Before having a chance to find any words, she spies Mari Simpson and Rev. Banks out of the corner of her eye. She turns toward the side door, and three people engrossed in conversation are blocking her only exit. She sighs and stands to greet them.

"Hey, girl!" Rev. Banks says, her hawklike eyes darting through Rookie's soul. "We thought you'd have a hard time comin' to the meetin' today, so we both came to get you. You ready?"

"I'm not dressed."

"If you're worried, you can change at home." Rev. Banks's dark eyes mischievously sparkle.

Rookie mentally kicks herself for moving in with the woman. At that point, Rookie can do nothing but head out to Mari Simpson's Echo. When they reach the house, Rookie changes into her faded secondhand Levi jeans and a red silk ruffled blouse. She knows Rev. Banks knows she is chickening out, so she decides to give it a try.

The beginning of the meeting, where everyone sings praise songs and testifies about their week, seems to drag on endlessly. Rookie can hear her stomach gurgle loudly. It comes to the time for speakers, and Rookie feels acid burn her gut as she isn't the first speaker.

"I'm Serena Watson. People call me Princess, and nine years ago, I...left my baby with my brother to be babysat."

It is the same lady Rookie has met before. The two have talked several times, but they have no idea that they have so much in common. She is pretty—as a matter of fact, very pretty—and refined with long manicured nails, perfect shoulder-length black hair, and a sleek pressed business-blue outfit with heels to match; yet here she is with this story.

"I didn't come back. I never came back." Her large hollow eyes search the room for understanding. "I...call every so often, but I haven't gone back."

Her story fades, replaced by Rookie's own. She cries with Serena, and she understands exactly what Princess says when she speaks the words "She'd never want me back, and I know my brother'll never forgive me."

In the past, Rookie would have been glad somebody was worse off than her; but this time, she understands why she has felt such a kinship with Serena and feels empathy for her friend.

Far too quickly, Serena finishes, and Rookie walks to the front of the meeting.

"I'm Rookie Simpson. I left many times…" She looks at Serena. "One day, I left and didn't come back. I don't know where all of the time went. I was just gone. I thought I was havin' a good time and had dumped the problems of those kids and that slow man that wanted me to be responsible, but I missed them."

Tears stream down Rookie's face, but she has to continue—has to finish.

"I missed them. Sometimes I'd call and just sit on the phone, sayin' nothin', and sometimes I'd write letters to them, about how much I missed them, about me, their lives, and the time we'd have together when I got home. But…I never mailed them, and I never got home." She feels Mari Simpson's eyes on her. "I left my babies. I loved having babies. They made me feel like somebody important, but I left them. The only time I ever did anythin' important is when I had my babies." She feels a tissue placed in her hand but doesn't use it. "I left my husband, but I knew I was holdin' them all back. I was their problem. I was *my* problem."

She glances at Perry, the gentleman from the first meeting she attended.

"At first, I wanted to pretend like everythin' was all right so that they'd take me back, but I was scared, and…they think I don't care. They think I believe they owe me somethin', but I owe them every-thin'!" She rubbed her face aimlessly with the tissue. "I want to say I'm sorry, and I will. I have to take the fact that they may not want me anymore, but I have to say I'm sorry and…that I love them, have always loved them, and won't ever stop."

At the end of the meeting, Mrs. Simpson looks searchingly at Rookie. The two grab each other and hug, engulfed in tears.

"Thank you so much. God has blessed me so much with all of the time He has allowed me to spend with you," Mrs. Simpson says to her.

"No, thank you. Thank you so much for being my friend. I know it's been hard, but thank you."

Chapter 30

"HEY, BABY." JEOFF SMILES AS he hears the familiar voice of Melasan.

"What's up, sunshine? I know you don't want me to come all the way to the house and bring you back to the city to pick up anything, do you?"

"No, not quite, but I do think you need to come home." Her voice sounds tight and worried.

"Why? What's wrong? You okay?"

"Yeah, I'm all right. It's Cha Cha. The school called, and they need us both to come in right away. They say there's a huge problem, and it's been ongoing, baby." Mel sounds on the verge of tears.

"I'm on my way. It'll only take me about twenty minutes, okay?" When she doesn't answer, he asks again, "Okay?"

"Mm-hmm," she says absently.

"I'll call you from the truck. I love you." He hangs up, tells his secretary, and heads home.

Melasan meets him at the front door. "Oh, baby!" Her face is blotchy from tears.

He hugs her, and the two return to the Suburban and pull into the parking lot of the school in record time.

The two walk quickly into the school and are ushered into the principal's office, where Mrs. Buckley, Cha Cha's third-grade English teacher, is also sitting.

"How are you today?" He shakes their hands.

They sit in the gray cushion chairs in front of his desk and stare at him with anxious faces.

"My wife tells me that you have some disturbing news for us, Mr. Sheehy?" Jeoff begins the conversation.

"Yes, I do. Your daughter Sienna has been disappearing from her third-grade classroom for long periods of time." He pauses. "At first, she was asking permission to go to the library, and Mrs. Buckley was allowing that. But I was informed that she would be gone from the classroom for twenty-five to thirty minutes at a time."

"Twenty-five to thirty minutes at a time?" Mel gasps.

"Calm down, baby." Jeoff grabs her hand. "Is this what has you so upset that you called my wife? I think we thought something more was going on."

Mrs. Buckley smooths her flowered-print dress and begins to speak. "There is more. I was allowing Sierra so much time because she seemed to be upset about something. Some of the time, she would ask to go to the counselor's office, and I was allowing that as well, and when that happens, we aren't supposed to be concerned with how long it takes for the children to return as long as they return with a pass from the counselor. But she has become very sullen in the classroom and short with everyone, teachers and students alike. Also"—she purses her lips—"today, she asked to go to the restroom. She was gone for more than twenty minutes, so I sent Sabria to check on her. Sabria also was gone for a long period of time, at least fifteen minutes, so I called another teacher into my room and went to check on the children myself. They weren't in the bathroom, and when I couldn't find them in the library or in our wing, I contacted Mr. Sheehy."

"She was frantic," Mr. Sheehy continues. "We shut down the school and put the teachers on notice that we thought we might have an abduction, and then we were contacted by the janitorial staff that Sienna and Sabria were seen outside of the building, past the parking lot talking with the migrant workers that work in the adjacent property."

"What?" Jeoff and Mel say simultaneously.

Mr. Sheehy and Mrs. Buckley nod, and Mrs. Buckley's face begins to get blotchy.

"There was nothing wrong with either of the children, but the things that could have happened to them leaving school property are unthinkable." She adjusts in her seat. "I told them to get back to

199

school property, and Sienna got furious and began to yell and tell me that I wasn't her mother and couldn't tell her what to do. I had to have Mr. Sheehy restrain her! I have never seen your child perform in such a manner, Mr. and Mrs. Simpson."

"Where is she now?" Jeoff questions.

"She is in the counselor's office."

Jeoff raises his eyebrows.

"We still haven't asked what they have been discussing in detail. However, Mrs. Chapulsky would tell us that it is an issue at home," Mr. Sheehy tells the couple. "I will have her bring Sienna in, and you can speak with her."

At that moment, he gets on the phone; and in a matter of moments, Cha Cha enters the room with the counselor. Jeoff's shoulders droop as he sees that she looks withdrawn and tired, her face a gray and sickly pallor and her eyes sunken. She appears to be a completely different child that is lying to him about the wonderful days she is having at school. They have no clue she is acting like this. She has been living the life of a chameleon. No wonder she is so tired.

"Come on, baby. Let's go home." Mel reaches out her hand.

Cha Cha holds it, then grabs her around the waist, drooping into her body. They drive home in silence while Cha Cha falls asleep in the small distance from the school to the house.

"I'll lay her down in her room," Jeoff tells Melasan.

He grabs up her limp nine-year-old body without effort, carries her to the bedroom, and lays her on her double bed serenely decorated with mauve sheer material hanging above it with a pink-and-green comforter set. The room, although shared with Adrienne, carries much of her personality. There is a three-tiered heart-shaped shelf with a healthy pink flowering hibiscus, and the small round table she shares with her younger sister has been painted to resemble the petals of a daisy. Needless to say, she has gained quite the love for plants and flowers and is a natural at nurturing them. If a person doesn't know any better, they'll think it is just her room due to similarities between her and Adrienne.

The younger child adores the older one and merely desires to mirror the effects that Cha Cha likes with her double bed decorated with a circular canopy with green sheer material, a small wandering Jew in a painted pot, and her animals hanging above in a corner in a pet hammock. No matter what, Jeoff has to marvel that he is still thankful that God has allowed the children their own space to expand in their own personalities.

"I told you it was bothering her," Melasan sadly states as the two stand in the living room.

Before Jeoff gets a chance to answer, they hear Cha Cha loudly screaming, "Where is everybody! Don't leave me! Please don't leave me!"

The two run down the hall. Before Jeoff gets a chance, Melasan sits on the bed, grabs Cha Cha, and begins rocking her.

"It's all right, baby."

"Why'd she have to come back?" she mumbles into Melasan's chest. "I hate her. I know God says not to hate, but I hate her."

Melasan continues to rock her, and Jeoff sits on the floor next to the two of them.

Cha Cha looks up. "I waited for her. Everybody had a mommy, and I wanted to know why I didn't have one."

She looks at Jeoff, and he nods, remembering.

"We talked about whether she was dead and that she wanted to come home, but…"

The three are still in Cha Cha's room when the others come home.

"I'll go check on them. You stay with her," Jeoff tells Melasan before leaving the room.

He lingers in the doorway looking at his child, the strain of the day written on his face. Finally, he turns down the hallway to greet the others.

"Daddy, Cha Cha wasn't on the bus. Is she sick?" Mari bombards him.

"I heard she hit a teacher," Jeoff answers before his dad can get in a word.

"No, a teacher probably hit her," Devon interjects.

"A teacher hit Cha Cha?" Adrienne incredulously asks. "They can't do that."

"That's right, Boo," Ni Ni tells her.

"None of that happened, children," their dad responds as they all head to the kitchen for snacks.

"Is she okay?" Ni Ni's eyes widen with worry as she looks at Jeoff.

"Yes, she's fine. She's sleeping."

"I'm gonna go see her," Adrienne says. "She probably needs me."

Jeoff smiles. "Don't wake her up, baby, okay?"

"I won't, Daddy."

"Did she see Miss Rookie? Is that what's wrong with her? I heard she was talking with some adult at the fence," Devon speaks quickly, too quickly for anybody to say anything.

The others look at him wide eyed, drinking in this false information.

"I heard it upset her, and that's when she hit the teacher." He holds a plum in his hand, contemplating taking a bite.

"None of that happened, son. Now y'all need to calm down," Jeoff Sr. tells them.

"What *did* happen?" they all say at once.

"Nothing, and she's fine. She's tired, but she's fine." He sits down.

The children get their snacks, dissatisfied with the conversation.

"I'm gonna call your grandparents over here because I think everybody needs to talk out their feelings about Miss Rookie being back in town."

"I don't got no feelin's." Devon quickly leaves the kitchen, with Jeoff Jr. trailing him.

"Does it really matter now, Daddy? She hasn't called or anything in a while, so we should just forget about her," Mari answers, looking at Ni Ni.

"I don't think it's that easy," Jeoff answers her. "A lot has happened in the short time period that she's been here, and we need to discuss it."

At that statement, he hears Duran close the front door.

"Hey, Dude, we're in the kitchen. I was just tellin' the girls that we all need to sit down and talk out this whole situation regardin' Rookie returnin' to town. Don't you think so?"

"Nope." He grabs the milk out of the refrigerator and pours himself a large glass. "I think it's hard enough on everybody that she's here in the first place. We haven't heard from her, so we should just forget about it."

Mari nods.

"We can't forget about her. She's here." Lines of stress appear around Ni Ni's face. "We've waited a long time to know where she was and if she was okay, and now she's here. We can't forget about her." She stomps out of the room with Mari on her heels.

Later that evening, in their bedroom, Jeoff sits on the edge of the bed. "I don't think I can handle all of this, baby." He looks over at Melasan.

"I know what you mean. Just like anybody, I wondered where she was and why she didn't call or something, but I never thought she'd wait this long, and nobody could know what it would do to our family."

"What am I supposed to learn from this? What are these kids supposed to take from this? I know we got blessed in all of this, but the purpose in her coming back after all this time, what's all this about? She's tearing those kids up!"

Melasan touches his back, and he slumps.

"I just wish I could talk to God face-to-face and find out why He's doing this to us. We ain't even too long been married, and this happens!" He sits quietly and then stands. "I gotta check on Cha."

"Baby, she's sleep with Adrienne. I think she's gonna sleep all night like that."

He sighs and sits back down. "I don't know what they'd do without each other. She's closer in age to Mari but has always been close to Adri. Makes no sense. Nothin' in life does, does it?" He looks at Mel again. "I love you, sunshine."

"I love you too, baby. It'll all work out."

"You know, I try not to harp on what's happened in the past, and I think our babies pushed it to the backs of their minds to function in this world. She did some pretty foul stuff, the worst bein' leavin' them behind like that."

"Maybe that's why she's back, J."

He looks at her with a confused look.

"Because everybody has to deal with it and heal from it."

He shakes his head. "I don't doubt a healing needs to happen. It's just the hurting that happens in the midst of it. I'm gonna have Daddy and Momma come over and talk to them because they're not all talkin' about it, and maybe they're talkin' about it with each other, but like you said before, they just don't seem like they're dealin' with it."

"Are you dealin' with it?" She leans on her elbows in the bed. "I mean, I know you've been prayin' about it, but it's almost like, when somebody dies, the one in charge of the family just makes it so that the rest of the family can grieve. Is that what you're doin'?"

"I guess in some ways because a part of me just wants to tell her off and send her on her way, but I have to let all of this play out so that they can be all right. I'd like to be able to pretend that she was never their momma, that it's always been you, but I have to deal with the fact that she walked out. I was embarrassed by it."

"Why, baby?" Mel asks.

"Because, at the time, I felt like it was my fault. Now I know it wasn't, but then I didn't. I have questions for her myself because I want to know what she was dealing with then, what made her do this." He lies back on the bed. "Lord knows I felt like leavin' before, but I couldn't do it, not to the kids. I just know how I feel about it, and I can't imagine what those kids feel, and I don't want them hurt. I don't want her hurting them, but she already has...by leavin' and by returnin'."

Chapter 31

THE NEXT MORNING, AS THE kids get onto their respective buses, the phone rings.

"Hey, baby, what's goin' on with you today?"

"Hey, Momma," Jeoff answers, recognizing the peaceful voice of his mother. "I'm not goin' into the office until later this afternoon for a minute or two. I'm with Cha today. You know she wasn't doin' too good yesterday. Why? What's up?"

"I was hopin' to spend a little time with you," she answers.

"I'll be here all day if you wanna stop by. Cha's been really tired, so she'll probably be 'sleep most of the morning. Why don't you come by? And I'll cook us up somethin'."

"You're gonna cook?" She sounds amused.

He laughs. "Not necessarily cook, but I'll make some sandwiches."

"Okay, I'll be by close to eleven."

Promptly at eleven, Jeoff's mother shows up and kisses him on the cheek.

"The navy in you wouldn't let you be late," he remarks, smiling.

"That's right." She smiles back at him, looking refreshing and casual in a yellow jumper with a blue belt and blue jean heels. "Where's my grandbaby?"

"She's still sleepin'. She woke up for a bit and watched a little TV but went back to sleep. The stress is a lot for her. I won't say it's too much for her, but it's a lot. We figured it was best to leave her out today and then just take it one day at a time to see when she needs to go back to school."

Mari nods.

"What brings you to our neck of the woods?"

"For one, I wanted to check on my grandbaby after you called about school, and then I knew that I needed to talk to you."

"Hold on. I have my sandwiches on, so come on in the kitchen, and we can talk after I fix your plate."

The two walk into the kitchen and sit at the large wooden family table. Jeoff takes sandwiches out of the oven and cuts them in half, placing chips and a pickle on each bright-blue-and-yellow plate. Mrs. Simpson raises her eyebrows, impressed.

"I told you Daddy can wiffle-diffle when he wants to." His eyes sparkle with a smile. "Mel ain't the only cook around."

He sets the plates on the table and then returns with juice and sits in front of his mother.

"Have you heard from Rookie?"

He shakes his head, chewing his sandwich.

"I have."

He raises his eyebrows.

"As a matter of a fact, we've been spending a lot of time together."

Jeoff puts his sandwich on his plate, and Mari takes a bite of hers, chewing slowly as though allowing him to digest the information. She swallows, takes a drink from the cobalt-blue tumbler, and resumes talking.

"I guess, about a month or so ago, she came by upset about Duran saying he didn't want to see her anymore and tried to invoke an argument."

"Sounds like her," Jeoff says, taking a drink. "What'd you do, lock her in y'all's basement?" He bites into his sandwich again.

She shakes her head. "No, baby. I took her under my wing, and she's been going to some God-filled meetings that have been helping her with her issues." She takes a drink and looks over her glass at Jeoff.

He looks shocked and then sits quietly, gathering his thoughts. "What do you want me to say? That you have my blessing?" He breathes in deeply and exhales. "When were you gonna tell me that you'd done this? Why did you do this?"

"Because I didn't have a choice."

He raises an eyebrow.

"I didn't want to help her at all. I didn't want her at my home, but God had different plans for her and for me. I think that helping her was for my healing, hers, and for this family."

She looks directly into Jeoff's eyes, and he lowers his, guarding them.

"I know you don't understand, and I didn't understand myself. I guess that's why I was in a mode where I felt like I was sneaking behind my family's back, but there is nothing to be ashamed of."

"Nothing to be ashamed of?" Jeoff looked at her, incredulous. "Do you know who this woman is? I mean, I'm sure you know who this woman is, but…after everything the kids have been through and are going through, you're gonna tell me that y'all have been in cahoots together?"

"No." Mari shakes her head. "Not cahoots, love. God has been using me to aid in the ministry to her and the healing of her heart and soul. So much pain and heartache."

"For who? Her?" He lifts up his glass as though getting ready to drink and sets it down, shaking the plum-tinted apple cranberry juice inside of it. "Whose side are you on, Momma?"

"God's side."

Jeoff sighs. "What do you want me to do?"

"I want you to pray, and I want you to forgive, really forgive."

"I don't know if I can. I have a child in the other room that I didn't even think remembered all of this, and she's traumatized. I have children fightin' with one another about not spendin' time with her. I have others holdin' in everything, and then you ask me to forgive, really forgive." He looks at her sadly.

"Yes, I ask you to forgive. I was comfortable not forgiving her, but we can't go forward if we don't."

"Momma, you're askin' a lot."

She nods.

"An awful lot. I'm still takin' in the fact that you've been spendin' time with her. I mean, I'm tryin' to not see you as a traitor, and I guess I can't because you've come to see me, but she's just—"

"She *was* just. The two of you will talk. It is important that you talk. It will help your marriage with Melasan, and it will help you move onward and upward." Her eyes look glossy. "J, God has allowed me to see something so amazingly awesome happen in my life and in hers, and I want you to see it too. I know that you need to see it too. You know I'd never lie to you, and I wouldn't lead you astray." She looks at him intently, holding his gaze. "It is time."

"I'll pray about it."

She stands. "That's all I can ask. Now I'm going to go see about my baby, and then I'm going to leave you alone with your thoughts and to talk with God."

Chapter 32

"Everything has been movin' so fast, baby," Mel speaks to Jeoff one morning, quickly pulling on her clothing, "especially the fact that I have overslept for work." She smiles sheepishly at him. "Between you and them kids, I can't seem to get the rest I need."

He walks to the bathroom to brush his teeth. "We haven't even been married four months, and everything has gone crazy. You sure you still want me?"

She follows him to the bathroom and hugs him from behind. "Of course, I still want you. We'll make it through all of this." She kisses his cheek. "At least Cha Cha has returned to school, and we haven't heard anything abnormal."

He nods.

"I wasn't expectin' everything to be normal. I just want you and these children."

"Oh, so you're sayin' I'm strange?" He snaps at her with a towel.

After Jeoff drops off Melasan at the hotel, he enters the shiny metallic doors of the elevator to his own job. The morning churns through quickly, and as he marvels at how much he's been able to accomplish, his cell phone rings. He checks the caller ID and instinctively tenses as the middle school's number registers.

"Jeoff Simpson here."

"Daddy?"

"Cha Cha, what's wrong?" He looks around the mahogany desk, grabbing for his keys.

"Nothin', Daddy. I'm sorry I was so sad." She pauses.

"It's all right, Choo Choo," he answers, calling her an old baby name and loosening the keys to prepare to leave if necessary.

"She hurt my heart."

Jeoff flinches at the frankness of his baby's words and nods even though she can't see him.

"I think she hurt herself even more than she hurts us, huh, Daddy?"

"Yeah, baby." Tears slide down Jeoff's cheeks. "Hey, Cha, where are you calling me from?"

"The office. I just told them that I needed to talk to my daddy."

He smiles, the tears still streaming.

"I am thankful for my momma, and I don't need this woman to be my momma. I don't wanna spend time with her, but I am all right with her comin' to our city. I can forgive her now."

"Me too."

"I gotta go, Daddy. I'll see you after school."

"God willin', Choo."

The phone clicks, and Jeoff immediately calls Melasan's office, relaying the whole conversation.

"How is it, Mel, in only a few days, she's stronger than I am?"

"It sounds like she let it go, J."

"How do you feel about her, about Rookie? We never discuss that," Jeoff asks.

Melasan thinks, remembering in the beginning the memories she had of the woman, and then she answers, "We're living a fairy tale. I didn't see it 'til Adrienne told me fairy tales have joy and hardships, and in the end, the characters overcome. We are overcoming."

"That's sweet. I think it's a telenovela though." Jeoff laughs.

"That's why you're my sunshine."

"I've noticed you haven't been eating much these past few days," she muses.

"I know, baby. Things on my mind."

"I would say you've gotta eat, but I believe you're building your strength, am I right?"

He says nothing.

"You could've told me, and I would've fasted with you."

"The Bible says, when you fast, do it solemnly and don't be broadcastin' it."

"I understand that, but I also know that it also mentions that, where two or three are joined in His name, then He's in the midst. Also—"

"All right, all right. I get you. I wasn't tryin' to keep anything from you. You forgive me?" he sweetly asks.

"Of course. Wouldn't have it any other way. I've been fasting with you anyway."

The two laugh.

"I love you, baby. I really do," he tells her.

"I know. Go on and get back to work and stay prayerful."

After a lengthy fight with his constantly crashing new computer program, Jeoff picks up the phone to call tech support, only to find his dad on the other end.

"Hey, bub!"

"That's strange. I was trying to call tech support, and here you are, but I knew you'd call sooner or later. Why don't you come by? I need to sit and talk with you." Jeoff tries his computer again with no response.

"I'd love to, but I'm headed to Destin to a conference. Just wanted to check on you. We haven't heard from you in a while."

"Yeah, I've been dealing with the kids and doin' some soul-searchin'. I'd like you to come by and talk to the kids about their feelings and whatnot."

"A little godly counsel?"

"Most definitely. A lot's been goin' on, and we need to turn it around so that the positive can be seen."

"Yes, yes. You know we'll be there as soon as I get back from this conference. That'll be Saturday if you're wonderin'."

He hears the smile in his dad's voice.

"In the meantime, your momma's at home. She couldn't come to Destin this time with me. She has other duties she has to attend to, so call and let her know what time'll be good for us to get there Saturday."

"I'm catching your hint with both hands, Pop. I'll call as soon as we hang up."

"Hey, Jeoff?"

"Yes, sir?"

"Before I get back, y'all need to be praying together. Remember, the family that prays together, stays together."

"Okay."

"Every day," Rev. Simpson asserts.

"Yes, sir."

With that said, Rev. Simpson loses his signal, and Jeoff makes his call to tech support to be filled with the promise that they plan to fix the problem right away. As he waits for them, he again picks up the phone.

"Hey, Momma."

"Hey, baby." She sounds a little relieved to hear his voice.

"I'll be headed to a meeting soon, but I wanted to make sure to call and let you know that I love you."

"Thank you, baby. I love you too, Jeoffy."

Chapter 33

By Saturday morning, Jeoff is feeling rejuvenated. He and his immediate family have implemented a morning prayer ritual before everyone leaves for their various tasks, and on a personal level, his relationship with God has grown as well. He attributes the renewal to the oneness with his wife and the godly strength she possesses as well as the naked honesty he has been sharing with his Savior. Rookie's disappearance years ago hadn't torn their lives asunder, rendering them powerless. It drew them closer to one another, making their family a strong fortress. He also realizes that Rookie's return made them each experience singular and collective growth. After just a couple days of morning prayer, the children are getting along better, and the house holds an exquisite peace.

Jeoff hums as he gets ready to help Duran cut the yard and direct the other children in their lawn chores.

"Dad, Duran and JJ cut the yard last time. It's me and Mari's turn," Devon asserts to his dad.

"I don't wanna turn," Mari interjects.

"Oh, I do, Daddy!" Cha Cha excitedly says.

Jeoff grins because Mari is scared of the lawn mower like a small child is of a vacuum cleaner, and Cha Cha is trying to wangle her way onto the Troy-Bilt Zero-Turn they own. He has given them each a chance to try it, but only the older children who've mastered it and he get to operate it. Otherwise, it's the push mower, loppers, rakes, and Weed Eater that are divvied out.

Ignoring the extra flack, he appoints Devon and Duran to grass cutting. He puts Ni Ni on the Weed Eater as she has become quite adept at the task and seems to enjoy wielding the lightweight machinery. Melasan simultaneously takes care of the herb and vegetable garden they have, and no amount of begging can make any child other than Adrienne help her with the weeding tasks. They have all been gung ho to plant everything under the sun yet likewise shy from the maintenance except Melasan, who's a dedicated soldier.

It's Adrienne that brings Jeoff the phone. "Hey, Daddy, I think it's a telemarketeer."

He grins at her mispronunciation and, grabbing the phone, asks her, "You ready to come over to the fun side of the house? I know Momma's weeds are borin'."

"I can't. She thinks I like it." She winks, skipping away.

Jeoff laughs, putting the phone to his ear. "Hello?"

"Hello, Jeoff."

"Hello, Rookie. I figured you'd call. I didn't know you had the house number."

"It was in the phone book. I ain't never used it because I was given your cell phone number, but your cell wasn't on," she explained all of this, surprising him with her calmness.

"It's not a problem for you to call the house phone. I don't turn on the cell phone on weekends."

"I think this is the nicest you've been to me here lately."

He says nothing.

She continues talking, "Um…I guess you're wonderin' why I'm callin'?" She struggles with her words.

"Yeah."

"But you said you figured I'd be callin', so you…had some idea?"

"Yep."

Jeoff's one-word answers are making her nervous.

"I wanted to ask if I could have some of your time, um, with the kids. I'm not tryin' to disrespect you or anythin'. Your wife can come too."

He detects the sadness in her voice. He pauses and then answers, "I don't think that'd be a problem. Uh, let's see. How soon were you thinkin'?"

"Today," she urgently states and then works to calm herself. "I need to do this."

He believes her. "All right. Later this afternoon, around three. We could meet you wherever you like." He fights the urge to ask her not to bring any of her usual mess, deciding to trust God instead.

"Jeoff, was it hard takin' care of the kids alone?"

"Yeah, it was real hard after you left," he answers.

She gets quiet, and he can hear the background noises of the street.

"I kinda meant while I was there."

Jeoff sits down in a lawn chair. He can tell the work is close to done as the kids have begun to chase each other and play. Duran stands in the yard fussing at them for order like a judge.

"Oh, I didn't know you knew."

"I didn't...not at first...but I do. I'm sorry."

Tears poke at the corners of Jeoff's eyes at the simple words.

"Thank you. I've waited a long time for that."

She sits silently, and he knows she's uncomfortable with this small display of emotion. He hears a faint sound like a sob.

Then Rookie speaks, "I'll see you at three at Rev. Idella's house. Your momma said you know where it is."

With that said, she hung up.

Making sure the children are done with the machinery and putting it all in its proper place, Jeoff heads for the garden.

"Did you buy me somethin' from that telemarketeer?" Adrienne bumps against him to ask.

Tickling her, he answers, "Nope, lovey bear, but you might wanna see what your brothers and sisters are doin'. I think you need to get 'em. They're actin' out."

She runs with purpose through the expansive yard, yelling bossy orders to the kids.

"Hey, baby." Jeoff leans down and kisses Mel.

"Hey back, lover." She smears dirt on his face, smiling mischievously.

"The telemarketer was actually Rookie," he informs her.

"What'd she want?" she asks, standing and yanking at a particularly cantankerous weed.

"Well, she wants to meet with us at three at Rev. Idella's house."

Mel ducks as the weed releases, slinging a spray of dirt.

"And…she apologized to me."

She tosses the weed into her wheelbarrow, glancing at her husband. "I can tell that made you feel good."

"Yeah, it did. It really did. She's not normally the apologetic type. You know that."

Mel nods.

"Well, after Momma and Daddy get here, we'll have lunch, chill out, pray, and then go to Rev. Idella's house. I like this seemingly calm change in her, but I still have to watch out for my family."

"True, true."

No sooner had they finished talking than Rev. and Mrs. Simpson pull into the long driveway leading to the house. The kids chase their grandpa's green Cadillac Escalade like farm dogs until they come to a stop.

"How're my grandbabies?" Mrs. Simpson gives hugs and kisses to the grandchildren and then takes bags out of the back seat.

"Now why you gonna go grabbin' at my stuff, woman? You're not takin' the credit for the things I bought for everybody on my trip!" Rev. Simpson grabs at the bags in the back.

Ni Ni and Devon snatch the bags, running into the house, leaving the two standing at the car stunned and laughing.

"We've been robbed," Mrs. Simpson says, looking at Jeoff and Melasan's direction. "How are you two doing? You look bright and happy."

They nod. "We are. Thanks for the input on praying together, Dad. It's made a world of difference."

The two hug as the ladies hug, and then they all walk up the wide steps, stopping at the porch swing.

"Dad? Rookie called today and wants us to meet her at Rev. Idella's house at three."

"Oh, okay. We won't take up all y'all's time today," he begins.

"That's not what we're sayin', Rev. We want y'all to come along too," Mel says.

Rev. Simpson nods his agreement as Jeoff speaks, "Besides, Momma, you kinda know her better than all of us."

Mari smiles softly.

"Where do y'all wanna talk to the kids?" Rev. Simpson asks.

"The yard is clean and pretty. Why don't we just sit on the patio and talk to them? We'll drink some of Melasan's homemade lemonade and just talk. How 'bout that?"

Everyone agrees, and they head through the yard around the house.

"Mel, how's the garden goin'? Am I gonna have any fresh vegetables to can this fall?" Mari asks.

"Oh, yes! Everything's comin' out so wonderful. I'm lookin' forward to us doin' it together."

"No doubt, love. Cee Cee usually comes home for that. She loves canning."

They end up on the patio and call for the children that aren't still outside to come and sit at the picnic tables and deepwater-protection-stained wooden patio furniture with them. Melasan loves being out in the yard. The deep-blue seat cushions with blue accents sewn by Ni Ni and Mari in an after-school sewing program are a sentimental joy to her.

"Hey, y'all call us?" Devon heads out the French doors leading to the kitchen with everyone else in tow.

"Yeah, we did, son. Have a seat. We need to talk to y'all."

Everyone takes seats, with Cha Cha and Jeoff Jr. racing for "favorite" seats and finally settling after some discussion.

"I asked Dad to come over so that we could all discuss our feelings about Miss Rookie's return to Alabama. The best thing to do is just start with the youngest and move upward." He looks at Cha Cha.

She shrugs. "I'm okay. Mari?" She looks at her sister.

"I'm older than Jeoff." She smugly states.

"You are not!" He screeches.

"Yes, I am, by three minutes. Daddy, tell him to respect his elders?"

She looks at her dad, and everybody laughs.

"She does have you by three minutes, so it is your turn, son."

Jeoff scoffs, mumbling, "I'm fine with it." He glares at Mari as she begins talking.

"I am okay with her returning. It doesn't really have much to do with us anyway."

Devon sits silently, and Jeoff Sr. looks at his dad.

"How do you feel, Devon?"

"I don't feel anything." He leans over and taps Ni Ni for her turn.

"I talked to her, and I feel all right, I guess." She looks sheepishly at Duran.

Jeoff Jr. stares at his brother.

"I think I've asked her all of the questions I had for her." He looks back at Jeoff Jr.

Their dad can swear he feels the old closeness returning.

Adrienne starts to cry.

"Baby, what's wrong?" Mrs. Simpson asks.

"Nobody asked me how I feel about Miss Rookie returnin'!"

Jeoff smiles. "Well, baby, how do you feel?"

Adrienne takes a deep breath. "I think that Miss Rookie had to be a pretty mean person to leave my family, but I think she is sorry for it because she came back." She crosses her hands on her chest as though pleased with her statement, then she turns to look at Devon. "If you don't forgive her, then God won't forgive you for stealing Duran's shirt and wearing it to school."

Everybody laughs.

Rev. Simpson speaks, "Well, I can't force y'all to have any feelings or speak on any, but forgiveness is on the horizon, and this happened for everyone's healing."

He looks at Devon's direction, but he won't meet his eyes. He talks to them for a while longer, and then they have prayer.

The children stand, relieved that the inquisition is over, and begin to head their separate directions.

"Simpson children, I need to tell you somethin'."

They all turn to their father's direction.

"At three, we're going to meet with Miss Rookie, so don't go far because it's almost one and we need to eat lunch."

There is an assortment of emotions displayed with grunting and groans, but Jeoff says nothing. They start the gas grill, placing on thick burgers which Mel glazes with a delicious teriyaki marinade the children love. They all sit down to burgers, chips, and lemonade, with the children eating solemnly as though their parents are taking them to slaughter.

"Hey, Devon, go check the mail please?" Mel absentmindedly asks.

He returns with several envelopes. "You got mail!" He smiles, handing out letters to all the children, himself, and his dad.

Chapter 34

Rev. Idella greets them into her home, kissing each of the children and telling them, "Don't be solemn. God has a great gift in store for you today, this very day."

Her excitement hasn't caught onto them yet, but Jeoff can feel that something important is about to happen. He looks at Melasan and sees that she feels it too. They all sit down around a large round mahogany table. There is fresh fruit sitting in the middle of the table, hearty wheat crackers, and thick slices of cheese; yet no one touches it. Jeoff continues to keep an eye on the children, praying for them.

"Where's Rev.?" he asks Rev. Idella, referring to her husband.

"Oh, baby, he'll be down directly. He's always got to take longer than anybody else, I suppose," she answers with a bright smile.

As though he heard his name, Rev. Banks makes his entrance. The small man with the fuzzy, almost-bald head stops at the stairwell, smiles as though coming into a party, and makes his way toward them.

"My favorite Simpson family!" he states, catching the kids' attention. He greets everyone with a kiss and then kisses his wife. "How are you, Rev. Idella?" He smiles.

"Wonderfully blessed, Rev. Banks."

Jeoff's not quite sure how old the couple is, but it seems they were bordering on old when he was a child. Now they're even older, but they seem to still carry a flame for one another. Her eyes gleam at him, and his dance right back at her.

The children begin to relax and talk among themselves but silence as Rookie walks into the room. Jeoff remembers her mere presence as being consuming and dominating; yet here she is, stripped of her once strikingly gorgeous facade, leaving her harmless in appearance. Her long hair is pulled back into a sensible ponytail, and her ankle-length brown sundress with golden accents seems out of character from the past. She sits beside the male Rev. Banks at the head of the table, glancing fearfully at Rev. Idella for direction.

"Let us begin this time with some help from up above," Rev. Idella tells everyone and nods at Rev. Banks to pray.

He gives a heartfelt yet quick prayer, sitting with a look at Rookie, who stands, placing her hands on the table, her gaze resting on the Simpsons.

"I'm not sure where to start, but I've learned, in our group, the beginning is best."

There's a general nodding of heads among the grown-ups.

"I left home because of only one person." She pauses, taking a deep breath, not noticing that she's caught the children's attention. "Me. I left because of me." She closes her eyes, and the words flow. "I loved every baby I had, but I hurt them just like I hurt my husband. I remember all of you. I remember the way you smelled when I had you, how you felt in my arms, and the cute things you'd do that made you different from each other."

She briefly opens her eyes, closing them again.

"I got tired of it all the time, but I knew he wouldn't leave. He was stronger 'an me, and I knew he'd always take care of all of us." She bites her lip. "I know I was supposed to come home. I was supposed to grow up and be a good mommy, but I was mad. I never had a good momma or a good daddy!" She opens her eyes, looking at the kids. "That's never been y'all's fault, never and never will. I just needed—need you all to be here to hear me."

She begins to cry and wills herself to stop.

"I shouldn't have acted like I was doin' y'all a favor comin' here." The eyes that match Ni Ni's perfectly close again. "I was scared and what people in the streets and in places I've been do when they're scared is act hard, act like you owe 'em somethin' so maybe you forget you don't and actually give 'em what they don't deserve." Her eyelids quiver with emotion. "I've done a lot of really, really bad things in my life, but"—looking at the kids again—"if y'all need to know about that, then I'll make myself tell it. I want to talk to each and every one of you, and I'm sorry for all of the hurt I've caused.

"When my daddy left, I always imagined he'd come for me. He'd let me live with him, and I'd have a red bike with tassels on the handlebars. He'd take me from the hell I was livin' in, tell me he loved me, and I'd be safe. That never happened, and even though I've come back and never shoulda left, I can't make y'all feel safe...You already are."

Rookie's hands shook on the table, and when she tried to steady them, her whole body shook with an earthquake no one else seemed to be aware of. She stood quietly for a few minutes, wiping her tears.

"I took away my own chance to raise y'all in a two-parent home." She looks at Jeoff, tears ever flowing. "I married you because you were my American Dream. You have two parents that love you and each other, and you were willin' to do that with me. I'm sorry I didn't know what to do with that."

Jeoff holds Melasan's hand, his own tears falling.

"You deserve happiness. You do. Babies, I don't recognize you as these beautiful people you've grown to be. I remember babies." Rookie smiles, suspended in memory.

The children stare straight ahead, paralyzed in their own emotions.

"I would be grateful for the chance to get to know you and to explain to you if you want that." She scans the crowd of children, eyes stopping on Devon. "I've got some things to explain to you."

He quickly breaks their gaze.

"When I finish talkin', I'll be sittin' right here, waitin' if you... if you wanna talk...to me. Thank you." She suddenly, without any other warning, takes her seat.

The grown-ups, along with Adrienne, leave quietly, leaving the room to Rookie and the rest of the children, who all sit quietly, staring at this strange woman, seemingly unaware that everyone else has gone. Cha Cha takes the initiative, walking over to Rookie.

"I'm Cha Cha. I'm the youngest." She surprises Rookie with a hug. "We got your letters today." With that stated, she leaves the room.

222

Mari is next. She walks over, looks at Rookie, and says, "I'm Mari. I don't have any more questions. I think you answered 'em. Thank you for the letter."

"You're Li'l Mari?" Rookie asks, her face reddening with embarrassment.

"Yes, ma'am. JJ, Jeoff Jr., is my twin. What are your hobbies?" she asks.

"I don't think I really have any. I take pictures. Rev. Idella says I'm a natural at it, and I like it." She thinks. "I've been crocheting with Rev. Idella, so I guess that's one."

"Me and Ni Ni sew. We've sewn a lot of stuff together. The last thing we made was some cushions for Momma."

"I wouldn't mind learnin' to sew," Rookie shyly hints.

"I can show you."

She gets excited, and the two talk longer with Mari leaving the room bubbling with a smile.

Jeoff Jr. walks her direction, pausing to quickly say, "I'm Jeoff Jr., and…I forgive you."

Duran stands with Devon. "We're glad you came to answer some questions. Devon has some for you though."

"We got off on the wrong foot, Duran. I'd still like the chance to know you."

He nods, and she glances nervously at Devon.

"Devon? I'm sorry about the janitor you met at school, the one I named you after."

"How'd you know about that?" he demands.

"I ran into him after I got back."

"Why'd you name me after him?"

"To make your daddy mad…" she answers sadly.

"Is he my biological?" Devon whispers. "You didn't mention it in your letter. I read it twice, and you didn't say a word about it." He searches her eyes for the truth.

"No, he isn't."

With that, Devon leaves with Duran, and Rookie sits alone at the table with Ni Ni.

"Did you ever write to your daddy?" Ni Ni asks quietly.

"No. I just cried a lot," Rookie answers. "Later I toughened up."

"I wrote you letters," Ni Ni states.

"I wrote you too," Rookie answers. "I brought 'em with me."

"I brought mine too!" Ni Ni excitedly tells her.

Ni Ni reaches inside of a plastic bag she has sitting on her lap and unearths a stack of letters in envelopes that merely say "Mommy" on the front, and Rookie moves to the back of the room, bringing out a large cardboard box.

"I wrote to all of you over the years and just never sent anythin'."

The two sit talking for what seems like hours until finally Jeoff ducks his head into the door.

"I'm glad that the two of you are having good conversation, but we really need to go so that everyone can have somethin' to eat. Rookie, would you like to go to Western Sizzlin' with us?"

About the Author

GINGER ROBINSON FELL IN LOVE with libraries and the smell of books as a child. She composed her first stories on the front porch with her grandma and has been writing ever since. Later in life, she achieved publishing with numerous publications such as the Columbia Missourian, Signs of the Times, Our Daily Bread, Beaumont Enterprise, and many others.

She is a mother of three, wife to one, and grandmother to four (wink!) who travels the country with her welding husband.